Lori M. Lee

First published in 2021 by
Page Street Publishing Co.
27 Congress Street, Suite 105
Salem, MA 01970
www.pagestreetpublishing.com

Distributed by Macmillan, sales in Canada by The Canadian Manda Group.

25 24 23 22 21 1 2 3 4 5

ISBN-13: 978-1-64567-210-4
ISBN-10: 1-64567-210-7

Library of Congress Control Number: 2020945229

Cover and book design by Laura Benton for Page Street Publishing Co.
Cover illustration by Charlie Bowater
Cityscape and spiderweb vectors © Shutterstock

Printed and bound in the United States

For the ones who dream of home.

ONE

The forest is still, the branches streaked in sunset. Weeds and shadows press at my heels.

The silence is a lie. I don't need my craft to catch the faint flutter of wings hidden behind broad summer leaves or the shuffle of small paws in the underbrush. But with my craft, every presence is amplified, like a dozen voices shouting at once.

My teeth clench. The souls are indistinct—I lack the control to separate them into individuals—and my fingers twitch restlessly. Magic burns through my veins, surging against my skin. With a frustrated exhale, I flatten my palms against my stomach and imagine compressing my craft into a burning ember of power at my core. It's like trying to stuff a storm into a cage. Still, my awareness of the souls dims enough that I can ignore them.

I draw a throwing knife from my belt, letting my other senses home in on the speckled hare digging for roots to my right. Before the blade leaves my hand, an arrow whizzes past my shoulder, finding my mark first.

Returning the knife to my belt, I face Saengo, who lowers her bow. "I had it," I say.

"You were taking ages, and I'm hungry." Her boots are silent as she moves past me through the deepening gloom to retrieve the hare. "No luck?"

"No," I say quietly. My gaze flicks in the direction she came from, toward camp where some three dozen Nuvali shamans and their familiars await.

Prince Meilek is there as well, having agreed to accompany us until the falcons he'd sent to Evewyn return. After betraying his sister, the queen, he's no longer safe in his own kingdom, not until he can confirm he still has allies.

For the last week, I've been trying to use my craft to hunt, as it was originally intended. But my first attempt ended in disaster when I ripped the souls of every creature within twenty paces. Since then, I've been trying to focus on individual souls, but it's been impossible without either physical contact or close proximity.

Heat flecks the tips of my fingers. It doesn't help that my magic seemingly *wants* to be used, straining toward every living thing within reach to loosen the tether between soul and body. It's disconcerting and keeps me on edge.

The Nuvali dislike that Saengo and I hunt on our own, but when they invited me to join them in the shaman capital, I made clear that I would keep my freedom to come and go as I wish. Thus far, they've tolerated it, but their grudging allowance is another reason to be cautious with my craft. I can't trust we won't be followed.

"You'll get it, Sirscha. You always do," Saengo says. Hare in hand, she wipes the arrowhead on some leaves and then returns it to her quiver.

I'm not so confident. My magic feels different, unruly. Before I fought Ronin at Spinner's End a fortnight ago, I struggled to even summon my craft. But to defeat him, I'd allowed the Soulless's power to flow through me and strengthen my magic. Even after the molten presence of his power faded, my craft never quite settled.

I haven't told Saengo. Hers is the only soul I can pick out without difficulty. She is always with me, a candle flame burning behind my ribs.

She hands me the hare and grimaces as I set about cleaning it. For all her training, she's surprisingly squeamish. I grin and consider flicking entrails at her.

"Don't you dare," she says, eyes narrowing as she backs away from me.

"What?" I say, laughing.

"Don't think I won't find something even more disgusting to leave in your bedroll."

I snort, grinning. "I would never underestimate you."

"I don't know how you can even see what you're doing." She indicates the quickening night.

"It's not fully dark yet. Besides, I'd make a lousy Shadow if I couldn't even do this. . . ." My voice trails off. I'd chased that ambition for so long—becoming Shadow to the queen of Evewyn, her royal spy and assassin. Sometimes I forget that, even if I still wanted it, it's now well beyond my reach.

Silence lingers for a beat, filled by the dull ache of old dreams. Then Saengo says, "We'll be to Mirrim soon."

I nod, crouched over my work. "Hopefully, we'll get some answers."

Mirrim, the capital of the Nuvalyn Empire, lies far to the east. Despite the risk, we agreed that going there was our best option. Posing as their soulguide is the best way to gain access to whatever information might be kept there about the Soulless. So long as my true craft stays hidden.

Besides Saengo, only Prince Meilek knows that I'm a soulrender, because he was present when I learned the truth. But we've another reason for venturing so deep into the Empire. Saengo is infected with the rot, and we've been promised Mirrim's best healers for her.

Part of me suspects, though, that she will never truly be healed until the Soulless is dealt with. His corrupted magic has infected her as surely as it's infected me, setting flame to my craft so that it burns beneath my skin. Always restless, always eager.

She fusses with the ends of her red sash, picking at frayed threads. "It's frightening, isn't it?" she asks softly.

"Me?" I fear my own craft, so why wouldn't Saengo? It was my power that turned her into a familiar. Now, she is bound to me—a spirit restored to shape and form in exchange for channeling my magic. Sometimes, I don't know how she can even bear to look at me, given what I've done to her.

"No, Sirscha," she says, exasperated. "Your magic."

"Me, my magic. It's all the same."

"Of course it isn't. You were you before you ever learned you were a soulrender."

I sigh. While I understand her meaning, it's not so simple. My powers are unsettling even to me. Souls are the source of shamanic magic. That a soulrender can grasp souls and destroy them is an attack against magic itself. Fear of what soulrenders can do—fear of what the Soulless did—is what drove the Empire to destroy them.

Aside from myself and the Soulless, no other soulrenders remain.

Finished with the hare, I stand and swing the carcass at

Saengo, who yelps and dashes out of reach.

"Get that thing to a cooking fire," she says, poking the air between us with one finger.

"At once, my lady."

She leads us back to camp, our boots whispering through the weeds. Somewhere overhead comes a sharp birdcall. Saengo looks up, grinning. Millie, her pet falcon, has been following us since we entered the Empire.

With her back to me, my smile fades. Holding the hare out at my side, I frown down at the faint spatter of blood on my pants. Although we're both in our old gray uniforms from the Queen's Company, there's little chance anyone would mistake us for fourth-years. Had I not discovered that I'm shaman-born, Saengo and I would have graduated from the Company a few weeks ago and been shipped off to some distant post to begin our years of military service. We probably would've been separated.

The person I was feels so far away that it might as well be a different lifetime.

Now, our uniforms are thoroughly travel-worn, washed and rewashed since we set out for Mirrim. I keep my hair in a braid for function, but Saengo's is short enough that the ends curl beneath her ears. She's a far cry from the reiwyn lady she's meant to be.

After the Soulless's awakening, no one had quite known

what to make of the surge of magic that swept from the Dead Wood. With no sign of the Spider King, no one was willing to enter a forest of vengeful souls to find out.

So the camps sent off their falcons and packed up. There'd been nothing else to do, and I wasn't about to risk Saengo's safety by volunteering the truth.

Sisters, this is hopeless. I draw a deep, slow breath and shake away the thought. The Soulless is just a man, same as Ronin. All shamans need familiars, something that bridges them with their magic. The Soulless can't be any different.

If we can find out what's connecting him to his magic, then we find the key to defeating him.

Two days later, we arrive in the trade city of Luam. Sitting at the confluence of two major rivers, the city sprawls around and above the water.

It is the largest city we've passed through. The previous towns were no more than a scattering of homes and buildings. I suspect our route was deliberate to keep word of my presence contained. There's no hiding here, though.

The sheer number of souls is overwhelming, and it takes several minutes for me to smother the surge of magic burning through my skin. I focus on the warm glow of Saengo's soul as she rides at my side. Exposing my craft wouldn't just put me and Saengo in danger. It would endanger Prince Meilek and the other Evewynians in our party. They only came this far at my request.

Boats pack the river from end to end. Some drift lazily along the banks and bridges, carrying goods to sell or trade. Others cut swiftly through the waves, a golden Nuvali sun painted along their sides and a uniformed waterwender at the helm. Broad bridges arch over the water. Buildings stand on thick stilts, crammed side to side, connected by wooden walkways.

Our procession is hard to miss as we enter the city, stalling foot traffic. At our lead is a lightwender priestess named Mia who met us on the road yesterday morning with a small party of lightwender guards. As everyone believes I'm a soulguide, the first to appear since the founding of the Empire, the Emperor had deemed it necessary to send an escort from the Temple of Light to ensure I reach Mirrim safely.

With the threat of war between the kingdoms, the Nuvali want me somewhere "safe." But I wouldn't have come if it didn't also serve my own purposes, and I'm only safe so long as they think I'm a soulguide.

After taking control of our group, Priestess Mia sent the Nuvali lord we'd been traveling with ahead to report to the Emperor. Aside from an awkward introduction, I've been doing my best to avoid them. I'm wary of questions I might not be able to answer.

Priestess Mia glances over her shoulder and gestures with one slick fingernail for me to join her at the head of our procession.

I smother my annoyance at being beckoned and nudge Yandor ahead. Yandor is a common drake with a sleek head and dark green scales. But Priestess Mia rides a snowy white dragokin, a species native to the Empire, with liquid black eyes and shining white horns swirled with gold paint. Like drakes, dragokins stand on two powerful legs but with shorter arms and claws, making them vicious companions in battle. Everything about Priestess Mia screams her status at the Temple of Light, where young lightwenders go to study and master their light crafts.

Priestess Mia herself is a petite woman with long black hair and warm copper skin. Her eyes are a luminous amber, the mark of a lightwender, and framed by sparse lashes accented with kohl. Gold dust streaks her lids. According to the murmurs in our party, she's a lightgiver. Lightgivers can transfer the light, or life, of one person to another—a power rarely used except in times of dire need.

White robes drape from her shoulders, the hem embroidered with golden sunbursts. A sheer golden sash cinches her waist, knotted elaborately to denote her rank.

"Priestess," I murmur as I join her and nod politely.

She returns the gesture. Her gaze passes over the two swords at my back and then to Yandor's saddle, where a third sword is wrapped within a long strip of cloth. She doesn't remark on why I'm carrying so many weapons.

Around us, people pause to watch as we pass. I fight the impulse to hide, to shrink into the shadows. Nearly everyone possesses the pointed ears and jewel-bright eyes of a shaman, although I've learned that even among the same Calling, the range of hues can vary. After two weeks on the road and numerous towns, I've seen lightwenders with every shade from the palest gold to vivid amber, and, in a trade city of this size, even some gray-eyed shamans who've never bonded with a familiar.

Familiars in the form of all manner of beasts accompany them. Birds flit from shoulders to rooftops, snakes and other smaller creatures curl around necks or ride tucked into satchels, their furred heads peering out from the openings. Lizards perch atop the brims of hats or burrow into the hoods of cloaks. Larger familiars—silver wolves, black foxes, and even a fire salamander—trot alongside their shamans. It's breathtaking to see so many creatures living naturally alongside people.

Among the boats that crowd the riverways, I glimpse the white hair and gray skin of the shadowblessed. I even spot brown-eyed humans with rounded ears like Saengo's. Like mine. To hide the truth of my parentage, whoever abandoned me to an orphanage cut my ears when I was a child.

"The governor of Luam is away on business, but he offered us the use of his home for the night," Priestess Mia says. Although her lips curve into a pleasant smile, there's a hardness in the way she observes me. Her luminous eyes lack warmth.

She must question the veracity of who I claim to be, and I don't blame her. I expect there will be others who feel the same in Mirrim.

"That was generous of him," I say awkwardly. I loathe making small talk and nearly glance back at Saengo for guidance. As the heir to House Phang, she is well versed in socializing with other reiwyn.

We cross a series of bridges, heading into the eastern part of the city. Beyond the bank of the river, built atop a rise half-covered in wild sunflowers, is a whitewashed mansion. It'll be a nice change from tents.

Priestess Mia runs her pale fingers along the reins of her dragokin. "There is one thing, however, about the Evewynian prince and his soldiers."

Her words steal my attention from the bustle around us. Prince Meilek and his small group of Eveywnians ride near the rear of our procession. A few days after setting out from the north, several of his Blades and servants caught up to our party, declaring their intent to remain with their prince. I recognized two of them from when Saengo and I were imprisoned at the Valley of Cranes.

After Prince Meilek warned the Nuvali and Kazan about his sister's attack in the north, no one objected to his presence. But while Prince Meilek agreed to remain with me until he's heard from his allies, I know he's restless. This deep into the Empire, the Evewynians have clung together, uncertain of their welcome and wary of a people their queen has fashioned into enemies.

"What about them?" I ask stiffly.

Priestess Mia speaks with a clipped matter-of-factness. "He and his soldiers are, of course, welcome in Luam. However, housing a fugitive prince within a government-issued home could be misconstrued. The Emperor has not decided how to respond to Evewyn's attack, and such a move might be seen as an escalation."

I was prepared to argue with whatever she said, but this is unexpected. It irks me that she has a point.

Still, Prince Meilek saved lives in the north. There's little doubt the Empire won't retaliate for Evewyn breaking the peace treaty long enforced by Ronin. But until the Emperor decides what that retaliation will be, they'll want to avoid anything that might imply the Emperor's approval.

Allowing Prince Meilek safe passage through the Empire

seems a clear enough stance to me, but what do I know of politics?

"Then I will find other accommodations with them," I say. Being able to speak with Prince Meilek away from the constant presence of our Nuvali escort will be welcome. There's too much we haven't discussed.

"You cannot," she says simply. "I have been entrusted with your safety."

"Not by me."

Her lips pinch, just the slightest. "By the High Priestess of the Temple of Light and the Emperor. Look at the manner of our arrival—within hours, everyone will know you're here. Luam is a city open to people from all over Thiy, including those historically at odds with the Empire."

I nearly snort. It's a delicate way of alluding to the ongoing hostility between the Nuvalyn Empire and Kazahyn.

"The governor's home is well protected. It's the safest place for you and your friend. But if you insist on remaining with the Evewynian prince, then my guards and I will have no choice but to join you," she says, her tone suggesting she'd rather dive into the river.

Saengo and I can take care of ourselves. As much as it would amuse me to inconvenience her, I wouldn't be able to speak freely with Prince Meilek, knowing she and her Light Temple guards are under the same roof. I can't trust them.

But there might still be a way.

"I'll speak with Prince Meilek," I say, and excuse myself with another bow.

Saengo lifts one eyebrow in question as I pass her. "Later," I mouth and make my way to Prince Meilek and the other Evewynians at the back of our party.

Prince Meilek rides flanked by two of his Blades, Evewyn's warrior elite and former members of the Queen's Guard. The rest of his group follow at his back, clustered together in this foreign city.

He has abandoned his pristine captain's look these last couple weeks. While the upper half of his hair is swept back into a ponytail at the crown of his head, the dark strands are mussed from a long day's ride, and a fine layer of dust coats his clothes. After the heat of the day, he's rolled back his sleeves and loosened the collar of his tunic. To blend in with the others, he's removed the golden hairpin that announces his royal blood, and the green sash at his waist is tied in a humble knot.

"Sirscha," he says, greeting me as I match Yandor to the pace of his dragule. His Blades make room for me.

I bow respectfully and quietly convey Priestess Mia's words. He doesn't seem surprised.

"I wondered how they planned to have me here without outright declaring their intent to oppose Evewyn. The attack in the north was an act of war. And now that the peace treaty is broken, the Empire will likely respond. But whatever they choose to reveal about their actions will be on their own terms."

"They owe you a debt," I mutter.

"She's right," one of his Blades murmurs, a tall thin man named Kou. "They disrespect you by—"

"They do what they must." Prince Meilek shrugs. "In truth, I'd planned to spend the night elsewhere anyway."

I frown. "You know someone in Luam?"

"A shamanborn acquaintance. There may be other shamanborn here as well. She'll be able to find us a room and a warm meal."

I don't like the idea of separating from my fellow Evewynians, who've offered a measure of comfort in their familiarity these last two weeks. Though I am loathe to admit it, Priestess Mia is right. As a soulguide, even a fake one, the Empire's enemies will view me as an enemy. If it were only me, I'd be willing to take the risk. But there's also Saengo's safety to consider.

Saengo falls back to join us, and we remain with them until we reach the path that winds through the sunflowers and up to the governor's mansion.

As we make our goodbyes, I pull Prince Meilek into a quick embrace and murmur in his ear, "We'll find you later."

"The Dancing Drake Inn," he replies promptly. He clearly knows more about the shamanborn in Luam than he initially let on.

I smile and bow. As Priestess Mia and the others continue ahead toward the mansion, Saengo and I linger on the road, watching as the flurry of traffic swallows Prince Meilek and the other Evewynians.

TWO

For a well-guarded mansion, it's laughably easy to sneak out once everyone has retired for the evening.

We dodge the guards by ducking into the sunflowers and then disappear into the buildings along the riverbank before crossing the next bridge into the city. There, some locals point us toward the Dancing Drake, which sits squarely over the Xya River. A small dock runs the length of the inn's eastern side, where patrons can dock and depart at their leisure.

Stilts at each corner support the inn, along with a thick central beam, which appears to be the general framework of most Luam buildings. As we approach, we practically hug the walls to avoid rickshaws barreling past, the wooden beams rattling beneath their wheels. A woman in a bright green tunic is parked alongside the walkway, selling layered tapioca cakes.

Saengo buys a bundle of them with coins I pickpocket from an elegant woman draped in silk robes.

The wooden caricature of a dancing drake hangs above the entrance, but the inn is otherwise unremarkable. As with most of the buildings in Luam, its construction favors function, not aesthetics. I quickly step aside, pulling Saengo behind me as the door flies open to unleash several patrons who are singing loudly and off-key. No matter the city or the kingdom, those who frequent taverns generally remain the same.

Inside, we're met by the clamor of noisy patrons. Heat rushes beneath my skin as my craft leaps to my fingertips, and I clench my fists. Like their voices, the souls blur into a bright, teeming mass. With effort, I breathe through the tension and imagine a wall between myself and the souls as I reel my craft back under control.

A girl standing near the bar shouts above the din. "Over here!" Flapping her hands at me and Saengo, she's doing a poor job of being inconspicuous.

I recognize her from Prince Meilek's party. Her name is Yen, a former servant within the Queen's Guard.

Saengo and I cross the room, weaving around a pair of musicians plucking enthusiastically at their instruments. Most of the people here are human, but I spot a few bright eyes and familiars flopped beneath tables looking bored. Once colorful drapes hang from the rafters, now dingy and tattered from time and the elements.

"Sorry, did you want one?" Saengo asks, having just finished her second cake. Sheepish, she holds out the last one.

"I'm not hungry," I say, amused. "You may continue stuffing your face."

"I do not *stuff my face*."

"You do, but it's very proper-like."

"What does that even mean—"

"Welcome!" Yen says, cutting off Saengo. She's not very tall, with black hair split into two sleek braids. Freckles spatter her cheeks and the bridge of her nose. She bows quickly and then gestures toward the stairs that lead up to the inn's rooms. "This way."

"Thank you," Saengo says before offering her the last tapioca cake.

"I couldn't possibly," Yen says. "I just ate. The owner is shamanborn, you see, and he was so honored to have the prince here that he isn't even charging us. Isn't that wonder—" She gasps as she trips on a step, and I catch her elbow before she can crash headfirst into the stairs.

"Are you all right?" Saengo asks, taking her other elbow.

Yen hunches her shoulders. "Sorry. I can't keep track of my own feet sometimes. Kendara used to call me a catastrophe."

My heart stumbles at the name, and I pause on the landing, my fingers tightening around her elbow. "You knew Kendara?"

"Oh, yes. Terribly ill-tempered woman. She used to come around the training yard for private sparring sessions with Prince Meilek. But since I worked with the Queen's Guard, I was often there running errands." She beams at this, oblivious to the turmoil churning my stomach.

I haven't seen Kendara for over a month. Even though she kept from me the truth that I'm a shaman and that she knew my mother, I miss her desperately. I swallow past the tightness encircling my throat and gesture for Yen to show us to Prince Meilek's room.

She leads us to the door at the end of the hallway and knocks once. The door opens almost immediately to reveal Kou, one of Prince Meilek's Blades. He pushes the door wider to allow us through but holds out an arm when Yen makes to follow.

"Thanks, Yen. Keep an eye out, will you?" he says.

She screws up her nose and thrusts out her bottom lip. She can't be more than a couple years younger than me, but she reminds me of the children back at the orphanage. "I never get to sit in on meetings."

Kou reaches out to tousle her hair, affectionate and familiar.

"Did you have any trouble?" Prince Meilek asks, sitting by the window and watching the street below.

Cards and half-empty glasses of amber liquid clutter a nearby table where the second Blade sits, waiting for the others to return to their game. As we enter, though, she stands and leaves without a word, joining Yen out in the hallway, and shuts the door. Only Kou remains.

"They gave us a room with a window," I say.

"At least she didn't have to break it," Saengo says. I broke a window at Spinner's End once for the sole purpose of snooping around the grounds.

"That was one time," I say.

"That I know of."

"That you know of," I agree.

The left side of Prince Meilek's mouth hitches. "Two weeks on the road together, and they barely even know you."

"Speaking of which," I say, turning to Kou, who is now leaning against the closed door. Although we exchanged introductions when they first joined our party, and Saengo and I remained close to Prince Meilek and the Evewynians during the journey east, we didn't interact much outside of the cursory. I imagine they were wary of me, given my eyes make me look like our Nuvali companions.

"Kou has been with me since before I became captain. I trust him with my life," Prince Meilek says.

But does he trust him with my life? Or Saengo's?

Kou straightens off the door. He's taller than Prince Meilek but thin and sturdy. His hair is cut close to his scalp, and thick eyebrows hang low over intense brown eyes. He's dressed in a muted green tunic with plain leather armor, and an unadorned sword hangs from his belt.

"Thank you for being here," I say. Saengo and I left Evewyn because we had no choice. Kou abandoned his home willingly out of loyalty and friendship to his prince. "I know leaving Evewyn must have cost you."

"My family is being cared for. Besides, they would want me to be here. My grandmother was shamanborn."

I frown. "Is she in the Valley?"

"She died before then, but her son—my uncle—was. He escaped in the prison break." His gaze flits to Prince Meilek. "I don't know what happened to him."

Maybe his uncle was one of the shamanborn Prince Meilek helped smuggle aboard a ship in Vos Gillis. Maybe he went north and is hiding in the Empire. Or maybe he fled east toward the Dead Wood.

A shiver runs through me at the memory of broken arms dragging a screaming body into the depths of a tree.

"May the Falcon Warrior protect him," I say.

Kou dips his head. "Thank you. My mother didn't inherit any shamanborn magic, so they didn't take her. Or me. Same with Yen." He nods at the closed door.

"She seems young," Saengo says, perched at the edge of a narrow cot in the corner.

"She is," Prince Meilek says. "I'm sending her back to

Evewyn in the morning with one of my soldiers. She still has friends within the Grand Palace, so she should be able to find work."

"You're making her a spy?" I ask. She's young, but that's not what gives me pause. I was younger than she was when I began training under Kendara. In the limited time I've known her, Yen doesn't exactly seem like the subtle sort.

"If necessary, yes. There are others like Yen and Kou whose families were taken when the shamanborn were imprisoned, even among the reiwyn, although they at least had the means of sending their relatives away to protect them."

"Are those the allies you spoke of?" I ask.

"Some. I served my sister faithfully until now, and I've forged a few friendships. Since I knew Luam would lie directly in our path to Mirrim, I asked that they send their correspondence here. My soldiers and I will remain here for the next few days, and then turn back for Evewyn."

I draw back at this news. "I thought we agreed you'd speak for Evewyn in Mirrim."

"You can do that just as easily," he says. He turns away from the window and leans his shoulder against the wall. "I'm sorry for not being completely forthcoming, but I'm not certain it's wise for me to be in the shaman capital. My soldiers feel the same. Luam isn't walled in, so we have an escape if necessary."

The Nuvali gave me their word that Prince Meilek and

the other Evewynians would be safe within the Empire, but I can understand the distrust. Evewyn and the Nuvalyn Empire have a strained relationship at best, made more so in recent years with his sister's hatred of shamans, despite that the Nuvali had nothing to do with the firewender who killed their parents.

"The Nuvali won't hurt you or Saengo so long as they believe you're a soulguide, but I can't give that same guarantee to my soldiers. Fortunately, we've friends here, so we'll remain until I've completed correspondence with my allies and established their loyalty. Once that's concluded, Priestess Mia has agreed to provide me and my soldiers with documents of safe passage through the Empire."

I scowl, annoyed that they'd arranged this without my knowing. "What do you mean to do then?"

"Whatever is best for Evewyn." He reaches for one of the drinks on the nearby table and empties the glass in one swallow. I don't recall ever seeing him drink before, but I understand the impulse.

Despite the vagueness of his reply, he's had plenty of time to think his actions through. He betrayed his sister, and the only way to regain his place in Evewyn is to remove her from the throne. This will be no easy task, and I'm not sure the prince is prepared to take such a step.

I consider my words for a moment and decide there's no

delicate way to phrase it. "Have you considered that what's best for Evewyn . . . isn't your sister?"

I suspect he'd gladly live in exile if it meant peace for his people. But peace isn't a possibility so long as Queen Meilyr is ruler.

Prince Meilek's jaw tightens. His gaze slides from mine as he sets the glass back on the table. "I've wondered that for far longer than appropriate for the captain of the Queen's Guard. But I always imagined I would be there to temper her. To . . . remind her of her duty." He rubs his fingers over his forehead, casting his face into shadows.

"His Highness hopes the queen will yet see reason," Kou says softly from his place near the door.

Prince Meilek tilts his head back. There's a tired look in his eyes. They've had this discussion before. "I've no desire to rule. You know that. All my life, I've known my purpose—to protect and serve my sister. It was my only duty, and one I gladly bore. Removing her from the throne is no small thing to consider."

"But you don't have a choice," I say, taking a step toward him. "There's no one else."

"Sirscha," Saengo says softly, voice strained.

At once, I retreat to the cot, wincing at my careless words.

Saengo's father, Lord Phang, has often said as much to her. Even now, she remains the heir to Falcons Ridge. Some nights ago, we discussed how Saengo would need to apprise her father of her circumstances, and how he would need to find a suitable replacement.

Despite running for years from the duty she's never wanted, she still cried for a life lost. How Saengo's father will respond is anyone's guess. She has cousins, but for Lord Phang, Saengo has always been his only choice. He will have no other as his heir.

"You know your sister best," I say, settling on the cot beside Saengo. "With Ronin gone, she's lost her strongest ally. What will she do next?"

His silence stretches between us, broken by the clacking of wheels outside and the hiss of boats sliding through water.

At last, Prince Meilek says, "Mei always liked the idea of power. She was eager to be queen. Her heart broke when our parents died, but I think she felt guilty for desiring the power suddenly handed to her." His gaze lifts to Kou's, and something passes between them, a quiet but shared pain. "So she directed that guilt toward punishing the shamanborn. It was an easy outlet. She'd never been comfortable with the idea of anyone lowborn possessing more power than her."

She sounds like she's always been terrible, but I refrain from saying so.

"The royal bloodline shares shaman ancestry," Saengo points out.

Once, the northern half of Evewyn was a separate kingdom, founded by a human slave who'd escaped the Empire during the chaos of the Soulless's rise to power. She tamed the first drake from the wilds of the north, and up until the domestication of drakes became common, she and her descendants were renowned as the Drake Queens. Her story has always been one of my favorites.

Some generations later, after the north unified with Evewyn into a single kingdom, the Empire offered Evewyn's queen a marriage alliance as reparations. Evewyn accepted the alliance on the condition that the Nuvali prince remain Prince Consort, without any true power. For a time, Evewyn's kings and queens had possessed magic.

"Hatred has no logic," I say, mostly to Prince Meilek. "It can't be reasoned away."

He doesn't react, well practiced in shielding his thoughts. "She fractured the kingdom when she imprisoned the shamanborn. None were spared, even among the reiwyn. It was not the wisest way to begin her rule."

"And now she's begun a war that few people in Evewyn want," Saengo says.

"You asked me once if my loyalties shifted," I say. Prince Meilek's eyes narrow. It was weeks ago; I'd been in Vos Gillis on a fool's errand to find Kendara and free the shamanborn imprisoned there. "My loyalty remains with Evewyn. Its people. Now, you have to make the same choice. What is Evewyn to you? Is your loyalty to your queen? Or to your people?"

He passes a weary hand over his face. "Mei is my sister. I never imagined I would have to choose between my family and my kingdom."

"Either way," Saengo says gently, "gathering your allies is a good idea. My father, for one, will condemn her actions, and others in the north will agree with him. Nearly every family on Phang lands has someone in the military, some of whom died in the attack at Ronin's gathering. Do you have paper and ink?" She rises from the cot as Kou retrieves the requested items from a desk drawer.

"What do you intend?" Kou asks.

She leans over the table, draws the lantern closer, and begins writing. "I'm asking my father to listen should Prince Meilek reach out. If it comes from me, he's more likely to agree."

Prince Meilek nods. "I appreciate that. Lord Phang would make a considerable ally."

"If my father sides with you, the other northern reiwyn will follow suit."

"Are you certain you won't come with us?" I ask. I tug at the collar of my shirt. It's warm, even with the window open. "It's not safe for you in Evewyn."

"I'll be fine, but I appreciate your concern. Are you hungry? I can have a tray brought up."

I shake my head. "There is something you could do for me, though, if it's within your power. I want to find out what happened to those at Spinner's End."

It's been weighing on my mind ever since we left the north. Priestess Mia confirmed that the Empire received correspondence from Spinner's End, so they're likely all right. But without Ronin, there's no way for them to leave the castle. And with the Soulless awake, I'm not sure how much longer they'll be safe.

"I know what happened," Prince Meilek says, surprising me. "I overheard Priestess Mia speaking with some of the other shamans. The shadowblessed sent a gate to retrieve what remains of Ronin's staff and soldiers."

Relief releases the tension in my shoulders. A gate is someone who can open shadow gates, allowing them to travel from one place to another in an instant. "When was this?"

"Last night. They were speaking in Nuval. I don't think they knew I could understand them."

After a few minutes, Saengo finishes her letter with a neat signature and then turns to me, one hand pressed lightly to her chest. My stomach lurches. Although I've been tending to her infection every evening to keep the rot in check, she says it still pains her sometimes.

"We should get back," I say, feeling suddenly awkward. It's bizarre speaking to Prince Meilek without Evewyn's rigid protocols. We aren't friends—at least, I don't think we are. But whatever our relationship, he is still my prince. And someday, my king. "Please . . . please take care of yourself. Evewyn needs you."

He remains in his seat, reclined against the wall, and half-obscured by shadow, but his eyes are alert and sharp. "And to you. All of Thiy needs you."

THREE

Mirrim is unlike anything I've ever seen.

Built into the side of a mountain, slim silver towers encircle the city, rising to such heights that it's a marvel they don't topple over. Multitiered roofs topped by spires crown homes that appear unevenly stacked atop one another, connected by sturdy, shining bridges and stairs that climb into the clouds. The city sprawls outward and upward in a way that defies logic.

The shaman capital of the Empire is easily thrice the size of Vos Talwyn. As we approach the gates and the outer wall, unease shivers through me. This is where we need to be, I assure myself. This is where I will find the answers I need to defeat the Soulless.

The land surrounding Mirrim is flat and lightly wooded,

allowing the watch towers a clear view of the horizon. Only a single mountain stands visible to the north. Mist drags along its jagged peaks. My craft stirs within me, and magic rushes to my fingertips, straining toward some unnameable power . . . a soul.

The lines of the mountain, the depressions of rock and earth, the trees that cluster around its base, the mist blurring its silhouette—they seem to shift, the entire mountain re-arranging into what could almost be a figure.

I blink rapidly and nudge Saengo. "Are you seeing this?"

When she doesn't respond, I glance over to find her watching the mountain as well, her mouth agape. So I haven't lost my mind.

"The Spirit of the Mountain," says Priestess Mia, a reverent hush to her voice. She slows her drake until she's riding alongside us. "When Suryal, the sun god, fell in battle, her remains gave birth to the three races of Thiy. The magic of the shamans, remnants of Suryal's soul, breathed life into the elements, awakening both the spirits of nature and the creatures that would become our familiars. The Spirit of the Mountain is all that remains of that ancient time. When Suri, the founder of our Empire, neared the end of her life, she sacrificed her magic to the mountain in order to create the barrier around Mirrim."

"So, it's true that only shamans can enter the capital." Although I'd read as much during my time in the Company, part of me wondered if the barrier was a lie the shamans had concocted to dissuade their numerous enemies from targeting Mirrim.

"It's true." She lifts her chin, her back growing ever straighter as she looks ahead toward Mirrim's looming white walls. "None may enter unless they are of shaman blood or given leave by the Ember Princess."

"So, if a shadowblessed merchant wanted to set up a shop within the city," I say, "or if a human relative wanted to visit their shaman cousin or some such, they would each have to go through the Ember Princess?"

"That's correct."

With such an inconvenience, it's a wonder anyone who isn't a shaman would want to visit the capital. "Why the Ember Princess?"

"Because she's also the current High Priestess of the Temple of Light. As a lightwender, you will be under her care."

House Yalaeng likely keeps that title close to the royal family. It's too powerful a position to trust to anyone else. Even if she wasn't the Light Temple's High Priestess, she's still one of the most powerful shamans in all the Empire. Once her brother, the Sun's Heir, takes the throne, she will become his First Advisor and the second-most-powerful shaman on the continent.

"The Spirit of the Mountain . . . she's beautiful," I say.

Clouds undulate around the mountain like hair billowing in a slight wind. Mist rising from a distant waterfall becomes the flutter of gauzy robes, treetops like emerald brocade. Then, the mountain settles, returning once again to indistinct patches of trees and ragged cliffs.

I can still sense her, though, a soul so immense and bright that it nearly eclipses my connection to Saengo. Curiously, I can also sense her soul's tether, but it isn't to a person. It's to the land. Her connection to the earth is too strong for me to break, allowing me the luxury of learning the strength and immensity of her soul without fear of ripping it from its mooring.

The low call of horns bellows from atop the city walls, announcing our arrival. The massive gates open. Carved reliefs of rearing dragokin resembling those ridden by the first and only true soulguide, Suri, flank each side. The connecting walls flow outward, the stones shaped like fish scales.

Saengo reaches for my hand. She is my anchor in a city bursting with souls. As our procession passes through the gate and I get my first unobstructed view of the city, my breath catches.

The streets teem with people and familiars, and every one of them is looking at me. I go rigid. Saengo squeezes my hand, and I remember to breathe.

The Nuvali don't cheer or shout. Instead, there's an

uncomfortable hush, as if they're waiting for something. The click of our drakonys's clawed feet against stone is loud in the strange silence. The Nuvali whisper to one another and point at me, the only other lightwender in our procession aside from Priestess Mia and the Light Temple guards.

Slowly, I force my body to relax into the saddle, although I can't control my heart thundering in my ears. Unlike in Luam, nearly all who've gathered are shamans. Gray-eyed children gawk as older shamans with jewel-bright eyes watch, their expressions ranging from curiosity to awe. Even their familiars pay attention, likely made aware of the strangeness through their shaman bond.

Something small strikes my leg. I instinctually reach for the swords on my back but quickly realize my mistake. I'm not being attacked. Another scatter of rice grains showers down on us, and I look up.

Nuvali crowd the wide lip of balconies and bridges that arch overhead. They grasp handfuls of rice from woven baskets, grinning as they fling the celebratory offering over our procession. This seems to free the others gathered along the streets, and their voices begin to rise in excitement. They speak in Nuval, so their words are lost to me, but I manage to pick out one word spoken again and again: *Suryali.* Little sun god.

I mentally cringe, but at least the general sentiment appears to be jovial. They've even decorated the streets for our arrival.

Thick ropes of woven sunflowers, hibiscus, and bamboo have been strung from building to building, forming a vibrant, fragrant canopy over our heads. Golden ribbons stream from nearly every window. Banners from the Temple of Light bearing brilliant golden sun rays adorn bridges and walls.

I attempt to appear pleasant, but really, I want to crawl into my own skin and shield the truth of my craft from their prying eyes.

Isn't this what you've always wanted? a part of me taunts. *To be acknowledged? To be seen?*

But they're not seeing *me.* What they see is a lie. Even the smile on my face is a mask, as thin and flimsy as the tether that holds a soul to a body. It's like I'm back at Sab Hlee with the shamanborn, their impossible expectations deposited at my feet. Except this is much worse.

Even as the murmur of the crowd grows, I can't help wondering how many of these people would gladly haul me to the executioner if they knew what I really am.

The streets are unnaturally smooth, probably the work of earthwenders. In fact, from the impossible towers of glass and bleached stone to the waterfalls cascading from hidden pools high above the ground, churning clouds of mist and scattering the evening sunlight, every part of the city boasts signs of shaman magic. Gilded birdfeeders hang from nearly every roof for familiars that can fly or climb. Flames burn in silver saucers without any noticeable fuel, and trees flourish on balconies, their flowering branches crawling over the walls and roofs in a strange mimicry of the Dead Wood.

The air is thick with magic and souls. It's too much. I lower my gaze, trailing my fingers down Yandor's cool scales. Something in the crowd catches my eye, the flash of an iridescent scale attached to a familiar scabbard.

It's there and gone in an instant. My heart climbs into my throat as I turn in my saddle and scan the crowd. I've never been allowed to touch Kendara's swords, but she wore them nearly always at her waist, and I would know them anywhere.

"What is it?" Saengo asks. Still gripping my hand, she turns to try and spot what I'm searching for.

I swallow back the surge of emotion—disappointment, anger, longing—and shake my head. I must have imagined it. "It's nothing."

The great gleaming dome of the Bright Palace rises in the north, capped by several huge spires. At the crest of the central spire is an elaborate sun with golden rays extending outward like an explosion of light.

The Bright Palace isn't our destination, though. Instead, we climb a gradually sloping path that weaves through homes of white-washed stone and vibrant blue roof tiles. The crowds grow thinner the farther we travel, although many follow in our wake, joining the procession.

At the top of the path stands a modest brick wall, and beyond it is the Temple of Light, a massive stone behemoth. White columns brace a multitiered roof, tiled in gold with ornate gables and an extravagant finial to rival the imperial palace's.

Figures dressed in pale robes move about the grounds, familiars trailing at their heels. Several kneel before the statue of a woman with long, loose hair and extravagant robes. She carries a sword in one hand and a sunflower in the other. A crown of golden rays circles her head. Another robed figure paces slowly about the temple, a censer swinging gently from her hand as curls of incense smoke lace the air.

Plain buildings stretch back through the temple grounds, but Priestess Mia stops our procession in the courtyard before the main temple. She dismounts smoothly, her movements as elegant as the rest of her. Her crisp white robes pool around her slippered feet. At once, a servant rushes forward to take her dragokin.

Saengo and I share a look—an unspoken agreement to watch our backs—and dismount. I roll my shoulders, taking comfort in the weight of my swords.

Those who followed us remain respectfully outside the temple grounds, draping garlands of sunflowers over the gates and calling out to me in Nuval. I wish I knew what they were saying, but part of me is glad to be spared the knowledge of their expectations. I'm thankful to escape them as Priestess Mia leads me and Saengo inside the temple.

The other priests and priestesses bow in deference as we pass. As far as I can tell, all of them are lightwenders. Even among those of the same Calling, I feel like a fraud.

Priestess Mia leads us past the statue of who I can only assume is Suryal, the sun god, and into the interior of the temple. We step out into a covered walkway that cuts through a walled garden. Lush trees and flowering bushes girdle a circuit of small connected ponds teeming with water lotus.

Gathered before one such pool is a gray-haired woman and a small group of five children, each no older than ten. Their familiars sprawl in the grass nearby, some of them eating lotus seed pods. The woman lifts her hands toward the sky, and warm sunlight fills her palms, bathing her face in golden light. The amber-eyed children clap excitedly, whispering and looking at their own hands.

"Light stitchers," I say, glancing at Saengo. Light stitchers can gather light in even the darkest of places. Many become renowned healers.

Although each Calling consists of three possible crafts, the Calling of Light is unique in that it has four: light stitcher, lightgiver, soulrender, and soulguide. The Light Temple hasn't been home to soulrenders for some time, and the founder of Mirrim is the only soulguide known to have existed. Even with only two crafts, the temple brims with shamans.

What had other lightwenders done when the Empire decided to eliminate an entire light craft? Did they stand aside, folding beneath the fear of retribution, as the humans did in Evewyn when the queen imprisoned the shamanborn?

To Priestess Mia, I ask, "Where are we going?"

"I'm taking you to your room."

"And then what?"

"Then," she says, arching one elegant eyebrow, "you will await the High Priestess."

Our room is a large chamber that opens directly into an enclosed courtyard.

Two beds stand at either wall, draped in layers of gauzy fabric. Thick rugs woven in eggshell blue and sunflower yellow cover the smooth tiles around them. The tiles continue into the courtyard where a glass-paneled roof arches over a domed stone pavilion sculpted in graceful swooping lines, like lace edging.

Beneath the pavilion, someone has prepared a modest spread. Steamed rice in bamboo baskets, fresh mango and papaya, saucers of thick coconut milk, and strips of seasoned meat, thinly sliced.

I set my bag on the rug and unbuckle my shoulder belt. I'm hungry, but I'm also exhausted, and the bed looks welcoming. But before I can decide which need to address first, our door opens.

A woman strides into our room followed by a sleek red fox with four bushy tails tipped in white. She doesn't announce herself, but I suppose there's no need. The Ember Princess wears an apricot spidersilk gown with sheer robes and a glittering sash. A crown of woven gold sits above her brow, and a thick band with cascading gold links and sunbursts hangs from her neck. Her eyes are a luminous amber, paler than my own, and her slick black hair is pulled away from her face into an elaborate braid threaded with gold ribbon.

She's beautiful in a way that doesn't seem real, like a painting brought to life. Precise streaks of crimson paint her eyelids, and her lips are stained in the same vibrant color as her gown.

Saengo recovers her composure first and dips into a deep bow. I follow suit, dropping my weapons at my feet.

Gliding past, the Ember Princess doesn't pause to greet us and heads directly for the pavilion. I watch, bemused, as she sits on a stone bench and arranges the considerable length of her robes around her so that she appears to be seated in a puddle of silk. Her fox familiar climbs onto the bench beside her and settles onto the silk, its tails fanning out around its slim body.

She smiles warmly and says, "Please, come sit. I've been in meetings all afternoon, and I'm starved."

Wary, I step out into the courtyard. The setting sunlight through the glass roof douses the corners of the area in shadow while bathing the rest in an eerie, orange glow.

The Ember Princess begins filling her plate at once, apparently content to serve herself. With a shrug at Saengo, I do the same. A wooden spoon with its handle carved to look like a crane rests atop the bamboo basket, and I use it to scoop the warm rice. It smells faintly sweet as if it's laced with honey.

"You may call me Kyshia," she says, lifting the pot of tea and pouring the steaming liquid into a dainty porcelain cup. It smells floral with an herbal undertone. Bangles of twisted gold circle her wrists, and delicate cuffs adorn the pointed tips of her ears. "Is this your first time in the Empire, Sirscha?"

Of course, she knows my name. Someone would have told her. "Yes. Saengo's as well."

Kyshia transfers her smile to Saengo. "I've heard of House Phang. Your falconers are renowned. You are both welcome in Mirrim." She pauses with her teacup halfway to her lips. "Is it true that you're a familiar?"

Saengo blinks once, clearly as puzzled about the protocol as I am. But, ever the reiwyn lady, she lifts her chin and replies calmly. "Yes. I am Sirscha's familiar."

"Remarkable," Kyshia murmurs, sipping her tea. Her other

hand caresses the red fur of her fox's head. "A human familiar has never before been recorded."

"We were promised your best stitchers once we arrived," I say. I saved Saengo from dying of the rot in the north, but it wasn't a cure.

"And you will have them," Kyshia says, which eases some of my uncertainty. "The infirmary is just north of the temple grounds. The Emperor's light stitcher will meet you there tomorrow."

"Thank you," I say.

She flicks her fingers as if it's a small thing. And maybe, to her, it is. "I'm not fond of the court's propensity to talk around a thing, or to soften a topic with pointless conversation, so I hope you'll forgive my bluntness."

I don't imagine she cares if I forgive her or not, but I say, "I appreciate that, actually."

I wonder how she and Theyen get along. They're still engaged, I assume.

"Then I'll get straight to it. I'm sorry to dampen the excitement of your arrival with ill news, but it can't wait. You'll recall what happened after the attack at Ronin's manor house when the Dead Wood . . . screamed, I believe is the word my advisors used." Her nose wrinkles in distaste, as if the Soulless's awakening is an undercooked chicken rather than the end of Thiy.

Saengo listens while taking delicate bites of fruit, and stomps her heel onto my toes beneath the table. My expression neutral, I jerk my foot out from beneath hers.

"Has the Spider King been found?" I ask.

"In a manner of speaking. There was a fire on the grounds, but his body was recovered. Murdered."

I push sticky grains of rice around my plate, my pulse quickening. There's no reason to believe she knows it was me. No one knows except me, Saengo, Prince Meilek, and Theyen. Her fiancé. But Theyen wouldn't have shared such a secret with her, not when he was at Spinner's End to dissolve their engagement.

"Murdered," I repeat, infusing the word with skepticism. "Who could have killed the Spider King?"

The Ember Princess dabs her mouth with a linen napkin and fixes her sharp amber eyes on mine. The slashes of color on her lids look like streaks of blood. Saengo's rising alarm rushes against my senses. The mental window I keep between us to block her emotions is firmly closed, but I feel her there, her panic fueling my own.

"This will sound ludicrous to you, but it was the very person Ronin once defeated," Kyshia says. Her sculpted brows lift as if daring me to argue. "The Soulless."

I affect a confused frown as the weight in my stomach lifts, and Saengo's alarm slowly recedes. After a length of silence,

I let out a small, disbelieving laugh. "That's impossible."

"He's been dead for centuries," Saengo adds.

"Actually, he hasn't. The Spider King has kept him asleep at Spinner's End for nearly six centuries. We've certainly tried to kill him, but nothing worked. To be honest, I think my predecessors simply accepted the situation as a working solution and left the problem for a future Emperor."

This time, my surprise is real. I throw up my hands in a plea for her to stop speaking because I'm still reeling. "Wait. You *knew?* You knew the Soulless was alive at Spinner's End this whole time?"

The Ember Princess brushes a grain of rice off her sleeve and sighs dramatically. "After centuries, we believed the danger had passed. Or if not passed, then had at least become manageable. And the secret had to be maintained to protect Ronin's power. Without him, we would . . . well. We would be right where we are now, with no one to control the Dead Wood and the Soulless, who's doubtlessly preparing to avenge himself."

My fingers curl into fists that I rest firmly on the tabletop to keep from doing anything rash. They knew.

She tilts her head, tapping her finger against her chin. An elaborate gold ring sits on both her middle and ring fingers, set with a series of glimmering yellow stones. "It's been so long since a Yalaeng has been to Spinner's End that I didn't quite believe it was even true. Until now, of course."

"Now that he's awake," I say flatly. Knowing the Soulless was alive, the Ember Princess must've suspected why Ronin was losing control over the Dead Wood. The Empire might have even surmised the Soulless was the cause of the rot.

And yet, even as familiars continued to die, they did nothing. Said nothing—all to protect an ancient secret that would rightly destroy their people's trust in them. I close my eyes briefly, long enough to compose myself and avoid betraying my anger. Beside me, Saengo is rigid, her blank gaze fixed at a point past Kyshia's shoulder. But her fury rivals my own.

Had House Yalaeng killed the Soulless when they had the chance, neither of us would be here.

Kyshia continues, her attention focused on rolling the thin meat slices to slide them whole into her mouth. "The Soulless must be dealt with quickly and quietly. Very few people know that he's risen. We've deflected questions about Ronin and what happened in the Dead Wood with half-truths. We must eliminate this threat before the secret is exposed."

She feeds a piece of meat to her familiar, who watches me through round golden eyes.

I straighten my shoulders, and some of my disgust bleeds into my voice. "So let me get this straight—"

"Sirscha," Saengo says. A warning.

I relax my jaw, reminding myself that I'm speaking to one of the most powerful shamans on the continent. As next in line to be the Emperor's First Advisor, she could bring the whole of the Empire down on us if she wished.

After her aunt, her father's First Advisor, died last year, the Ember Princess took on much of a First's duties, acting as her father's voice and hands beyond court. But, due to the Empire's traditions of succession, she's unable to claim the title until her brother takes the throne.

Kyshia glances up at me through the thick fan of her lashes, a smile curling her stained lips. Anger burns in my throat.

I ignore Saengo's heel digging into my foot and say, "House Yalaeng knew about the Soulless for centuries, did nothing about it, and now you want me to fix it for you."

"You're a soulguide," Kyshia says simply. "The first to appear since Suri founded Mirrim. And now, one of the most powerful enemies the Empire has ever faced has awoken. This is no coincidence, Sirscha. You were meant to help us. And you'll have the whole of the Empire supporting you. You won't be alone."

I nearly roll my eyes at this ridiculous assertion, but stop myself. There's no need to draw suspicion to the possibility I'm not a soulguide.

Saengo saves me by saying, "Can you tell us what you know of the Soulless? If Sirscha is to defeat him, then we need as much information as possible."

"Did he have a familiar?" I ask.

A line appears between her brows, and she rests her hand between her familiar's ears. "Shamans and familiars share a sacred bond. Attacking another shaman's familiar is a grave sin. You risk angering the gods, and your soul would wear that stain even into the afterlife."

It's a sacrifice I'm willing to make if it means curing Saengo.

"Regardless, I don't know what his familiar was. Priestess Mia is our Scholar of History at the Temple of Light. She'll have read any surviving texts from that time, so you'll want to speak with her. Something Scholars have argued about, though, is whether he extracted his soul and hid it within a talisman so he couldn't be killed."

Thus the title of the Soulless, I suppose.

My fingers close around the collar of my shirt as if the mere thought might loosen the seams of my soul. The idea makes my skin crawl. I find it hard to believe the Soulless powerful enough to rip out his *own* soul and survive, and I'm reluctant to accept anything Kyshia says without proof.

"Ronin was supposedly in possession of the Soulless's talisman when he subdued him," she continues.

Meaning, if it exists, the Soulless would've recovered it. "Has anyone actually *seen* this talisman?"

"We've only written accounts to rely on," she says.

I glance at Saengo, who sips daintily at her tea. Though the shamans would see it as sacrilege, severing the Soulless from whatever connects him to his magic is the best means of defeating him.

Wouldn't Ronin have done that, though, if it were so simple? What if the Soulless's familiar is trapped within the Dead Wood alongside all the other souls? It would be impossible to find. One soul among countless others.

As a sower, Ronin wouldn't have possessed the ability to sense the Soulless's magic, nor his familiar.

But maybe another soulrender could.

FOUR

The sun has fully set by the time the Ember Princess leaves, and a servant clears away the meal.

Saengo and I eagerly bathe in the adjoining washroom and then change into clean clothing we find in the armoire. I slip on a simple gray tunic and loose pants with matching robes, over which I knot a plain white sash. It's the same outfit I'd seen others in the Temple wearing, but the soft fabric feels indulgent compared to the coarse fibers of our old Company uniforms.

"Let me take a look," I say, gesturing for Saengo to join me at the edge of her bed.

She makes a face, fingers fidgeting with the troll-bone bracelet at her wrist—Kendara's last gift to me. Depending on the creature whose bones are used, talismans have a number of purposes. The troll-bone talisman is meant to protect against magic, so I gave it to Saengo to help slow the rot's spread.

Born of the Dead Wood, the rot emerged from the Soulless's corrupt magic that seeped so deeply into the trees and the souls trapped there that it spread to others, namely familiars. In the decades since the disease first appeared, no light stitcher has been able to cure it.

Saengo tugs down her collar. The rot is a livid knot of bright blue veins extending from the center of her chest. The sight always makes my gut tighten with fury and fear. Saengo releases a soft, shaking breath as my fingers brush her skin as if I could sweep away the infection. Her soul's candle flame brightens within me as I grasp it. She stiffens, inhaling sharply. Her hands grip my shoulders hard enough to sting, but neither of us pulls away. There's no fear of ripping her soul free. She's tethered to me, our connection shimmering between us, strong and sure.

My magic flows into her, filling the cracks in her soul where the rot has worn her away. Her fingers dig into my skin, biting through my sleeves.

At last, she sags against me before tipping onto her bed with a sigh. "I know it's necessary, but it always feels so strange."

I lean over her, pulling at her collar again. The blue lines of infection have diminished into a tight bundle at her chest.

She smiles wearily and slaps my hand away before brushing damp hair off her cheek. "Will you rest?"

Although I'm tired, after speaking with Kyshia, my thoughts are too restless to find sleep. I kneel beside my things on the floor. Phaut's sword, still wrapped in cloth, is tucked beneath my bag. I pick it up, hefting its weight. Brushing back the cloth from the pommel, my fingers find the ornate curls and rivets of the metalwork.

I'd found the sword near the riverbank where Phaut died. I could've sent it on with the party who returned her body to her family, but it hadn't felt right. Her death is my responsibility. I need to return the sword to her father, even if that means facing his judgment.

Prince Meilek, who recovered Phaut's body, assured me that her family would be informed of the circumstances. She died defending the soulguide, a worthy end for a warrior and an honor for her family. But I doubt her family viewed it as such. In their position, I wouldn't. Phaut should not have died in the first place. I should have protected her.

Standing, I grip the sword and turn to face Saengo. At the sight of it, she slowly sits up.

Her brows pull together, pain and regret tightening the skin around her eyes. "Do you think she would have forgiven you for killing Ronin?"

In truth, I don't know. Phaut had been my friend, but she was also loyal to the Spider King. I'm not sure she would have believed me had I told her the truth of his plans.

"Doesn't matter now," I say quietly, wishing it were otherwise. "I couldn't save her, but I can do this, at least."

Saengo nods and slips on her boots. I do the same, tucking my pant legs into my knee-high leather. Then, I strap my swords to my back and belt Phaut's at my waist.

Although we're forced to take a pair of Light Temple guards with us, no one objects to us going into the city. That's something, I suppose. Part of me wondered if they meant to confine us to the Temple of Light.

Phaut once mentioned that, after she pledged her service to Ronin, her father sold the farm and moved to Mirrim with her sister. She described a view of the Temple of Wind and how her father found work as an assistant to a cartographer. While the Light Temple guards aren't familiar with the cartographer, they know how to reach the Temple of Wind. They guide us through the city's winding streets, illuminated by the soft glow of lanterns.

Although the sun has set and the crowds from earlier are gone, the city hasn't yet quieted. Carriages clatter past, pulled by drakes. Soldiers bearing the Nuvali sun on their breastplates patrol in pairs. Shamans on a corner perform a show with streams of glimmering water and ribbons of fire, as onlookers toss coins into a metal tin. Familiars scamper between feet and along rooftops, moving freely through a city that reveres them. Shopkeepers haul their wares indoors, closing for the evening as taverns and teahouses throw their doors open in welcome.

In our Light Temple clothing, no one seems to suspect who we are. We're generally ignored as we pass beneath bridges lit by floating lanterns and trees strung with tiny silver bells that sing every time the wind shifts.

"What did you think of Kyshia?" Saengo asks. She's squinting at the shining dome of the Bright Palace that rises above the curling roof tiles.

"Criminally beautiful," I say, quiet enough that the Light Temple guards won't overhear. Saengo suppresses a grin. She's probably blushing. "But I'm certain she uses that to her advantage. I think she likes catching people off guard to see how they'll react."

"With all this talk of war between the kingdoms, I can't imagine the Nuvali will embrace a Kazan prince as her husband. They seem like they would have a . . . volatile marriage."

I laugh. "They would murder each other within a week."

Saengo shrugs one shoulder. "Maybe they wouldn't. Maybe they'd grow to respect one another. Or even fall in love."

The idea of Theyen and Kyshia falling in love is so absurd I almost snort, but I catch the wistful twist of Saengo's mouth. So instead, I reach out and hook my arm around hers.

"Once you're cured—"

"Don't," Saengo says, pulling away. She averts her face, letting the short ends of her hair shield her eyes. "Who would have me as I am, Sirscha? I'm not even real."

The guilt that hangs ever around my neck coils tighter. "Don't say that. Of course you are. And anyone with a heart would have you. The Ember Princess herself would be lucky to have your attention."

Saengo begins to shake her head, but then one of the guards says, "There's the Temple of Wind."

Sure enough, a wooden gate blocks a path leading up to a temple nearly the size of the Temple of Light. Its roof tiles are arranged in undulating waves, ebbing downward from a central spire. A statue of a woman, her hair and clothing caught in an invisible wind and arm extended toward the sky, stands in the courtyard. A massive bird of prey is perched on her forearm, wings outstretched as if preparing to take flight.

"The statue is of Cua," one of the guards says. "She was a member of Suri's inner circle of shamans from each Calling. Together, they founded Mirrim and established each of the temples. It's said that Cua could fly on wind currents and ride the clouds."

Magic must have been more powerful then, back when it could animate the elements and bring to life the spirit of a mountain.

"Can windwenders still—" Something flashes at the edge of my vision, and I turn in time to catch the glint of serpent scales and the curve of a pommel before the cloaked figure, and their familiar sword, vanishes into shadows. It isn't my imagination this time. "Stay here."

"Sirscha?" Saengo calls, but I'm already moving.

I dart across the street, leaping onto the nearest ledge and then up to the roof. Behind me, the Light Temple guards shout, darting after me, but they're too slow. My boots whisper over the ridge of the roof. My heart pounds.

When I reach the lip of the building, I turn in a circle, scanning the alleys below, my breath loud in my ears. A shadow slips behind a gate, and my feet race into motion again. I swing from the roof, finding purchase on a terrace before dropping to the ground. Then I'm running, the darkness a familiar friend as I burst through the gate to see the flutter of a cloak vanish around a corner.

Breathless, I give chase, frustration building with every turn, every dead end, every alley, empty save for the rustling of nocturnal birds.

Finally, I collapse against a brick wall and slam my fists into the stone. My heart climbs up my throat. With a furious inhale, I hiss the name I'm too afraid to hope for: "Kendara."

"Hello, idiot girl."

FIVE

A figure stands at the end of the alley, her hood lowered around her shoulders.

"Took you long enough," she says in that beloved rasp. My throat closes, emotion rising hot in my cheeks. "I thought I taught you better."

The meager light from a distant lantern outlines the crown of her head, where her hair has been pulled tightly back. As ever, the upper portion of her face is concealed beneath a black handkerchief. The rest of her is obscured in shadows save for the gleam of her favorite swords at her waist. She'd been in the crowd earlier today, watching our arrival.

I swallow thickly, a myriad of emotions bubbling in my gut. Joy. Pain. Anger. My fists remain balled at my sides, still stinging from striking the wall.

"Are you going to say something or just stand there like a buffoon?" she asks, stepping closer.

The tightness in my chest is unbearable. I want to hug her. I want to scream at her. I do none of these things, as even now, I know she wouldn't tolerate it.

I somehow manage to speak with only a slight waver of my voice. "When you fled Evewyn, you came here?"

You left me, a voice inside me shouts. It sounds small and childish. *You left me to deal with all of this alone. You were supposed to look after me. You made a promise.*

I press my lips tightly to contain the words. *Get it together, Sirscha.*

"Obviously," she says, crossing her arms. Despite her years, she stands straight and tall, her strength as unwavering as it has always been. Yet, everything about her, who I believed her to be, has changed.

Even the handkerchief concealing her face and the barest edges of scarring beneath takes on new meaning. Kendara's blindness isn't a façade. But has she always been blind? Or did she give up her eyes—the irrefutable proof of a shaman—when she left for Evewyn? If I dared to look, I'd probably find scars along the curves of her ears, much like my own.

"Who . . . who are you? Really." What was her Calling? Her craft? Did she have a familiar, or did she give that up too? Kendara is more than capable without magic, but did she miss it while she was in Evewyn? There's so much I don't know about her.

Kendara snorts in disgust. Part of me wants to lower my head and apologize, to please her even now. But she's no longer my mentor and has no control over my future or my choices.

"Wouldn't you rather know about your mother?" she asks.

I close my eyes, only for a moment, hesitant to look away should she vanish again into the night. I do want to know about my mother, but I need other answers first.

"I'm asking about you right now," I say.

"Then you'll be disappointed. I left that person behind a long time ago. I chose this life, knowing it would cost everything because I wanted to serve a greater purpose."

As everything is with Kendara, her words are a lesson. If you set yourself on a path, you must be willing to make the sacrifices to see it through. I think about what still lies ahead, of what I need to do to face the Soulless—of what sacrifices I might yet need to make. A weight sinks in my gut.

"So you did what was necessary to pass as a human and won the place of Shadow to King Senbyn, and then to his daughter. And all that time, you remained loyal to the Empire."

"The Shadow is allowed information and freedoms no other Evewynian can match," she says. "It was the ideal position."

A faraway voice rises above the rooftops, shouting my name. I frown, feeling the frantic currents of Saengo's emotions.

I want to go to her, but I can't let Kendara leave. Not yet.

"Saengo Phang," Kendara says, plucking her name like she's criticizing the syllables. "After how long I've lived, I'm not easily surprised. But when I heard you turned your friend into a familiar, I was truly shocked."

I stiffen. "How do you know about that?"

She waves a dismissive hand. "Don't sound so surprised. You're not a complete twit. You know it's my job to uncover secrets."

"I noticed," I mutter. She's always known things she's no business knowing.

"It won't end well between you two."

I scowl and push away from the wall, angry for allowing such weakness before her. "You're wrong," I say, proud of the conviction in my voice.

Kendara shrugs. "You always preferred to learn things the hard way."

I shake my head. It's pointless to argue. Kendara is a realist, which I grudgingly admit is part of why I love her. She never glosses the truth as she sees it, though sometimes I wish she would.

"Like the fact that I'm a shaman? Why didn't you ever tell me? After I awoke my craft, why didn't you find me? You just disappeared and left me with a letter rather than face me yourself."

Even though her letter claimed she loved me, I don't think I can believe it. In all the years I was her pupil, she did her best to smother any signs of affection between us.

Kendara's tone is biting. "I was your mentor, not your keeper. I taught you what you needed to take care of yourself. When Ronin discovered the truth, he and the queen plotted against us both. So I left."

If nothing else, it's reassuring to know she didn't tell the queen about me. But Kendara hasn't revealed herself to me now because she misses me.

"Why are we speaking then?" I ask, crossing my arms to mirror her posture.

"Because you still have time to make a choice."

"What choice?"

Again, Saengo's voice calls from nearby, closer now.

Kendara makes an impatient sound. "Whether you want to hear it or not, I need to tell you about your mother. She was my friend."

I snap my mouth shut, swallowing my retort.

"My last friend, the only one who refused to be cut from my new life. She was a soulrender, and when her family discovered her craft, they moved her to the countryside. They kept her powers hidden, so she never trained to control it. After she accidentally exposed her craft, she was jailed to await an imperial escort for her execution in Mirrim."

"You saved her," I say, trying to reconcile that with the hard-edged woman standing before me.

"How could I not? At the time, I was still in training to become the next Shadow, but I'd left her means to contact me. After receiving her plea, I hurried back to the Empire and caught up with her escort before they could reach Mirrim."

My fingers find the pommel of Phaut's sword. She used to touch it when she felt uneasy. "And the rest of her family?"

"Dead," Kendara says without inflection. "Following the law of the Empire, they were executed for birthing a soulrender. I meant to go back for them, but it was too late."

I swallow, bitterness coating my tongue. I assumed my mother was shamanborn. The thought of finding family in the Empire hadn't even occurred to me until this moment. Yet, the loss of what could have been swells through me. Saengo is the closest person to a family I have. And Kendara, much as she seemingly wishes to disavow me.

"And your friend?" It's too strange to say "my mother" out loud. It doesn't feel real.

"I left her somewhere safe and checked in on her as often as I could until I found the fool girl pregnant. I offered to kill the man responsible, but she insisted it was consensual and that she wanted you. She refused to leave you the way she was forced to leave everyone else."

I want to believe that the harsh rasp of her words is to

disguise the emotion beneath. But I've always wanted to read more into Kendara's words and actions than was actually there.

I reach up to trace the faint scars lining my ears. "But she did."

"Not by choice. The Empire found her shortly after you were born. She died refusing to tell them who helped her escape. In return for saving her life, she saved mine." Anger lingers beneath her voice, the resigned ire of old wounds. With each word, her voice grows quieter. "I hunted them down and silenced them before they could reveal to others that she'd had a child."

"It was you," I whisper, my fingers still hovering at my ears.

"I had no choice. I didn't know who else might know about you. If more shamans came looking, they would mistake you for human."

I always thought I was abandoned at the orphanage. Unwanted. A girl with no true name save what the monks gave me in mockery. I'm not sure how to reconcile Kendara's story with the one I've always believed.

My mother had loved me. If the Empire hadn't found her, what sort of life might I have had? I push away the thought. There's no use lingering on what can't be changed.

An ember sears beneath my ribs, but I don't know where to direct my anger. Kendara killed those responsible. But they were sent by the Empire. By House Yalaeng.

They would kill me without hesitation if they knew the truth, just as they have whole families. All because of one shaman. I lower my hands before me, palms upright, as if I might see the truth of my craft peering out from beneath the lines.

My mother accidentally revealed herself because she never learned to control her craft. What if what's happening to me isn't because of the Soulless? What if it's just me . . . losing control?

"You should've told me all of this sooner," I say, dropping my hands to my sides. Saengo's voice calls my name again, close enough that I can also hear the voices of the Light Temple guards.

"I hoped to never tell you. It wasn't important then."

Her words ignite that ember in my ribs, burning away the ache and sadness, leaving only anger. "You knew who I was, and you lied to me. You've lied to me from the moment we met."

Kendara huffs, annoyed. "Clearly, my lessons about containing your emotions didn't take. I didn't lie about everything. You're a gifted fighter, Sirscha. And you are tenacious as well."

I hate the way her words settle within me, taking root. All I want is to tear them loose. Even after all the lies, a part of me still aches for her approval.

"It was for your protection. I don't expect you to understand," she says.

"Stop talking down to me," I hiss. "I deserve the truth."

"I'm not your mother, and I don't owe you anything but the promise I made to her. I prepared you as best I could. You think you know everything now, and that you're ready for every truth just because you murdered someone?"

I flinch. I'm not sure if she's talking about what I did at the teahouse or if she knows I killed Ronin. But to hear her snap about not being my mother stings like a physical blow. Of course she isn't, but she's the closest to one I've ever had, which she damn well knows.

Slowly, spitting every word through my teeth, I say, "Murder is what you taught me to do."

Kendara is silent for a moment. Then she turns on her heel and pulls her hood back over her hair. "You stupid girl," she says roughly. "I taught you to *survive*, not to throw your life away for an Empire that would sooner see you dead than thank you."

She's angry, which catches me off guard. My own fury dampens. I've rarely seen her angry.

She glances over her shoulder. "It isn't too late to walk away. You still have a choice."

"This is the choice? You said you taught me to survive. To prepare me."

She throws up her hands and looks away again. "It's a pity you didn't pick up the wisdom to know when to act and when to walk away. You're too damn stubborn. Still too afraid that walking away means failing."

"So you'd rather me and Saengo just . . . disappear? What about the Soulless? Saengo isn't healed yet, and we can't leave until he's dead."

Kendara nods once. "You were never tied up in all of this with oaths and secrets, not like me. But if you mean to stay, then I won't have any part in seeing you throw away the life your mother died to give you."

She strides up the alley, back toward the shadows.

"Kendara," I say, my voice breaking.

She doesn't stop. A fresh wave of betrayal burns up my throat and scalds my eyes. I've always hated leaving Kendara because it was never guaranteed that she would call me back. Now, watching her walk away, it feels like an ending I'm not prepared for.

"Your cartographer is here," she says, gesturing to the back of the nearest building where the glow of a lantern flickers within a second-story window.

Then she slips around a corner, and she's gone.

SIX

Saengo and the Light Temple guards find me a minute later, alone in the darkened alley.

Blood roars in my ears, every muscle in my body coiled tight, ready to spring after Kendara and demand . . . what? That she stay? It's an unreasonable and childish reaction, and I know it. Her only obligation to me was the promise she made to my mother, and she fulfilled it.

When Saengo sees me, she pauses for a heartbeat. She doesn't ask for an explanation, only rushes forward and puts her arms around my shoulders. I push down the anger, the self-pity, and the pain that squeezes at my throat. The Light Temple guards linger at a distance, uncertain of what's happened.

"The cartographer." I force out the words and inject my voice with a sense of calm I don't feel. "I found him."

To their credit, the guards don't complain about my running off. They simply follow us from the alley, watching me warily. At the front of the building, we find a bookshop. The wooden likeness of a partially unfurled scroll hangs above the door alongside a lantern and the name Winimar Books.

I grip the hilt of Phaut's sword. I have a task to complete, and I can't dishonor her memory by wallowing in my own troubles. I'm meant to be doing this for her.

"It's open," Saengo says, turning the knob. A bell chimes above the entryway as she pushes the door wide.

Inside, the shop is cluttered but warm. Every wall is lined in bookshelves and piles of scrolls spill out onto tables. Sconces burn at either side of the back wall where a map of the Empire is mounted and framed. Beneath it sits a table, littered with parchment, bottles of ink, and stacks of books, some lying open as if someone was reading and then walked away.

An emerald and magenta hummingbird rests within a wooden birdhouse hanging from the ceiling. Presumably a familiar. The shaman it belongs to sits behind a counter, scrawling notes into a ledger. His neat black hair dusts the collar of his plain, navy robes.

He says something in Nuval, probably a reminder of their closing time, but one of the guards cuts him off in Evewal. "We're on an errand from the Temple of Light."

The man lifts two bushy, graying eyebrows, and with an

air of resignation, lowers his pen and rises from his chair. Emerging from behind the counter, he drops into a bow, and replies in stilted Evewal, "How can I be of service?"

"Are you Winimar?" I ask. When he confirms that he is, I continue. "I'm looking for a man in your employ. I'm afraid I don't know his name, but he has two daughters. One of them goes by Phaut. Can you tell us where he lives?"

Winimar's smile wilts, something like pain pulling at the corners of his mouth. He seems to struggle to find the words in Evewal but manages to say, "I hate to be the bearer of ill news, but Phaut . . ."

"I know," I say gently, unbuckling her sword from my belt. "This was hers. I wish to return it to her father." And apologize for failing to protect her.

Winimar only shakes his head and lowers his eyes in genuine sorrow. "He left Mirrim to see to her burial and stay with his brother up north. I'm afraid I don't know when he'll be back."

"Oh." I lower the sword, disappointment spearing through me.

"But!" he adds quickly. "His daughter Juleyne works as a guard at the Bright Palace and stops by to check in on me once a week. I'd be glad to give her the sword for you. What did you say your name is?"

I don't like the idea of passing on the task to someone else.

Phaut's family will have been told how she died, but I was there. I wanted to tell her father how brave and loyal she was, how she became a friend and defended me to the end.

But maybe that's selfish. Maybe by trying to make amends, I would only be putting him and the rest of his family through more pain. I don't know what the right thing to do is, but if he won't return for some time, there isn't much choice.

With reluctance, I hand him the sword. "My name is Sirscha."

His eyes widen, those thick brows shooting up his forehead. "As in, the soulguide?" He hastily bows again, lower this time. "You honor me with your presence."

I try not to grimace. "Please, it's quite all right. I'm sorry to have troubled you."

"Not at all." He turns away, gently setting the sword on the counter, and then makes a broad gesture around his shop. "Is there anything else I can help you with? Anything at all."

"There is one thing," Saengo says, stepping forward. "Would you happen to have any books about the Empire from around, say, six hundred years ago?"

Winimar taps his fingers against the counter, considering. "I don't think so. But if you're interested in old texts, you might like this."

He rushes to the back of the shop and grins as he slides out a framed diagram from beneath a pile of parchment. It's much smaller than the map on the wall, but he hands it over proudly.

"This is one of my oldest specimens. I should really organize this." He gestures at the table.

"What is it?" I ask, holding it up so the others can see. It looks like a crudely drawn floor plan.

"An early draft for the construction of the Temple of Light," he says.

"Really?" one of the guards says, peering over my shoulder. "It looks different seeing it from the top like this."

I tilt my head at the shape of the main temple, the connecting corridors, and adjoining rooms. "Is it me, or does the arrangement almost look like someone sleeping on their side?"

"You've a sharp eye," Winimar says. "That was deliberate. Whoever designed the Temple of Light wanted the entire building to be an homage to Suryal the Sleeper."

"Sleeper?" I repeat, handing him back the diagram. "I've never heard her called that."

"It's an archaic title." He sets the diagram on a nearby shelf for display. "It fell out of use during Emperor Orin's reign, about a century after the construction of the five temples. You know the story of the Fall of Suryal?"

Saengo and I shake our heads as the Light Temple guards nod. We weren't taught Empire history or mythology at the Company, certainly not with Queen Meilyr's hatred of shamans.

"It's a long story. The pertinent part is that nearly all the world had been destroyed by the Devourer, a creature born of humankind's greed. Only Suryal took pity on the realm and challenged the Devourer. And while she succeeded in destroying it, the battle took her life as well. As she lay dying, she willed the last of her magic to restore humankind. From her blood came the shadowblessed, from her bone the humans, and from the fragments of her soul, the shamans were born.

"Although she fell, part of her consciousness, some essence of her soul, lived on, which is why some of her followers began calling her the Sleeper, as they believed she would awaken someday. Sometimes, the very lucky are even blessed with dreams about her."

Winimar tells the story with buoyant energy, but I'm unable to summon the same enthusiasm. Instead, there's a sick feeling at the back of my throat. Suryal. Suryali.

It's an uncomfortable comparison, and one wrongly made. I'm not even a soulguide.

Here, in the heart of the Empire, I must be careful to contain my magic and my words.

Maybe Kendara is right. Maybe I'm still too afraid to fail. Not only in regard to Saengo, but in what the shamans want of me. Otherwise, why would I risk coming here?

I rub my forehead and thank Winimar for his help. Saengo links her arm with mine, at once reminding me of our purpose here. What anyone else expects from me doesn't matter. I'm not their soulguide. My only task is to defeat the Soulless and save my best friend.

I wish I knew what the Soulless even wants. The most powerful evils can only be driven by something equally powerful. Like fear. Or love.

Maybe he doesn't want anything at all. Maybe he'll remain at Spinner's End and enjoy the rest of his days in peace and solitude. And maybe I'll sprout wings and a tail and go live with the wyverns.

I close my eyes, leaning into Saengo as we make the trek back to the temple. We rest our heads together, exhausted from a long day.

If only I could speak to the Soulless so that I can be better prepared for whatever he has planned. But that would be too easy. Admittedly, I want to speak with him partially out of morbid curiosity.

What would a shaman that old and powerful have to say? If the history books are to be believed, the Soulless went mad. But, knowing how the Empire has hidden the truth, I'm learning to be skeptical of what history books say when written by those with the power to alter them.

SEVEN

The lucky are blessed with dreams of Suryal. My dreams aren't blessed. They're cursed.

The souls went quiet in the aftermath of the Soulless's awakening. I'm not sure what that means, and I imagine part of it is the distance I put between myself and the Dead Wood. Still, after so many nights plagued by restless souls, I've learned to distinguish when I'm dreaming.

It's not like before, nebulous and dark, with hands grasping from a shadowy maw. Instead, I'm standing inside the greenhouse at Spinner's End.

It looks much the same, overlaid in dust and in disrepair. Fibrous webbing covers the windows in patches, and columns run the length of either side. The difference is the spider's web at the opposite end of the greenhouse. It's thicker and larger than before, sprawled across the ceiling and floor, thick ropes of white webbing stretching from wall to wall.

At its center hangs the Soulless's cocoon, half speckled with moss that has blackened into rot, shedding shriveled flower petals. A bright red stain streaks the front of my tunic. I'm wearing the same clothes from the night I killed Ronin.

The cocoon begins to tremble. Heart pounding, I back away and reach for swords that aren't there. All the energy and fear of that night rushes back, sending my pulse racing and thinning the air in my lungs. The cocoon's casing stretches and distorts like something inside is trying to break free.

Panic seizes me. I turn to run, but in place of the door is only a seamless expanse of wall, laced with cobweb. I slam my palms against the stone, skin stinging, and then turn again to face the cocoon.

This is only a dream. Only a dream.

The cocoon rips open. Loose dirt spills from within, cascading to the floor. Spiders explode from the tear, dozens of them, small and quick, skittering in every direction. I step back, my heel bumping the wall, as gaunt fingers emerge from the cocoon. They push at the ragged opening, spilling more grave dirt and bits of broken roots.

A face follows, pale and hollow-cheeked. It's the same face I'd seen when I first opened the cocoon, but within the dream, he looks altered. Long black hair, matted with earth, winds around his neck and shoulders like a tattered shawl. His veins streak green and stark beneath his ashen skin as if the dregs of Ronin's venom still linger in his blood.

He thrusts one arm free, and then the other. His shirt is frayed, eaten through by decay, and crusted with rot. Whatever hue it might have been has long since faded to a colorless gray.

"Sirscha." His voice is a whispered rasp that scrapes my nerves.

I close my eyes and press my palms to my temples. "Get out of my head."

"But you wanted to speak to me."

My eyes fly open, something sick and sinking opening in my stomach. "No. You're not real."

"As real as any dream, and I've known nothing but dreams for a very long time." He climbs from the cocoon, his movements strained and jerky, as if he's relearning his own limbs. Spiders flee from the folds of his ragged robes.

The entire web begins to shift and extend. Threads loosen and sag, slowly lowering the cocoon to the floor of the greenhouse. When the Soulless at last steps free of his prison, his foot touches solid earth.

He takes one slow, quivering step away from the cocoon and then another, a pale specter trailing grave dirt. Somehow, he's more terrifying than the broken bodies spat from the depths of the Dead Wood. Yet, beneath the fear lies a tremor of what I'd felt back in Spinner's End—the call of a nameless power, beckoning me to answer.

I back up until my spine presses against cold stone, wishing for nothing more than the ability to flee this nightmare.

"What do you want?" I ask. This is only a dream, yet all of my senses feel the weight of this place and of *him*. My boots scrape over stone gritty with dirt. A trickle of cold sweat teases the back of my neck, and there's a bitter aftertaste in my mouth.

The air smells dry and musty. Once, when Kendara sent me down a mineshaft in the Coral Mountains, the air smelled like this. Old. Stale. A pocket of trapped time.

Whatever this dream is, it's a well-wrought illusion.

The Soulless doesn't move, but his bloodless lips stretch into a smile. Everything about him is pallid and unnerving, save for the vibrant, crystalline sheen of his amber eyes. He makes a small gesture to the room. "In my position, what would *you* want?"

"To rest in peace?"

He laughs, a dry scraping sound. "How can I rest in peace when the people who created me still hold power in the Empire?"

Created? My thoughts snag on the word, and suddenly, terror transforms into purpose.

If this is really happening, if he's somehow speaking with me and this isn't just a wild concoction of my imagination, then I'd be a fool not to take advantage. Determination straightens my shoulders, shaking loose from the grip of fear.

I push away from the wall, fists clenched. "What do you mean by that? What is House Yalaeng to you?"

"They've ruled for as long as Nuvalyn has existed. You don't hold on to power for that long without a few buried skeletons."

"Skeletons like you," I say. His magic scours lightly at my mental walls, hooks dragged over flesh just waiting to catch. There are secrets hidden within that power, teasing the unknown. I lift my chin, willing away the sensation.

A tremor races through him, and his form ripples like a pebble disturbing still water. I blink to clear my eyes, wary. His jaw tightens, the veins bright and ghastly beneath his skin. Then everything realigns, and he's whole again, those amber eyes fixed on me.

Realization strikes. He is weak. Weak enough that he's struggling to maintain this illusion, this dreamscape fashioned by the bridge of our craft.

When he speaks, his voice is barely above a whisper. But his gaze is intense and consuming, like I'm the sun and he's been starved of light. "Ask yourself why House Yalaeng kept my presence here a secret. Do you really think an Empire built on conquest, again on the brink of war, did it to keep the peace?"

"Because Ronin lied about killing you. But he was the only person who could control the Dead Wood and keep you asleep. They had to uphold the lie."

"That would make sense if you knew little about soulrenders and House Yalaeng," he says.

"Then enlighten me."

My sarcasm seems to amuse him. He tilts his head. A crust of dirt slides from the tangle of hair that twines around his neck. "Most soulrenders aren't strong enough to rip human souls. The power is rare, and every time we do, it costs a little bit of our own souls. Our craft was never meant to be used against humans. But House Yalaeng has never accepted that they couldn't do something. They have always seen our powers as a weapon of war."

The only human soul I've ripped was the knife thrower's, back at Ronin's northern holding. I hadn't done it intentionally—he'd been strangling me at the time. But had taking his soul cost a bit of my own? The thought is unsettling.

"History says you ended the Yalaeng Conquest when you turned against your own side and gave the kingdoms a common enemy. You went mad with power and killed every person on that battlefield, friend and foe. If that was a fabrication, then tell me what really happened."

The scholar in me can't help the small thrill that shoots down my spine at hearing from a direct source. But I remind myself that the Soulless isn't a reliable one. Whatever story he chooses to spin, the only person who could have refuted or confirmed it was Ronin.

"Maybe," the Soulless says, "when you're ready to hear it."

"That's convenient."

He smiles again. Even ravaged by time in that cocoon, there is something distinctly disarming about him. His magic is a corruption of our craft, and yet there's an allure that seeks purchase in my darkest, weakest thoughts. A promise of unmatched power. Of never again fearing that I am not enough.

I shake my head and press one hand to my chest, thinking again of the piece of myself I ripped away when I took that knife thrower's soul. I know my worth. I do. Yet, fear is not a river, crossed once and then overcome. It is a sea, and every storm weathered is armor gained against the next to come.

"I can't trust anything you say."

"Then trust in what others might tell you. Ask the Ember Princess how the Empire created me. See what version of the truth they give."

I sneer at the challenge. I mean to seek the truth not to prove him right but to defeat him. I have to know who he was.

He takes one unsteady step toward me. His eyes are clear and bright, and the knowing edge to his smile makes my shoulders bunch. "Ask them," he says again, "about my brother."

My pulse jumps beneath my skin. This is the first I've heard of the Soulless having a brother. In fact, the history books never mention anything about who he'd been or what family he might've had.

However curious I might be, whatever game the Soulless is playing is only a distraction. I need to know what he has planned.

"How do you plan to strike at House Yalaeng when you're here, one person in the middle of a dead forest, and they're at the other end of the continent, protected by the largest army on Thiy?"

He flicks dirt off his fingers and says, "You'll see soon enough."

That sounds ominous.

He turns away slowly, and I catch the scent of earth and decaying leaves. The edges of our dreamscape begin to blur.

"What about the rot?" I ask quickly. "Can you cure it?"

"I might be the source, but I am not the cause. You can thank Ronin for that."

"Can you cure the rot?" I repeat, louder.

"Possibly. Ask me again the next time we speak."

My fists clench, and I shout at his back. "What's the point of coming to me if you won't answer anything I ask?"

"I didn't come to answer your questions, Sirscha Ashwyn," he says evenly. The greenhouse begins to fade, dissolving into formless gray. "I came only to hear them and know where your thoughts lie. And now I have."

I straighten. Heat surges in my chest. He'd given me no answers, and yet my questions had provided him everything he needed to know about my intentions. I'd allowed him to manipulate me like a complete imbecile. Kendara would be incensed.

"We'll meet again," he says, and then he's gone.

I gasp awake, blinking rapidly to focus my eyes. Early morning light brushes gold over the ceiling mosaic and the silks draping my bed. My hands are clamped around the sheets at my side, and there's a slight ache in my temples.

Bent over me, Saengo nudges my shoulder. "Sirscha. Wake up. You need to see this."

I follow Saengo, my mind still split between the unsettling dream and the urgency in her steps.

Our slippers are quiet over the marble floors as we dart up a flight of stairs. I recall the temple's floor plan and how it resembled a figure lying on their side. We're somewhere along the lower spine, but the next corridor takes us toward the shoulder and then the upper arm.

A balcony overlooks the main courtyard, which is lined with statues and topiaries in the shapes of cranes. The stone balustrade resembles flowering ivy. Every few seconds, the blossoms shrink into tight stone buds before slowly unfurling again into full bloom, revealing a gleaming jewel hidden within the flower head.

It's still early. Two shallow saucers of hammered brass hang from hooks at either side of the balcony, cradling flames that burn without oil.

"What were you doing up here?" I ask as Saengo tugs me onto the balcony.

"I couldn't sleep. But look who just arrived."

I rub away the last of my drowsiness and lean over the balustrade to see the courtyard below. It's filled with people and drakes. Sun warriors stand guard as servants wait beside several finely adorned dragokin. A small procession of mounted warriors in light armor takes up most of the courtyard. All of them have snowy white hair and gray skin. Their cloaks bear the symbol of a burning crown: the Fireborn Queens.

"Theyen." I scan the group of warriors, but he isn't among them. He must already be inside the temple with whoever arrived on those dragokin. "Come on."

We rush from the balcony, heading toward the main prayer chamber with the large statue of Suryal. There are few guards within the Temple of Light as, this early, only the priests and priestesses have risen for morning prayers.

Voices drift down the corridor, and I grab Saengo's wrist, pulling her through an open door. We wait, backs against the walls, as a flurry of booted feet pass. I recognize Theyen's and Kyshia's voices. For Theyen to be here in person, their meeting must be urgent.

Once they've passed, Saengo and I follow discretely. Kyshia and Theyen, flanked by Light Temple guards and attendants, are speaking in Nuval. Frustration pinches at my temples. I need to speak with Priestess Mia about finding someone to help teach me and Saengo the language here.

Even from the back, Theyen and Kyshia make a glittering pair. Despite the hour, the Ember Princess is resplendent in layers of gold silks that trail behind her. Her hair is woven into a crown of gilded leaves and crimson rubies, and gems drip from her around her neck, matching the glint of red in her ear cuffs. Beside her, Theyen is dressed in blue with silver embroidery at his wrists and collar. A silver sash is cinched around his waist, over which rests a belt of interlocking silver links encrusted with white gems that match his crown.

There are no familiars present. Despite their alliance, trust is still a fragile thing between them.

At the end of the corridor, guards open a door into a large circular chamber. Kyshia and Theyen step inside alone. All of their attendants bow as the guard makes to shut the door after them. Beside me, Saengo gives me a shove.

"Wait," I call out, hurrying past the attendants.

The guard pauses, giving me a puzzled look, likely due to

the fact I'm still wearing my nightclothes. At least I'd thrown on a loose linen robe as well and a hastily knotted sash. The guard hesitates and then pushes the door open again, allowing me through.

Inside, the room is larger than I expected, with full-length windows spanning half the wall and framed with heavy vermillion curtains. The ceiling overhead is a glass dome, revealing a brightening sky streaked with wisps of clouds.

Five other shamans are seated at a table, and each of them stands to bow at Kyshia and Theyen's arrival. Judging by the elaborate quality of their clothes and the fact that each shaman in the room bears a different eye color, I can assume these are the High Priestesses or Priests from other temples. This must be an important meeting indeed.

Kyshia moves to sit at the head of the table and spots me just as she finds her seat. She doesn't react other than with the rise of a single perfectly arched eyebrow.

The others note my presence, murmuring to each other in Nuval. Since Kyshia hasn't objected to my presence, I pretend like I'm meant to be here. I lean against the wall and relax my shoulders. Theyen's back is to me, but he glances over to see what the others are looking at. Surprise flits behind his eyes for a heartbeat, and he turns away again without a word.

"Thank you for coming on such short notice," the Ember Princess says in Kazan, likely for Theyen's benefit, but I'm grateful to understand the conversation. She smiles, that same irritatingly amused smile she wore at our first meeting. The room falls silent. She commands the instant attention of even Mirrim's elite. "Hlau Theyen has come with urgent news."

She nods to Theyen who says something in Nuval, a greeting of some sort. Then in Kazan, he says, "I won't leave you in suspense. Evewyn's navy has surrounded a Kazan port at our southern border. Queen Meilyr is demanding access to the Xya River that will allow her ships to pass through the mountains and into the Empire, putting her within a day's march of Mirrim."

EIGHT

The shamans listen, grim-faced, as Theyen details their numerous attempts to communicate with the queen and turn Evewyn away without bloodshed. The queen has not yet responded to their falcons.

You'll see soon enough.

Could this be what the Soulless meant? Without Ronin, would Queen Meilyr have made a deal with the Soulless instead? If so, by allying with Evewyn, he has an army at his command.

How many in this room know about the Soulless? Somehow, I doubt Kyshia has shared her knowledge with the other temple leaders. She might be a fellow High Priestess, but she is the Ember Princess first.

"Where is His Imperial Highness?" a sapphire-eyed man asks

Kyshia. The High Priest of the Temple of Water is a middle-aged man with dark brown hair graying at his temples. He slams his palm onto the tabletop, his thick bracelets jangling loudly.

Kyshia replies breezily, "My brother has already been apprised of the situation."

Judging by their mild reactions, His Imperial Highness's absence must be customary. I vaguely recall Kendara mentioning how the Empire's current heir lacked political acumen. I suppose it's safe to assume that between the two siblings, the Ember Princess wields the true power.

"This cannot be allowed to stand," the High Priest continues. "We should have marched on Evewyn the moment they attacked in the north. You see how our inaction has been met? She grows too bold. We must retaliate."

The High Priestess of the Temple of Wind, a young woman with amethyst eyes, nods her agreement.

"Do you plan to join our soldiers in battle, Lord Elwyn?" Kyshia says. "If not, don't be so eager to endanger Nuvali lives." There's a bright lilt to her voice at odds with her words. Lord Elwyn sits back, lips pressed tight. The hand he removes from the table curls into a fist in his lap.

Kyshia wasn't lying when she said she preferred to speak plainly. It's certain to have earned her enemies at court. I recall my conversation with Theyen at Spinner's End about what would happen if the Ember Princess died. She has several siblings. She might hold one of the most powerful positions in the Empire, but she can also be replaced should anything happen to her. It's no wonder she spends all her time at the Temple of Light rather than the Bright Palace with her father's court.

Theyen says something else, and I refocus on the issue at hand. Why does the Soulless need an army if what's said about him is true—that he can decimate an entire battlefield with a wave of his hand? He claims to be targeting House Yalaeng for unspecified crimes, but does he mean to attack them head-on? Having removed all the shamanborn from her armies, Queen Meilyr wouldn't even be able to enter Mirrim.

Unfortunately, I can't say any of this out loud.

"Why bring this to us if it is Kazahyn's border under siege? Can your clansmen not fend off such a small kingdom?" asks a shaman with a thick black beard.

Nothing changes in Theyen's posture, but when he speaks, it's with a slight bite. "In the past, Kazahyn has held off a much larger kingdom for far longer than a few days. Be assured that isn't why I'm here."

The shaman's cheeks flush, but I smother a smirk.

"I've brought this before you because Evewyn's attack in the north was against all of us, not just the Kazan. If this alliance is to succeed," he says, pausing long enough to share a measured look with Kyshia, "Nuvalyn and Kazahyn must answer as one."

Evidently, without Ronin's influence, Theyen has made peace with his future marriage. Guilt pricks at my spine.

"Hlau Theyen is right. The Empire must respond swiftly and decisively," another shaman says, a woman with hard ruby eyes and dark black hair that transitions to white at the tips. She wears a high-necked gown, giving her the look of an ostrich. The others nod in agreement.

"And we will, Lady Iya," Kyshia says. "Let us discuss how best to proceed, and then I will take our suggestions to my brother and the Emperor."

She pauses here and gestures to a guard in the corner. The guard moves to open the door, and then bows to me, waiting. I'm being kicked out. Possibly, Kyshia only allowed me to stay long enough to avoid making it known I'd overstepped her authority and joined her meeting uninvited.

"Hold on now," says Lady Iya. "Is this the soulguide? We've not had proper introductions."

"Introductions can be made tomorrow evening when she is presented to the Emperor," Kyshia says.

This is news to me. My stomach immediately drops at the idea of taking my lie before the Emperor of the Nuvalyn Empire, but I don't allow the surprise to show on my face.

Out in the hall, Saengo is waiting alone, all of the servants and attendants having cleared out. She rushes over, eyes wide.

"Well? What's happened?" she whispers.

"Come on," I say, pulling her back toward our rooms. "We need to get a letter to Prince Meilek."

Saengo contains her questions until the door to our room is closed and locked. I quickly relay what I learned as I withdraw writing materials from the dresser beside my bed.

Items in hand, I move to sit beneath the pavilion in the courtyard. "If Queen Meilyr is on a ship outside a Kazan port, there's no better time for Prince Meilek to gather his allies in Evewyn."

Saengo paces, digesting this news as I pen a quick letter with the information. "What if he's no longer in Luam?"

"Then Millie will find him."

Once the message is folded and sealed, Saengo takes it from me. "Last I heard, Millie was terrorizing the other falcons in the aviary. I suppose I'll go rescue them from her."

Millie is technically wild, so she comes and goes as she pleases, but I'm grateful for her. I couldn't trust any other falcon to deliver the message.

It seems Prince Meilek has not yet finished in Luam. Shortly after noon, just as we're preparing to leave for our appointment with an imperial healer, Millie returns through the single window at the back of the enclosed courtyard.

"He wishes to meet," I say, skimming the brief message. "The evening after tomorrow if we can make it."

"We'd have to leave tomorrow to be there in time, and I

doubt we'll be allowed to miss meeting the Emperor. Even if we snuck out afterward, we can't be gone for two days without explanation."

"Maybe we don't have to be gone for two days," I say, feeding the message to the lantern that sits on the pavilion table. The flames devour Prince Meilek's words within seconds.

Saengo's lips twist to the side. "A shadow gate would be perfect, but do you think he'll help us? After what happened at Spinner's End?"

"Only one way to know for sure."

The following day, Priestess Mia and a veritable army of maids arrive to help us prepare for our evening at the Bright Palace.

They draw us baths of scented water and rub oils into our skin and hair. Afterward, the maids sit us before two large mirrors they'd hauled into our rooms along with an endless assortment of pots, brushes, and lotions. Laid out on our beds are gowns I'm only allowed to glimpse before Priestess Mia nudges my head, forcing me to turn back to my reflection.

"When you arrive, you will be presented to the Emperor and Empress," Priestess Mia says. She clasps her hands at her waist where a shimmering gold sash is knotted. A bright red streak slashes across her lids, and a single amber jewel adorns the corners of her eyes to accent her irises.

At her words, my gaze finds Saengo. She's across the room, her back to mine, but our eyes meet through our mirrors. She tries to smile, but her anxiety presses through me, seeping past the mental window between us.

We'd met with the Emperor's healer yesterday as planned, but even an experienced imperial healer, with years of studying human anatomy and pushing the boundaries of her craft, couldn't stave off the rot. I expected this, but the disappointment still hit like a wave, dragging me under, made worse by the despair lurking behind Saengo's eyes.

If nothing else, at least we now know for certain that the only path forward is to eliminate the source of the rot.

Priestess Mia continues in that steady, cool voice. "You must not speak unless spoken to and address the Emperor only as 'Your Imperial Majesty.' Look only at his feet, and excuse yourself as quickly as possible. There will be many others who will want the honor of the Emperor's attention."

I nod as a maid gently dries my hair. Another removes the lids from several pots before dipping a brush into one. The dark bristles come away coated in shimmering gold dust. I close my eyes as she applies the dust to my lids. Someone else grasps my hands, tutting softly at the calluses and scars. I do not have the hands of a pampered reiwyn lady. They're the hands of a warrior, every mark hard-earned.

Something cool touches the tips of my fingers. A quick peek reveals she's applying oil to my nails. When the maid doing my makeup clears her throat, I close my eyes again.

"Priestess Mia," I say. "I've some questions I was hoping you could answer."

The priestess has been scarce since she brought us here two days ago, making it difficult to do much more than sift through the stacks of scrolls and bound parchment in the Temple of Light's archives. Everything was written in Nuval, which neither Saengo nor I can read.

On top of that, only a handful of people within the Temple of Light can speak Evewynian beyond cursory greetings. Simply trying to find the archives was an adventure.

"Of course," she says, but there's a new edge to her tone, a wariness.

I open my eyes again to catch her reaction. "Princess Kyshia says you've read all the surviving texts from the time of the Yalaeng Conquest."

Her shoulders go stiff beneath the crisp white of her robes, but only for a heartbeat. "That's true, but very little has survived. The conquest was nearly a thousand years ago. The Scholars then didn't prioritize preserving such texts. Unfortunately, we simply don't have as much information as we would like."

"Even so," I say pleasantly. "What can you tell us about the Soulless?"

At his name, all the maids go still, their eyes widening a little. Priestess Mia doesn't hide her distaste. Her lip curls, and her chin jerks higher. She clears her throat pointedly, and the maids quickly resume their work. "Not much is known of who he'd been before he became an imperial soldier. But he went mad during the war against the Kazan and turned against his own."

"And what of his familiar?" I ask.

Her brows lift. "To my knowledge, such a detail was not recorded. He must have had one, of course, but no soldier would march into battle with their familiar. Whatever it was, he kept it well hidden, well enough that it's been forgotten to time."

"And the Dead Wood?" Saengo asks for me, as the maid is now painting my lips with a deep stain the color of pomegranate seeds.

"The Dead Wood as we know it didn't exist until after his death. Since souls are the source of our magic, some Scholars believe the Soulless could use them as you would a talisman, growing his power. He bound them to a forest surrounding the ruins where Spinner's End now stands."

As soon as the maid sets down the brush, I ask, "How?"

In Evewyn, we were taught that the souls took root in the trees of their own accord. Unlikely, given the Soulless never died, as we believed.

Priestess Mia hesitates for the barest of breaths before saying, "I don't know. The Soulless's magic wasn't like other soulrenders. He wasn't bound by the usual restrictions."

Ronin once said that when a shaman reaches a certain level of power, the limitations of shamanic crafts begin to bend. The Soulless, and Ronin himself, is a clear example of that phenomenon. Still, Priestess Mia's hesitation makes it clear she knows more than she's letting on.

Two maids paint my nails with gold lacquer as another dusts my shoulders and collarbones with shimmering powder, and yet another pins up my hair, weaving the strands through a magnificent headdress of golden rays. As Priestess Mia speaks, they cast nervous glances at one another, visibly uncomfortable with our conversation.

"After his death, the souls had no escape. With every year, the forest died even as it continued to grow, claiming new souls and creeping outward, impervious to all attempts to destroy it. No one but Ronin could control it."

It's been six hundred years since Ronin defeated the Soulless. A very long time for the Dead Wood to become a danger, not just to travelers but to all of Thiy.

"I'm afraid there really isn't much more I can tell you," she says as the maids step back to allow me to stand.

"But there has to be more than that," I say.

"You're free to explore the archives for yourself," she says, which annoys me.

"They're written in Nuval." Which she certainly knows.

"Are there translations?"

"The Empire doesn't make a habit of sharing our historical accounts with neighboring countries."

That's a no then. Frustration pinches at my temples, but I push it away for the time being and allow myself to admire the exquisite spidersilk gown the maids bring forward.

Hand-sewn crystals swirl across the bodice. Layers of translucent gold robes edged in gossamer lace drape my shoulders, and a maid ties a brilliant emerald sash around my waist. She knots it in an elaborate style I'm unfamiliar with, but that I certainly don't deserve. When I glance at Saengo, I find her similarly garbed, her robes embroidered in swooping silver falcons as a homage to her House.

As they affix two small, perfect sunflowers into my hair at the base of my headdress, Priestess Mia lightly rolls her shoulders and says, "I must excuse myself to finish my own preparations for the evening. I'll see you again soon."

Unless I'm mistaken, she seems eager to take her leave.

When the maids set me once again before the mirror, I'm momentarily breathless. But the small thrill dancing along my spine is quickly chased away by the reminder that all of this is for the Emperor.

Suddenly, all I can see is the lie, a pall that dims the grandeur. I'm wearing a costume, nothing more, and if I'm to survive the evening, I'd best play my role.

The Bright Palace is possibly twice the size of the Grand Palace in Vos Talwyn. It feels like an extravagant fortress, with a massive gate and high, white stone walls enclosing the grounds.

Elaborate lanterns of blown glass in the forms of fantastical beasts hang above our heads as Priestess Mia leads me and Saengo through a glowing colonnade. Beyond that is the imperial gardens, which have been lit with what must be hundreds of magnificent lanterns. A massive expanse of manicured grass stretches before us, with sculpted hedges, stone fountains, and flowering trees strategically placed throughout.

Shamans dressed in layers of silks and lavish jewelry stand at either side of a path created entirely of rose petals in sunset hues. Their familiars lounge in the grass or the trees, filling the branches with luminous round eyes and vibrant feathers. The path runs the full length of the vast gardens, leading up to a marble courtyard and a glittering deck where two figures stand.

At my side, Saengo straightens her back and lifts her chin, likely drawing on every lesson she's ever received as the heir to a reiwyn house.

I repeat the instructions given to us earlier. Don't speak unless spoken to. Address the Emperor as 'Your Imperial

Majesty.' Look only at his feet. Excuse yourself as quickly as possible.

Easy enough, if not for the way my heart hammers at my ribs. My palms go damp. We step onto the rose path, our slippered feet crushing petals in vibrant saffron, lemon, and coral. The flowers catch in the trains of our robes.

Shamans watch us pass, murmuring to each other as they lounge beside fountains of water that spin and dance in unlikely patterns. Some point and whisper behind their hands as they flock beneath the fan-shaped leaves of ginkgo trees strung with golden lanterns. Our arrival was already announced, so there's no doubt that every person here knows who I am.

I draw a slow breath through my nose and paste a pleasant smile on my lips. My stomach churns, my craft racing in time with my pulse, but I keep my head high and meet their gazes. These are the most influential shamans in the Empire, and I refuse to shy away from their stares. Instead, I search their ranks, seeking a familiar head of white hair.

As a visiting prince, there's no reason why Theyen wouldn't be present. I told Saengo that the best time to speak with him would be this evening, assuming I'm not exposed as a fraud and immediately imprisoned. Saengo was not amused.

I spot Theyen's guards first. There are four of them, all dressed in shining silver tunics to accent their gray skin and white hair. They stand apart from the Nuvali, clustered beside a stone bench, curved like a bow. Lounging on the bench, looking perfectly—and likely deliberately—at ease is Theyen. He's as immaculate as ever in a deep moss green tunic with silver embroidery and matching sash.

His eyes find mine and I hold his gaze hoping he understands I need to speak with him. All too quickly, we pass him and the other shadowblessed, and I look ahead again.

The march through the gardens is both excruciatingly long and over too quickly.

We stop before the marble courtyard. At the other end, overlooking the whole of the imperial gardens from a high stone deck, stands Emperor Cedral and Empress Lyryn. They're dressed in gold and crimson, with magnificent crowns of twisted metal and crusted jewels nearly twice the height of their heads. Standing over their right shoulders is a man I assume is the Sun's Heir, Emperor Cedral's eldest child. To their left is Kyshia.

More of their children and advisors stand at the back of the deck, along with an impressive guard of sun warriors in full armor. I want to linger a moment on the exquisite metalwork in their breastplates and spaulders, but with so much attention on us, it's impossible to focus on them for long.

An attendant gestures to the other end of the courtyard and says something in Nuval, presumably permission to approach because Priestess Mia bows her head and leads us forward. The area is lit by more lanterns, each more delicate than the last.

My fingers, painted in swirls of shimmering gold, clutch at the layers of spidersilk. I school my breathing to a calm, even pace. Everyone here believes I'm a soulguide, and I can't give them any reason to doubt that.

We pause at the end of the marble courtyard. As instructed, we keep our eyes down, which is easy with the Emperor and Empress standing well above our heads.

Priestess Mia lowers to her knees, and Saengo and I follow suit. My gown pools around me in a sea of lace and spidersilk. I bow over my knees until my forehead nearly touches the ground.

"You may rise," comes a low, resonant voice from above. To my surprise, the Emperor speaks in Evewal.

I stand again, glad for Saengo's nearness as she edges closer to me. Her fear underscores my own, the tension thickening the air.

"Welcome, soulguide, to the Bright Palace. You honor us with your presence," says Empress Lyryn.

"The honor is mine, your Imperial Majesty," I say, demurely. Priestess Mia gives me a tiny nod of approval.

The Empress continues. "Suryal shines her light upon us with this gift. The Nuvalyn Empire has not seen a soulguide since the time of Suri. This blessing speaks to the Empire's might in victories to come."

I force my muscles to relax despite the way her words put me on edge. They remind me of what Ronin said when we first met—stories about soulguides have been passed down from the time of Suri, but that one should again appear could only be taken as an omen. If the Empire knew the truth, they would pray for Suryal to strike me dead.

"We've heard the story of how you saved your familiar from the rot, recounted by a sun warrior who witnessed the miracle," Emperor Cedral says. "She spoke of how your familiar glowed as if she contained the light of the sun beneath her skin. It's said that Suri could also illuminate the souls of others simply by touching them. We would be honored if you could provide a demonstration of your craft on the priestess."

This time, I can't help the way my entire body goes still. My heart lurches into my throat. Beside me, Saengo's eyes dart to mine, widening just enough to hint at her panic. Throughout the gardens, those of the Emperor's court who understand Evewal begin to murmur excitedly.

Priestess Mia steps aside with another deep bow and gives me a cool, expectant smile. She's clearly not thrilled to be used as a demonstration, but she's hardly going to object.

I wipe the alarm from my expression as my mind races for how to respond. I open my mouth and quickly close it again. When I say nothing, Priestess Mia's smile grows strained, a question in her eyes.

"Soulguide," the Emperor says again with the barest hint of impatience.

I look at Saengo, dread spreading cold and sharp down my back. Then, I dampen my lips and say, "I'm sorry, Your Imperial Majesty, but I can't."

NINE

At once, a collective silence falls over the gardens.

Priestess Mia's eyes widen, a mixture of surprise and horror loosening her jaw. I don't need to look around to know the rest of the court wear similar expressions.

Above me, the Emperor speaks again, repeating my words in slow mockery. "You. Can't."

There's no mistaking the threat in his voice.

I swallow with difficulty, my throat dry, even as annoyance begins to creep into my shoulders. What was it the Soulless said? House Yalaeng has never accepted that they couldn't do something. They're not used to being told no.

Movement at the edges of my vision catches my attention. Imperial soldiers shift on their feet, hands closing around the hilts of their swords.

I'm reminded of Evewyn's strict protocols in the presence of royalty. Before the fire at the inn when everything changed, I would have never dared to raise my voice or my sword to the prince of Evewyn. I've since done both, but while I've no desire to lower my head and submit to yet another person who believes they're my superior, I'm also not a fool.

So long as I can avoid putting myself or Saengo in danger, the Empire's customs must be respected. There are two knives strapped to my thighs beneath my gown because I'd refused to walk into the heart of the Empire unprotected. But they are a last resort. Until then, I'm a guest here, which I'd do well to remember.

As Kendara tried to teach me by forcing me to join the Queen's Company, sometimes it's better to be underestimated.

"What I mean to say, Your Imperial Majesty, is that I don't know how." I lower myself again to my knees, bowing deeply. "What I did with my familiar was from desperation and instinct rather than skill. Please forgive my ignorance."

The silence begins to ebb, giving way to a flurry of whispers. I remain on my knees, awaiting judgment, my gaze fixed on the marble gleaming in the light of hundreds of lanterns.

To my surprise, Kyshia speaks. "Your Imperial Majesty, you are a kind and just ruler. The girl has only known she's a soulguide for a handful of weeks, and as Her Imperial Majesty said, there hasn't been a soulguide since Suri. She has no means of learning her craft. Surely, with your guidance, she can become a most valuable servant."

I try not to bristle at the assertion I would serve the Emperor. I'm not a Nuvali shaman. I am an Evewynian shamanborn. That hasn't changed just because they think I'm a soulguide. I am not a thing to be claimed.

"This woman beside you is your familiar, is she not?" the Emperor says. "If you might demonstrate your healing instead. My personal healer tells me you've been able to keep her infection contained."

A second wave of whispers ripples through the assembled crowd, louder than before. I grit my teeth, anger breaking past the fear. He might as well have told the whole of the Empire that Saengo is my familiar. Kyshia said that harming a shaman's familiar is a grave sin, but I can't trust that every shaman feels the same, most especially not House Yalaeng's enemies.

I want to refuse. I want to remind him that Saengo and I are not his subjects, and even if we were, we're not pets trained to perform at his command.

But I'd prefer to survive the evening. So I say, "Of course, Your Imperial Majesty."

Slowly, I rise to my feet and face Saengo. She looks calm, but her fear and outrage echo over the bridge between us. Even so, she reaches for my hands, which are frozen at my sides.

"It's okay," she whispers.

Fury surges within me again. Word of this will spread, and anyone who views me as a threat will now know who to target. I can't hide Saengo away like other shamans might their familiars. She is my friend.

My craft responds, blazing hot beneath my skin. Every soul around us sharpens briefly. My hands tighten around Saengo's as I push down my anger.

"Soulguide," the Emperor says again. From the tone of his voice, I know this is my last warning.

With a nod, I unfurl my fingers and press them gently to Saengo's chest, above the silk collar of her gown. I close my eyes to block the stares as heat flares through me and Saengo goes rigid.

When it's over, the entire garden is deathly silent. Saengo brushes her palms down the front of her gown as we turn again to the Emperor and Empress, our heads bowed.

"Remarkable," says Empress Lyryn in a hushed voice. "Thank you, soulguide. You have blessed us this evening."

"Indeed," the Emperor agrees, sounding appeased now that he's had his way. It makes my teeth clench with irritation. "The Temple of Light is at your disposal. See that you learn what you must quickly."

"His Imperial Majesty is as generous as he is kind," I say as I bow again. Beneath the color brushed over her cheeks,

Priestess Mia looks ashen and slightly awestruck, her painted lips pinched.

I back away, hoping to escape.

Fortunately, the Emperor lets us go.

Once Saengo and I are clear of the marble courtyard, we're eager to disappear between the hedges of the imperial gardens. The shamans watch me with wide eyes. Some of them make to approach us. I grab Saengo's wrist, darting behind a cluster of ginkgo trees where two shamans sip wine on a stone bench. We leave Priestess Mia behind, ducking around a fountain to avoid another shaman who looks intent on speaking with us.

At last, we find a quiet spot between two hedges where the light of the lanterns doesn't quite reach. We collapse into the grass, arranging our skirts to avoid staining them.

"Let's not do that again," Saengo says, fanning her face.

"I agree. The next time the Emperor summons us, we'll just tell him we're busy."

She smacks my arm with a small silk purse hanging from her wrist. My heart has yet to calm beneath my chest, and every beat sends a rush of magic and blood coursing through me.

"Are you all right?" I ask, taking her hand. "I'm sorry that happened." Damn the Emperor and his disregard for Saengo's privacy.

"It's not something we could've kept hidden anyway. There

were witnesses in the north, remember? The truth would've spread eventually."

"I thought for certain you were going to stab someone," a voice says.

My head jerks up to find Theyen leaning over the hedges, sneering.

"That is how you tend to deal with conflict," he adds.

I'm too relieved to see him to feel annoyed by his insult. I rise to my feet. "I need to speak with you."

His snowy brows twitch upward. "I thought as much, but I believe I made the nature of our relationship clear the last time we spoke."

"And yet here you are, delightful as ever," I say before I can stop myself.

Saengo glances between us, looking exasperated. "Please forgive her, Hlau Theyen. We only need a moment of your time."

I wince and nod. "Yes, I'm sorry. But you'll want to hear this."

"I doubt that." He glances over his shoulder at two shamans watching us and whispering furiously. They keep their distance, though, as Theyen's four shadowblessed guards linger just out of earshot.

"Then why did you seek us out?" I ask.

His lip curls and he speaks softly enough to avoid being overheard. "I'm truly cursed when you're the least vexing thing in this whole city. I've endured enough Nuvali politics in a day to last me a decade."

"Hlau Theyen, we need to speak," Saengo says, adjusting the fall of her gown and brushing a bit of grass from her sleeve.

He rubs lightly at his temple. "Fine. Let's find somewhere less exposed."

We make our way back through the colonnade and into an antechamber that leads into a vast room. Even with sconces, the lighting doesn't quite reach the high ceilings. Portraits line the walls, along with what appear to be suits of armor. It must be a collections hall of some sort.

"I'll keep watch with these four," Saengo says, indicating the other shadowblessed.

I make a face at her for abandoning me, but she only flicks her hands at me and then introduces herself to his guards.

Theyen continues ahead into the large hall, his boots echoing quietly over the smooth marble. With a sigh, I follow.

"Has it been decided how Nuvalyn and Kazahyn will respond to the queen's actions?" I ask, catching up with him.

He doesn't answer. Instead, he says, "Might I point out that this is exactly the scenario I feared when you decided you'd be better suited at keeping the peace than Ronin? The Fireborn Queens will be forced to act should this come to war."

"I suppose I could've let Ronin kill me. Then you'd be facing war with him instead of the Soulless. That is if you hadn't been murdered in his manor house first."

Theyen gives me a long, indecipherable look. When he doesn't laugh or say anything caustic, I take this as a good sign and continue. I tell him about finding the cocoon inside Ronin's greenhouse, and how House Yalaeng has known all along that the Soulless was still alive but kept it a secret to preserve Ronin's power.

"So the magic that swept from the Dead Wood after the attack . . . that was the Soulless awakening." He sounds skeptical, and I don't blame him. Had I not seen the Soulless with my own eyes, or felt his power sink its talons into me, I don't know if I'd be able to believe it either. "I suppose that would explain why the gate sent to Spinner's End hasn't returned."

I frown. "Wait, what? Are there people still trapped at Spinner's End?"

"I only learned a few days ago. The gate managed to guide over a hundred people from Spinner's End before she abruptly stopped. I mean to go there myself once I deal with everything here."

The idea of anyone left at Spinner's End, trapped with the Soulless, makes me ill. But if one gate is already missing, sending another isn't an option.

"You can't do that. It's too dangerous." As terrible as it sounds, the best way to help them is to ensure we have a means of defeating the Soulless. "I have a suspicion that

Queen Meilyr's move against Kazahyn may be at the Soulless's request. There's no reason to march on Mirrim when she can't enter the city. The Empire and Evewyn have never been on good terms, but—"

"Conquerors need no reason to subjugate their neighbors other than because they wish to," Theyen says.

We stop beneath a portrait of a stern-looking woman with gray hair and steely crystal-blue eyes. She's dressed like a warrior, perhaps a Yalaeng ancestor who fought in the Empire's numerous wars.

"That's true, but Evewyn is a small kingdom. I don't think she'd move against two larger kingdoms on her own. Not without an equally powerful ally." What I don't understand is why Queen Meilyr would risk trusting another shaman after what happened with Ronin. Once the Soulless regains his strength, what's to keep him from breaking their deal? Even with the whole of her army, she wouldn't be able to control him. All of Thiy once tried and failed.

Theyen mulls this over in silence. His crown catches the low light, flecks of orange dancing along the cool silver. "And you say my dearest fiancé knew about this. A promising sign for our marriage to come. Why are you telling me this now?"

"Prince Meilek is in Luam. He has information from his allies in Evewyn and wants to meet tomorrow night."

Theyen turns away from me, but not before I catch the

disgust that twists his mouth. "Let me guess. You need my help. I'm beginning to understand why you don't have many friends."

I flinch. "That's hypocritical."

"I am selective about who I offer friendship, but I admit, rare as it is, I sometimes choose poorly."

His words sting, much as I wish they didn't. It's true I'm not good at making friends, far worse at keeping them, and I don't offer my trust easily. For half the time I've known Theyen, I've suspected him of wanting me dead. How could I have known he didn't send that shadowblessed assassin after me at Spinner's End?

"I'm not asking you as a friend," I say. Aside from Saengo, I don't know how to be a friend anyway. Phaut was my friend, and I failed her. "I'm asking as a potential ally. I've given you vital information. All I request in return is your help for one evening."

"Because your keepers won't let you leave the city?" he asks.

My jaw clenches. "Not without their escort, and I don't trust them."

As much as I dislike agreeing with anything the Soulless said, he was right that the Empire was built on war and conquest. An Empire of Sun, bright enough to conceal its darkest shadows.

Ask yourself why House Yalaeng kept my presence here a secret.

Priestess Mia didn't seem to know about the Soulless being alive. Even if she had, she certainly wouldn't have confirmed it. She's hiding something, though, and so is Kyshia.

I doubt details like who the Soulless was before the Yalaeng Conquest or whether he had a family would survive the passage of time without being recorded. Given how critical it was for House Yalaeng to keep the truth of the Soulless a secret, any such archives they might've kept would be securely locked away. The Bright Palace would be my first guess.

Unfortunately, breaking into the palace to find them probably isn't an option. I wouldn't be able to read them anyway.

"I can't just create a gate and show up anywhere I like, you know," Theyen says, strolling farther into the hall, toward the suits of armor displayed against one wall. "I have to know a place or a person well enough for it to work."

I follow on his heels, glancing at the exit where Saengo and the guards wait. "Have you ever been to Luam?"

"Yes. The river the queen wants access to is the Xya River, which cuts through the Fireborn Queens territory and into the Empire."

"To Luam," I say, glaring at the back of his head. "So, what's the problem?"

He pauses at the first suit of armor, head tilted to observe the elegant designs worked into the leather breastplate. There are curious embellishments, ribbons of pale brown that wrap around the chest like a rib cage. All of the armor pieces on display have similar details.

He runs his fingers along a leather vambrace and doesn't reply.

I lift one eyebrow, impatient. "What are you doing?"

"This armor," he says, a question in his voice. "I think this is the Hall of Heroes."

I look again around the vast chamber, seeing it with new eyes. "I've heard of this place. Nuvali heroes from the Yalaeng Conquest."

"Enemies to the Kazan," Theyen murmurs, moving to the second set of armor.

I reach out, passing my fingers down the breastplate, and then snatch my hand away. "Are these . . . ?"

The pale brown ribbons felt like the talisman Kendara gave me, and like the palisade circling Spinner's End.

"Bones," Theyen confirms. "These were fashioned from creatures called sunspears. They were a species of wyvern native to the northern mountains."

"Were?"

"There are none left on Thiy. But this armor would've been worn in the war against the Soulless."

At this, I step back to take in the collection. There are dozens on display. Each one is unique, with designs worked into the leather and scraped into the bone, beautiful and grotesque.

"A whole suit of armor as a talisman," I muse. "Why? What did these bones do?"

"Sunspears' bones are dense and heavy, impractical for long battles. But their bones acted like a cage for their souls. A sunspear was the one creature whose soul a soulrender couldn't rip."

My craft stirs. Magic rushes through my limbs, circling the tips of my gold-painted nails. A creature whose soul I can't rip. "A weapon of war against the Soulless."

"Scholars say they were hunted to extinction during the war, but I don't believe that. I've lived with wyverns all my life, and they're too intelligent to allow themselves to be picked off. I think they abandoned their mountains and left Thiy." He gestures to the numerous suits of armor. "Wyverns live in colonies far larger than this. The creatures must've fled before any more could be killed."

My thoughts fly to Kendara and her last words. She wanted me to flee as well. I ignore the ache inside me and shake my head at the horror of what must've been done to these creatures. "Good. Thiy wasn't worthy of them."

Something in Theyen's face softens then. "You asked what the problem is—the Kazan don't answer to a single ruler. The city Queen Meilyr has surrounded belongs to the Silverbrows, who are allied to the Fireborn Queens. We need all of our allies, including the Nuvali, because we have enemies as well, even among the Kazan clans, many of whom wouldn't mind seeing our clan brought low. Some of them don't believe allowing Queen Meilyr access to the Xya River is a threat to Kazahyn. They might even support her if it meant a blow to both us and the Empire."

"Then let Prince Meilek count among your allies. Help him take his sister's throne, and Evewyn will no longer be a threat."

He closes his eyes and rubs one finger at his temple. "I can't say I've missed your stubbornness. I recall how it ended the last time I listened to you and crept into places better left alone. But if Prince Meilek has information from within Evewyn that will help, then I've no choice."

TEN

Slipping from the Temple of Light unnoticed is a simple matter. Only two guards watch the gates. Further precautions aren't needed within the shaman capital.

Once Saengo and I clear the courtyard and the outer wall, we meet Theyen beneath the shelter of nearby bamboo trees. Wordlessly, he extends a hand. I take it, and he guides me first through his shadow gate.

The moonlight and the singing of the cicadas fade to nothing. Silence encloses us, oppressive in the utter darkness. I clutch Theyen's arm, an anchor in the void. Although it only lasts moments, it feels like longer before the darkness recedes and my feet find solid ground again.

We emerge into a small room lit by candlelight. After the sightless, soundless horror of the gate, I suck in lungfuls of air to calm my racing heart. It takes me a moment to uncurl my fingers from around his arm.

"How are you able to stomach that every time?" I ask hoarsely.

"I grew up with the shadows," he says, watching me with disdain. "I know them as I know myself. I'll be right back."

He doesn't say anything else as he disappears again into the shadow gate to retrieve Saengo. I shake out my hands, annoyed by how my fingers have gone cold, and warm them above the candle flame. The room is sparse, with only a short table pushed up against the wall beneath a shuttered window.

I adjust my cloak to conceal the dual swords belted at my hips and then crack open the shutters to find a familiar city-scape of wooden buildings propped on stilts above the river's surface. Bridges and walkways twine and intersect, and boats crowd the waterways. The governor's house is visible in the distance, raised on a hill overlooking the city.

Behind me, the shadow gate opens again. Theyen steps out, pulling a pale-faced Saengo with him. She gasps for air as if she's been holding her breath, and her knees buckle. I hurry to her side and cup her face.

"You weren't exaggerating when you said it was awful." Her fingers squeeze my wrists.

"And I thought you were the dramatic one," Theyen says. Since he's helping us, I don't glare.

"Where are we? Is this an inn?" I ask, helping Saengo to her feet. Beside the candle on the table, there's a pitcher of water and a beaten metal cup. I fill the cup and hand it to Saengo.

"Kazahyn Trade Embassy. Most shadowblessed looking to trade stay here."

"I'm surprised the Nuvali even allow Kazan into the city," I say. Saengo sips the water, color slowly returning to her face. I inspect the lines of infection below Saengo's collar. I've already treated it today, but there's no telling how the infection interacts with shadowblessed magic or walking through gates.

Theyen stands by the door, head tilted as he listens for movement. Tonight, he opted for a simple black tunic and sash, although he still wears a plain silver circlet. When he seems satisfied we're alone, he says, "Our kingdoms aren't technically at war, despite the border conflicts. Even the Empire isn't dense enough to stop trading with Kazan clans."

The mountains of Kazahyn are home to plants and precious metals found nowhere else on the continent. And the gems mined by the Kazan are exported all over the world, including to both Evewyn and the Empire.

"Will you come with us to meet Prince Meilek? He would make a valuable—"

"I've already spoken with him," Theyen says, catching me off guard. "After I left the palace last night, I came here to verify his presence."

"And you what? Told him you're a Kazan hlau? And he simply . . . believed you?" I can only imagine how Prince Meilek and his Blades must've received the arrival of a random shadowblessed claiming to be a prince.

Theyen's lips quirk in amusement. "He knew who I was based on your description of me."

I don't recall telling Prince Meilek anything about what Theyen looks like. Instead, I said Theyen is a peacock, albeit a trustworthy one when he isn't being completely unbearable.

"Is that so?" I say, sharing a smile with Saengo. "And did you come to an agreement?"

"We did. Speaking of agreements, the Emperor approved sending a regiment of Nuvali soldiers to Kazahyn as a gesture of goodwill and trust between our peoples." He snorts, making it clear what he thinks of the Empire and their "trust." "You should go now while it's quiet. Even if Luam allows the Kazan to trade here, a shadowblessed in the company of a shaman and a human would still draw attention."

"We'll be back soon."

Saengo and I slip out, blending into the late evening crowds. We keep to the shadows and pull our hoods low over our faces. Finding the Dancing Drake is a simple matter of using the governor's mansion as a fixed point and tracing our steps from there.

Inside the inn, patrons mill about, deep into their drinks.

The barkeep yawns as he wipes up a spill. It's quieter than the last time we were here. We weave around the tables and climb the stairs. As I step onto the landing, a door on our right cracks open.

Kou's face appears before pushing the door wider and gesturing for us to enter. The room is nearly identical to the previous one. Prince Meilek paces before a window, the curtains drawn, pausing only long enough to greet us before his feet are moving again. He must feel confined, so far away from Evewyn and the ability to do anything about the impending war.

"I heard you met Theyen," I say. "Did that go well?"

"It did. I like him."

My eyes narrow. "Really?"

Saengo's brows pinch as she finds a seat at the table beneath the window. "Really?"

Prince Meilek laughs, easing some of the tension in his frame. "He cares about his people, which is a fine quality in any person." He flashes a crooked smile and adds, "I have better hair though."

I almost laugh, but Saengo does, and the sound is a balm to my worries.

"Thank you for coming," Prince Meilek continues, the mirth fading from his face. "I have important information that I couldn't trust to a falcon, not even Millie."

Kou gestures for me to sit, but I shake my head and remain standing. Prince Meilek's restlessness is infectious. On the road, Prince Meilek and I sometimes spent evenings sparring, partly to stay busy but mostly to keep our reflexes sharp. Although it hasn't been long, my body is in want of exercise.

"My sister's new captain of the Queen's Guard remains loyal to me. I received word of Evewyn's naval fleet in the south just before your message arrived. She also mentioned that my sister sent a falcon to Spinner's End upon returning from her defeat in the north."

"Probably to find out why Ronin abandoned her in the attack."

"Yes. All communication with Spinner's End stopped after news of his death surfaced. Except my sister's falcon received a response. She's since continued contact with someone there."

I lean against the door, arms crossed. "So it's true that she's allied with him."

A muscle jumps in his jaw. "It's possible, but we don't have proof. Why would the Soulless even need an ally?"

I recall my dream and the Soulless's slow, unsteady movements. "He may be powerful, but he's also been poisoned and trapped in a cocoon for the better part of six centuries. He hasn't regained his full strength. I'm not sure what will happen when he does. Until then, he needs your sister to act in his stead and report what's happening around Thiy. I just don't understand why she would risk making a deal with him. He's too powerful to trust as an ally."

"My sister would want a guarantee of his loyalty, especially when she's gambling his strength against both the Nuvalyn Empire and Kazahyn."

I frown. "But there's nothing—"

The window shatters. Flames and glass explode around us. Pain shears my cheek as I lunge for Saengo, dragging her to the ground. Her eyes are frantic as she paws at her cloak, which is on fire. I tear it off her shoulders and toss it aside.

The scent of grease and acrid smoke fills the room. Whatever smashed through the window was soaked in oil and set aflame.

Kou rises from where he'd thrown himself over Prince Meilek and wrenches open the door. Heat and smoke pour into the hallway. I pull Saengo to her feet, and she stumbles along beside me as we escape the raging flames. Others have emerged from their rooms, shouting in alarm and waving through the smoke to see what's happened.

More of Prince Meilek's soldiers crowd around him, guiding him down the stairs. Saengo and I follow closely. My heartbeat drums through my ears, blood rushing hot and furious in my veins.

Chaos unfolds as patrons escape the inn. The fire is spreading, the smoke growing thicker. Another Blade takes Saengo's other hand, directing us outside. I look around at the panicked faces, at the spot of blood trailing down Saengo's jaw from a shard of glass, and then at Prince Meilek, whose sleeve is torn and blackened, his skin beneath angry and red.

"Stay with her," I tell the Blade. He gives me a confused look, but then his lips tighten in understanding, and he nods grimly.

"Better hurry," he says.

Saengo begins to protest, but I don't give her the chance.

I dash into the night and leap onto the nearest ledge, pulling myself up onto the roof of the burning inn. The moonlight offers little illumination, and thick black smoke distorts my vision. It's begun to drizzle, which doesn't help. I hold my breath and dart over the roof tiles.

With a leap, I cross onto the next building over, rolling to absorb the impact before I'm back on my feet. My gaze sweeps the rooftops. We were in a room on the second floor, and the buildings are too closely packed. The way the glass exploded meant whoever was responsible had thrown the object from a higher vantage point.

Movement in the shadows catches my eye—a figure darting behind a chimney. Anger burns in my lungs as my craft blazes to life. I move on instinct, my body flying over the ridge of a roof as I give chase.

The light rain thickens into sheets of water, slicking the

tiles beneath my feet. I grit my teeth and hold my balance as my boots try to slip out from beneath me. The figure ahead is fast and slim, but as they leap between buildings, the light from a lantern below flashes over a shock of white hair beneath a dark hood.

I draw one sword. The figure flips onto the ledge of a taller building, and I fling the weapon. The blade slams into the wood above their fingers. The figure jerks back, falling, only to land easily on their feet. But by then, I'm there, my fist meeting a startled face.

Their hood falls back, revealing a woman with short white hair and light-gray skin. She snarls, shaking off the punch. She draws a knife from her belt. I dodge the swipe of her blade before landing a kick to her side. She doubles over and then lunges for my legs. We both go down, rolling over the tiles, and nearly slide off the edge. But I catch myself in time, gasping as pain digs into my ribs.

I reach down and find a small shard of glass embedded in my skin. Gritting my teeth, I yank it loose. Rain slides down my forehead, gathering in my lashes. The shadowblessed woman struggles for balance a few feet away. With a flash of silver, she dives for me. Her knife burns a line down my arm, but I twist in time to avoid being stabbed. The smell of blood mixes with the scent of fresh rain.

With a curse, I strike my elbow to her temple. She topples

to the side, rolling against the edge of the roof. Her eyes go wide as the momentum carries her over. I grab her wrist.

Every muscle in my arm and shoulder screams as she nearly pulls me off the roof with her. But my boots find purchase, and my body jerks to a stop against the ledge. The shadowblessed woman dangles from the ledge, my grip on her wrist the only thing keeping her from plummeting into the frothing river below. Her knife is lost to the dark and the rain.

"Who sent you?" I shout over the roar of the rainwater pelting into the river's surface.

"Let me go!" she shouts, trying to yank herself free.

"Oh, no, you don't," I say through my teeth. Magic surges beneath my skin, reaching for her soul. I could force her to talk—grip her soul and make her spill all her secrets.

I shove away the temptation. No one can know what I am.

Instead, I reach down with my other hand to pull her back up. With a cry, she swings her legs and kicks her feet against the side of the building. I grapple for purchase as I begin to slide.

Then, hands grab my waist. My head snaps back to see Saengo crouched beside me, drenched in rain, her teeth bared from the effort of dragging me back onto the roof. Once I'm secure, she drops onto her stomach and reaches down to help me grab the woman who's still twisting and kicking.

Together, we manage to heave the struggling woman back

onto the roof. The moment her legs are beneath her, she grabs for the other sword at my waist. Thoroughly spent, I smash my knuckles into her cheek. She flops back over the tiles, groaning. I punch her again for good measure, and she goes limp.

Prince Meilek and his two Blades await us on the walkway below. His arm is hastily bandaged. The Blade I left with Saengo heaves the shadowblessed woman's body over his shoulder, and I collapse against a damp wall, my muscles aching.

"Are you okay?" Saengo asks, searching me for injuries. I hiss when her hands pass over the cut on my arm. She scowls.

"I'll be fine." I bat her away. "Prince Meilek. We can't let the Nuvali have her."

With the downpour, the river has cleared of boats, and the walkways are quiet. Several streets away, the glow of the burning inn is a soft haze through the rain. Prince Meilek watches it with his jaw clenched, a quiet rage building behind his eyes.

"This could delay the Nuvali from sending their soldiers to Kazahyn," he says, understanding my meaning.

If the Nuvali suspect the shadowblessed woman was sent by Theyen's allies, this could not only ruin their fragile agreement to send aid south but also threaten their whole alliance. I won't let that happen.

"Then what do we do with her?" Saengo asks. Her short hair is plastered to her skull.

"We give her to Theyen. He can take her back to the Fire-born Queens for questioning," I say.

Prince Meilek says, "She knew which room we were in. I've been rotating rooms every night since we arrived. If she was meant for me, then she's been watching us closely without our notice."

"And if she was meant for me, then she's been waiting for us to return to the city." I scowl. How could I have failed to notice someone tailing us through Luam's bridges and walk-ways? Kendara would be disgusted. Then, I remind myself that it doesn't matter what Kendara would think anymore.

He nods and addresses Kou. "We can't stay any longer. We've put everyone at risk by lingering. We return to Evewyn as soon as we've gathered our things."

Kou bows his head. "Yes, my prince. I'll make the arrangements." He strides off through the rain, vanishing into the night.

Conscious of how exposed we are, the rest of us rush over a bridge and into the shadows beneath an awning. It's meager shelter, but there's no helping it.

"What are you going to do?" I ask Prince Meilek.

Some of that rage lingers in his eyes in the fierce way he scans the night. "Everything I've ever been, everything I've ever trained for, was to serve my sister and my people. Now the two are at odds, and I haven't yet reconciled what to do about it. Either way, it's time to leave Luam." His eyes settle on me. "What will *you* do?"

I look at the woman, remembering the shadowblessed assassin at Spinner's End who'd chosen death in the Dead Wood over capture. This has to end.

"If Queen Meilyr is in the south, then that's where I'll go. I need to know if she's helping the Soulless, and, if so, why she would risk it. You said she'd want a guarantee of trust. If one exists, then I have to find out what that is." And, if possible, use it for my own gain.

"Don't kill her," Prince Meilek says. He reaches out, his fingers closing around my wrist. "Promise me."

My lips compress, anger surging. I want to tear my arm free and tell him that she deserves to die after everything she's done.

"She will face judgment for her crimes against Evewyn," he says. "But it must be done justly. I cannot take the throne of Evewyn with her blood on my hands. I will not."

I close my eyes. Rainwater spills from my lashes. Prince Meilek is my future king, and I must honor his request. With reluctance, I nod.

ELEVEN

In my dream, I'm standing in the garden maze outside the greenhouse.

Overhead, wispy threads of clouds stretch across a gray sky, a spiderweb encasing the earth. Just as I remember, the dirt underfoot is cracked and dry. Weeds wriggle from empty flower beds, and the skeleton veins of ivy clamber over stone walls.

Where the path that led to the greenhouse had been, the Soulless reclines on a gnarled wooden throne carved into the massive trunk of a withered tree. Rot mottles the pitted gray bark. Branches extend in all directions, twisted into the unsettling cast of dismembered arms. Featureless faces strain and stretch the bark like insects working to break from their cocoons.

Within the trees at either side of the Soulless, fractured fingers thrust outward, grasping at the dusky fabric of his sleeves, digging for the flesh beneath. Above his head, the torso of a screaming man arches against his wooden bonds, spine twisting into impossible angles.

I look away. "Why are you here? What do you want?"

"Is it not enough that I wish to know more about you? We're two of a kind, you and I." His voice is no longer a quiet rasp. It has depth and resonance. A slowly awakening strength.

But he doesn't move from his place on the throne. He sags into the wood as if the souls are trying to absorb him into the tree with them.

"I'm not like you," I say.

"Aren't you? Would you not do anything to protect the ones you call *family*?"

The word is a bruise. Whatever family I may have had is gone. There is only Kendara, who's washed her hands of me, and Saengo. Though Saengo isn't a blood sister, it's true that I would go to unimagined lengths to protect her.

"Whatever wrong House Yalaeng did to you, that was a dozen lifetimes ago. Who do you think waging war against the Empire will protect, other than yourself?"

His head tilts, his gaze appraising. "You should protect yourself better. What do you think House Yalaeng will do to you when they learn the truth of what you are? You want to protect your friend, but what else drives you to such danger? I can sense it within you—a hurt and a fear."

"You don't know anything about me." My fingers flex, wishing for the grip of my swords. In this dreamscape, my wounds from Luam are gone, but I'm dressed the same in plain dark clothes and boots spattered with crusted mud.

Whatever he can sense in my soul, I can sense something in his as well—an ache and a longing. And a deep, fathomless rage.

"But I will. Fate could not have better designed our meeting." His fingers curl into the wood, where the snarling faces shy away from his touch. "You were meant to awaken me. Who else could have sensed my presence at Spinner's End? I was mistaken before, but now—"

"Before?" I ask. I don't believe anything he's saying about fate, no matter how his magic probes at the chips in my mental armor. But that word, 'before,' means something.

"Ronin didn't tell you. There was another before you—a soulrender at Spinner's End. I hoped she would awaken me, but I see now she was only a bridge to someday connect me to you. Your magic is similar enough that I assume she was related. A mother, perhaps?"

All the breath rushes from me. When Kendara fled the Empire with my mother, she took her to Spinner's End. Why wouldn't Kendara tell me? How many more secrets is she hiding? Anger with her, and everything that's happened since that night at Talon's Teahouse, presses at my temples. I'm so tired of feeling overwhelmed with all the things I don't know how to fix.

"Crafts can be common within a bloodline," he continues. "My brother was a soulrender."

"And what happened to him?" I ask.

"The Empire happened to him." The throne ripples around him, the souls thrashing in a sudden frenzy. It only lasts a few seconds, but I fight the reflex to step back.

"Is Queen Meilyr moving against the Empire on your behalf? You've waited centuries for your chance to strike at House Yalaeng. Why let her do it for you?" I move toward him. Every step is deliberate. I will not be cowed by his attempts to unnerve me.

His anger transforms into an amused twist of his mouth. "What's a few weeks more?"

"I imagine she keeps you informed of what's happening beyond Spinner's End," I say, stepping beneath the shade of the massive tree. The souls writhe, mouths shrieking soundlessly, baring the pits of their throats. My skin crawls, the memory of coming within arm's reach of those trees skittering through me.

Without warning, the Soulless's hand shoots out. His fingers seize my wrist. His grip is like steel, and his skin is so cold it burns. Pain radiates up my arm, and fear spreads through me like frost over glass, but I don't give him the satisfaction of flinching.

"You're weak," I whisper, despite his nearly crushing grip. But I know it's true. Otherwise, he'd do more than taunt me in my dreams.

His eyes glint with malice. "I know your weakness too, Sirscha Ashwyn. I feel her connection to you even now."

With a snarl, I wrench my wrist free. I'm not sure how I can feel pain in a dream, but my entire forearm throbs as I back away.

"Don't speak of her," I say, infusing my voice with every ounce of hatred I can muster. I made her a familiar, but he's the reason she's dying.

"Her soul is strong, but she will never be our equal. Your friendship won't last. Everyone and everything I knew has become dust and ash, and, someday, so will your bond."

I scoff. "What do you know of our bond?"

"Maybe not your specific bond, but I know of friendship." With distance between us, he sags again into the cradle of his throne. Black sap slides down the rivets of bark, pooling at his shoulder. "I know of brotherhood. I've watched House Yalaeng break souls in ways worse than you or I ever could."

"What are you talking about?"

"I told you to ask the Ember Princess about how they created me. You haven't yet come to the truth. Ask them again,

Sirscha," he says, a challenge in his voice. "Ask them, and then you will come back to me by choice."

I sneer. "We'll see."

First thing in the morning, Millie wakes us with a message.

"It's from my father," Saengo says, skimming the message. She sits at the foot of my bed, legs crossed, and bare feet buried in my blanket. Her cold toes press against my calves where my nightgown has ridden up my legs.

Having delivered her message, Millie relocates to the top of the pavilion's dome and watches us with those dark, intelligent eyes.

"He's been in contact with Prince Meilek, but . . . he doesn't like that the prince is working with you."

I roll my eyes. Could Lord Phang not swallow his superiority to save his own kingdom? "Because I'm not reiwyn."

Saengo winces and twists her finger in the sleeve of her nightgown. "Because I told him about . . . what I am now."

My mouth snaps shut. "Oh." That *is* a good reason not to trust me. In his position, I would also balk at allying with the shaman who turned my daughter into a familiar.

"I had to tell him." She lowers her gaze to her lap. "So he can find a proper heir."

A familiar guilt leashes tight around my chest. "Saengo—"

"But we'll need his help if we're to turn the north against the queen," she continues, lifting her chin again.

"We'll think of something," I say. I've no idea what that something is, though.

When I push back the blanket to rise from the bed, something on my bedside table snags my attention. A folded slip of paper is tucked beneath the corner of the unlit lantern. My throat goes dry as I reach for it.

Back in the Company, I'd find notes left in my things, as if by magic, whenever Kendara wanted me to meet her somewhere. It always vexed me how she could do it without my noticing—proof that I might never hope to match the skills of a proper Shadow.

"What is it?" Saengo asks.

I unfold the note. At the sight of Kendara's handwriting, the tightness in my chest rises into my throat. Some stupid, foolish part of me hopes it might be a request to meet as if we were still mentor and student.

It's not too late to leave if you can overcome your stubbornness. If this helps your decision, I'm taking my own advice. Spies rarely live long enough to see old age, and I've given enough. I'm leaving Mirrim and can only hope you'll do the same.

But if you choose to follow your idiot sense of duty and stay, then seek out the Sleeper and take her hand.

For long seconds, I can only stare at the words, not quite processing their meaning. Then, I crush the paper in my fist and clench my jaw tight against the heat rising in my face.

"She's left Mirrim," I whisper. "Damn her."

I expected her to leave, and yet part of me held on to the hope she might have remained in the city—that she might seek me out again. But, as ever, she has abandoned me to wade through this alone, taking all of her secrets with her. Is this her idea of love? If so, I don't want it.

I fling the crumpled note onto my desk and stalk into the courtyard. The morning sunlight bears down on my head and shoulders, warm and reassuring. But it does nothing to soothe my anger.

My eyes sting, and I swipe at them. I won't shed tears for a woman who has never shown me an ounce of tenderness, who left me behind, more than once, without a second thought. Wordlessly, Saengo retrieves the note and smooths it out. Once she has finished reading, she lights the lantern and feeds the message to the flames.

I focus on trying to breathe. A moment later, Saengo approaches me from behind and wraps her arms around my shoulders, resting her cheek against my back. My lips press tight. I feel like that helpless child back at the orphanage, discovering once again that the people meant to love me the most were the ones who left me behind.

But I'm not a child. I'm not helpless. And new as it might be, I know my mother didn't abandon me out of a lack of love.

I focus on the steady flame of Saengo's soul. On the certainty that I am more than what Kendara made me.

"I'm sorry," I say, turning to face her. "This isn't about me. It's about saving you." What right do I have to feel sorry for myself when I've stolen so much from Saengo?

She takes my hands in hers, holding our clasped fingers between us. "It's about all of us. It's natural to feel betrayed by her leaving. Caring about one thing doesn't mean you don't care about another."

I manage to smile at that. "How terribly wise, Lady Phang."

Saengo peers down her nose at me, a look perfected by all reiwyn. "Don't sound so surprised, Ashwyn. Some people are simply too dim to appreciate my enduring wisdom."

I snort loudly, which makes her laugh. And then we're both laughing, and the vise around my throat loosens.

"We'll do this together, okay?" she says, still grinning. "You don't have to answer that. You're stuck with me regardless."

Her words are meant to be lighthearted, but something

about them bothers me. "Saengo, you do know that just because you're my familiar, that doesn't mean you *have* to do this with me, right? You don't have to put yourself in danger."

She rolls her eyes, even as her smile takes on a sad tilt. "I know. But I choose to be here."

"You can change your mind at any time. I'm your friend, not your keeper."

She cups my face, amusement creeping back into her voice. "Sirscha, dearest. You're being exasperating. We do this together. I watch your back, and you watch mine. Promise?"

Sighing, I nod. "Promise."

"Good. If we can't get answers from Kendara directly, we'll need to follow her clue. She said to find the Sleeper and take her hand. What do you think that means?"

I shrug and return to my bed, flopping onto the blankets. "No idea. We know the Sleeper is Suryal, so maybe the message is supposed to be some metaphor for religious conversion. She knows I keep faith with the Sisters." Although, admittedly, I'm not the most devout of followers. It was one of my many disappointments at the orphanage.

Saengo disappears into the washroom to clean up first. Over the sound of running water, Saengo calls, "Did Kendara care much about religion?"

"Not that I know of," I say. I doubt her message has anything to do with religion, which makes it all the more baffling.

Millie takes flight from her perch above the pavilion, lands neatly on the ledge of the window, and then vanishes into the sky. Through the window, which is too high to provide much of a view, the back of a stone head is just visible.

I bolt upright as Saengo emerges from the washroom. "Statues!" I say, which earns me a bemused look. "You can't walk twenty paces in this place without running into a statue of either Suri or Suryal."

Realization sparks in her eyes. "Then we've got a lot of exploring to do."

Once we're both washed and changed, we begin our search within the main prayer room of the Temple of Light. With the map of the temple's floor plan firmly in mind, we make our way methodically from head to spine to limbs. We pass Light Temple novices praying before a statue of Suri, young lightwenders practicing their crafts in quiet gardens beneath the press of the sun, and priests and priestesses hurrying about their daily routines. The temple residents bow respectfully when I pass, but leave us to our task.

Although there's a statue of Suryal in nearly every wing of the temple, checking the god's stone hands results only in frustration.

Following my mental map of the temple, we turn down a corridor leading into the leg and come upon a set of double doors. Beyond lies a large room with five statues gathered in a circle at the room's center, but none of them are Suryal.

"Suri," I say, gesturing to the first statue. If the likeness is accurate, Suri was tall and wiry with the build of a warrior. But there's a gentleness in her face, whether true or artistic choice.

"These must be the other members of Suri's inner circle." Saengo twists the troll-bone bracelet around her wrist, her fingers restless.

The other four founded their respective temple for their Calling, but all of them played a role in helping Suri build Mirrim. And, if history is to be believed, they were all friends as well.

"Did you know that some Scholars suggest Evewyn's faith originated here, with Suri and her inner circle?" I ask, moving from statue to statue. The Sanctuary of the Sisters is an old religion, and I can't help wondering if there's any truth to the theory. All the statues are of women, and two of them even appear similar enough that they could be twins.

"My father would call that sacrilege," Saengo says, running one finger along the pommel of a stone sword.

I imagine most Evewynians would be incensed to be told they're worshipping ancient Nuvali shamans. I move to the back wall, where a stunning mural is painted across the stone. "This isn't right. The original floor plan indicated that this wing goes farther."

"So it's been walled off?" Saengo asks, joining me before the mural.

It's a rendering of the Fall of Suryal. Whoever painted this did so with exquisite detail. The sky is a riot of colors, a brilliant contrast to the ravaged earth below. Suryal lies atop a rise, her body sprawled at the base of a massive tree, and her black hair strewn about her face, concealing her features. She wears armor painted in flecks of gold and amber, an aura of light cast about her. One hand rests beside her head, the other over her stomach.

She looks like she's sleeping.

"The Sleeper," I say, touching the mural. I frown and drag my fingertips lightly over Suryal's form. "Take her hand."

The hand lying beside her head rests atop the roots of the tree. I peer closer, running my fingers repeatedly over the spot. There's no mistaking it—there's a slight ridge in the wall.

"There's a seam," I say, following the edge of that seam up the wall and then down to the floor. "It's a door."

It's well hidden behind layers of paint and the lines of the tree and sky. I wouldn't have known it was here at all if not for Kendara's clue.

Curious, I give the door a shove. It doesn't budge.

"Kendara wouldn't send us here to find a door we can't open," I say, stepping back.

"Take her hand," Saengo repeats, reaching for Suryal's other hand, the one lying on her stomach. The artist painted her wearing shining gauntlets bearing the mark of a golden sun. With the tip of her nail, Saengo presses against the symbol of the sun.

Her nail slides through the paint. She draws back, delight spreading over her face, as my stomach lurches with realization—directly above Suryal's hand is a keyhole.

TWELVE

Thank the Sisters that, no matter how much time passes, locks generally remain the same.

It doesn't take me long to pick the lock with hairpins I retrieve from our room. There's a scraping click, rusted metal parts objecting to movement. Saengo and I share a look. Even if we're caught, I have to know what's behind this door. Why did the Temple of Light close off this wing? What does Kendara want me to find?

It takes both of us, but we manage to push in the door. The slow sound of grinding stone is uncomfortably loud. The density of old air rushes outward, a sigh of release from the room hidden beyond.

The door cracks open enough for us to slip through. Saengo removes two golden lanterns from the walls. Within the glass, flames burn without any noticeable fuel source. Holding the light out, I squeeze through the gap first.

At once, my magic stretches and strains beneath my skin, heightening my senses, and sharpening my awareness of the souls around me. There's me and Saengo and the distant gleam of temple residents, but there's something else too—an awareness gathering around me like a rising tide.

There are no souls here, but there is a presence all the same. A memory of souls. An imprint, powerful and many and pained.

The lantern is warm in my hand. I hold it higher as my boots cross a stone floor of interlocking tiles. Whatever colors they'd once been are faded to gray. No one has been here for a very long time, yet the souls' impressions linger, swirling around me and making my craft blaze and burn in my veins.

I've watched House Yalaeng break souls in ways worse than you or I ever could.

A pit grows in my stomach. What happened here?

The room is small, empty save for the dust and cobwebs gathered in the corners. At the other side of the room is another door, left ajar.

I push the door open with the toe of my boot. Beyond, the glow of our lanterns spills into a vast chamber. The room stretches into the darkness, wide and long, its walls on either side lined with plain, wooden doors. Tables run down the center, half-eaten by decay. They look like they might crumble into dust at the barest touch.

"What is this?" Saengo whispers, crossing slowly toward the first door at our left.

"A buried skeleton," I murmur, repeating the Soulless's words. The memory of pain lashes at my senses. My craft sears within me, but there's nowhere for it to go, no souls to grasp.

I follow Saengo, peering over her shoulder as she raises her lantern to illuminate the space beyond. It reminds me, strangely, of the barracks at the Company. Narrow, doublestacked cots cram the space, the mattresses long bare of sheets. If the other rooms are like this one, then this wing must've once housed dozens of shamans.

The impressions left by those who once occupied these beds press tightly around me, the tide closing over my head. It's too much. "Let's get out of here."

Saengo gladly retreats. We return the way we came, eager to escape. My thoughts blur together, uncertain where to focus with this discovery.

We squeeze back out through the door in the mural and are met with a furious Priestess Mia, looking flushed and ruddy as if she just ran the length of the temple grounds.

"What are you doing here?" she demands. Usually a pinnacle of decorum, she presses her palms anxiously down the front of her robes. Her voice shakes, and her eyes shoot wildly between us and the mural, now broken by the partially opened door.

"What was all that?" I counter, gesturing toward the hidden rooms. "Something terrible happened in there. I could feel it. What are you hiding?"

Priestess Mia's nostrils flare as she draws a sharp breath. Perspiration dampens her hairline. The gold-and-garnet butterfly in her hair, which I assumed to be an ornament, flutters its wings—her familiar.

"You shouldn't be here. How did you even—"

"No." I stalk toward her. To her credit, she holds her ground until I'm glaring down my nose at her. "You're going to tell me what those hidden chambers were used for. You're the Temple of Light's Scholar of History, and you came running the moment we opened this door, so don't pretend you don't know anything."

She lifts her chin and, even through her nervousness, gives me a look to rival any reiwyn's. "I can't just—"

"I wonder what the Ember Princess will do to you when she finds out you allowed us to discover the temple's hidden chambers?"

Her cheeks darken with color, and a droplet of sweat slides down her neck. Whatever secrets this wing contains must be considerable if Priestess Mia fears reprisal.

"Tell us what you know, and the Ember Princess never needs to be aware of this."

"We just want the truth," Saengo says, more softly.

At last, Priestess Mia's shoulders slump, and she turns to close the double doors behind her. She locks them with a key hanging from her sash, sealing us inside with the statues of Suri and her comrades. In her hair, the butterfly's wings flutter faster, hovering above her head for a moment before settling again.

"This part of the temple was closed off long ago," Priestess Mia says, wringing her hands at her waist. When she realizes what she's doing, she drops her hands to her side and attempts to recover some of her usual poise. "It hasn't been in use since the conquest."

"What did this have to do with the conquest?" I ask. Something tugs at me, a certainty that I'm missing something important.

"The war with the shadowblessed was long and difficult. It stretched on for over a decade before the Emperor sought new means of quickening our victory."

I suppose it never occurred to the Emperor to abandon his pursuit of conquering all of Thiy. An entire people can't carry the blame for the crimes of their leaders, but it's not difficult to see why the shadowblessed clans hate the Empire, or why the Soulless wants House Yalaeng brought low.

House Yalaeng has always seen our powers as a weapon of war.

My eyes widen. The anguish steeped into those buried

places wasn't left by physical torture. That kind of pain—the kind that soaks into the stone and fuses to the floorboards so that you can't even breathe without inhaling the caustic stain—comes from a deeper place. It comes from breaking someone's soul.

"Soulrenders," I whisper.

Priestess Mia, standing with one hand pressed to Suri's stone arm, startles in my direction. "How—"

My fingers tighten around the lantern's handle, the metal edges biting into my palms. "The Empire kept soulrenders down there. If it was during the conquest, then it was before soulrenders were hunted." That room with the beds wasn't a prison. It was a barrack.

"But why?" Saengo asks. Priestess Mia can't meet our eyes.

"New means of quickening their victory," I repeat with a mocking laugh. "The Temple of Light trained them to be used against the shadowblessed."

Priestess Mia turns to face the statue of Suri, her eyes closed as if in prayer. "Our predecessors needed a new tactic. They believed if they could train an army of soulrenders to . . . to destroy their enemies, all without even having to touch them, they would be unstoppable."

The Soulless is said to have lost control on the battlefield, killing both friend and foe. But his madness began here, at the Temple of Light, where House Yalaeng forced the soulrenders to push against the boundaries of their magic by ripping human souls—whose souls, I wonder—and fracturing their own with every attempt.

"How?" I ask.

"Something to do with their familiars," she says, grimacing.

To become powerful enough to defeat the Soulless, Ronin consumed the blood of his familiar. He made himself an abomination. But that had been his choice, terrible as it may have been.

"Did any survive?" Was this the secret to the Soulless's power, as it had been Ronin's?

Priestess Mia shakes her head. "After the Soulless came to power, specific details about individuals were destroyed, and this section walled off. All I know is they devised . . . experiments to alter the relationship between familiar and shaman. They believed that if the soulrenders were less reliant upon a familiar, they would be less vulnerable.

"Diminishing a familiar's role as a conduit might also mean allowing the shaman better access to their own magic, and, in turn, grow it. Or, in failing that, perhaps the opposite—binding the soulrender to more than one familiar in the hopes of amplifying their magic. Whatever the method, the strain of trying to extend the limitations of their craft proved too much for some."

Shamanic crafts begin to bend when a person reaches a

certain level of power, but not every shaman can be pushed that far. Those who couldn't bend, broke instead. Then, after creating the monster who would become the Soulless and end the conquest, the Empire punished every soulrender who came afterward for their own sins.

"That's horrific," Saengo whispers.

"And what of the Soulless and his familiar? I asked you that before, and you claimed ignorance."

"I wasn't lying," she insists. "As I said, specific details were destroyed. Whatever happened to him, no one can answer."

Disgusted, I gesture to the exit. "Open it. We're done here."

But Priestess Mia only lifts her chin. "You must understand that happened centuries ago. The Empire is a force for good, and we've learned from past—"

"Have you?" I snap. "Is that why you keep this part of the temple blocked off? Or why the truth of the Soulless's rise to power remains erased from history?"

"Be careful how you speak of the Empire. You're here by their allowance, and there are eyes and ears everywhere. As a soulguide, you're granted certain privileges, but I advise you against testing them. At present, you are an ally."

I hear the threat clear enough. I cross the short distance between us and snatch the key from her waist. "The Empire is *my* ally. I advise you against forgetting *that*."

When the Ember Princess appears at our door the following afternoon, I wonder if Priestess Mia confessed to our discovery of the hidden barrack. But she doesn't accuse us of trespassing. Instead, she informs us that the Emperor and his counsel will allow us to accompany Theyen south. We're to prepare to leave at once.

Queen Meilyr's ships still surround the port at Kazahyn's border. At least for now, I need her to remain there. I have to know if she's working with the Soulless and why. Any advantage against him that I can uncover will be of help.

There's also the question of what the queen plans to do if granted access to the Xya River. Humans can't enter Mirrim, but there's no limit to the destruction an invading army can unleash. If the queen invades the Empire, the Emperor's armies would have to meet her before she ever nears the capital.

Hopefully, if negotiations succeed, that won't happen. According to Kyshia, having the soulguide along, even an untrained one, will help reassure Nuvali soldiers uncertain about entering Kazan territory and prove the Empire's commitment to their alliance with the Fireborn Queens.

At least in theory. Within a day of setting out, Theyen and the Nuvali leader, a woman named Lady Ziha, have broken up three different fights between shamans and shadowblessed, forcing the ranks to be suitably divided to prevent further interaction. Fortunately, none resulted in bloodshed, but we've several days ahead of us, so there's plenty of time.

The following morning, a Nuvali soldier marching behind me calls out, "Suryali. What say you about the Empire coming to the aid of a Kazan clan?"

I'm riding Yandor, who has been rightly spoiled this past week by Light Temple stablehands, and Saengo is on a borrowed drake, so it's easy for us to turn and spot the soldier on the ground. As expected, when heading into battle, all familiars were left behind. Save for Saengo, that is. I'm about to tell the soldier that it's the Empire's duty to aid their allies when another shaman shouts over the rumble of plodding feet.

"We should be marching to war. Our people were killed in the north. By not retaliating, we bare our bellies to our enemies."

"We have an alliance with the Fireborn Queens, and we will honor that," another says. "We're not oathbreakers."

Some mumble agreement, but all fall silent when Lady Ziha rides past, her sharp gaze cutting through the ranks.

There's some truth to their discontent, though. Queen Meilyr broke the peace treaty and killed Nuvali and Kazan alike. In previous reigns, the Empire would've already retaliated in full force. But Kyshia and the Emperor seem to favor caution, and I can't say I'm not grateful.

"Sirscha," Saengo says, gesturing with her chin. "Am I seeing things or does that soldier look a lot like . . ."

It doesn't take long to spot who she's referring to. Marching farther ahead, a soldier peers over her shoulder at us. Her hair is cut to her scalp, and she has gleaming emerald eyes. She looks like a younger version of Phaut.

My breath catches. Winimar mentioned Phaut's sister worked as a guard in the castle, but she must've been reassigned to accompany us. Her name is Juleyne, I think. Realizing we've spotted her, she quickly faces forward again.

I want to speak to her, but I doubt she'll welcome my company.

We're to reach the hills outside Luam tonight. In the morning, we'll board boats and make the rest of the journey by river. With tempests and vortices to hasten the waves and the wind, we should reach the Kazan border within days.

Prince Meilck left the morning after our disrupted meeting in Luam, and I haven't had the opportunity to ask Theyen what the Fireborn Queens have learned about the attack. Maybe it's silly, but with Prince Meilek and the other Eveywnians gone, the Empire feels less . . . secure. Now it's only Saengo and me, foreigners in a kingdom I will never call home.

The idea of home sets my chest to aching. Sometimes it's the places I miss—the meandering streets of Vos Talwyn, the curling green rooftops, the imposing statues of the Sisters, and all the hidden nooks where small shops sell fresh bread rolls filled with plum jelly. For a time, it was home. Some days, the yearning cleaves me in two.

Other times, it's the people I miss. The sense of belonging. I remember a shopgirl who blushed and slipped an extra sweet bun into my purchases every weekend. There was an older fisherwoman with only one good tooth who told tales of the Sisters to anyone who'd listen on warm evenings, and children who loitered on dusty street corners playing knucklebones with smooth pebbles. And Kendara in her tower, a fixed point forever displaced.

"What are you thinking about, Sirscha?" Saengo asks. She's been watching me.

I sigh and pat Yandor's neck. He's my only other friend here. "I was thinking about how nice it'd be to go home."

Saengo's eyes unfocus. I can sense the same longing within her. "It could yet happen," she says softly.

If Prince Meilek takes the throne from his sister. If the Soulless is defeated. If the kingdoms don't go to war. If. If. If.

But I only say, "It could."

The rest of the journey passes without any further harassment from either side. After a fight on the first evening, resulting in the responsible shaman and shadowblessed spending the whole next day mucking out the boat with the drakes, everyone else fell in line.

Our small fleet of boats travels swiftly down the Xya River, aided by shaman crafts. It isn't long before Theyen announces we've crossed into Kazahyn. What we can see of the land is breathtaking—ancient forests and harsh gray peaks. At one point, nothing but sheer rock braces either side of the river, so high the sun remains hidden for hours. After, though, the cliffs give way to lush valleys teeming with flocks of cranes. Most of the shadowblessed live underground, leaving the surface generally undisturbed save for the occasional farm.

I also find a few minutes alone with Theyen, long enough for him to confirm that the attack in Luam targeted me, not Prince Meilek, to sabotage Theyen's alliance with House Yalaeng.

The assassin wouldn't have been able to enter Mirrim, not with the magical barrier around the city, so she waited for me in Luam. The only reason she might suspect I'd return to Luam is if she knew Prince Meilek was there as well. She must've watched the inn for days.

A reasonable conclusion is that a rival clan of the Fireborn Queens sent her. But if it's true that Prince Meilek switched rooms every evening, how did she know where we would be? The curtains were closed.

I suppose she could've been inside the inn and observed my arrival. Or, she had help from someone among Prince Meilek's followers. It's unlikely, given how much they adore him, but it's something to consider.

Sometime after noon on the third day, we reach the port city of Tamsimno. It's smaller than I expected, certainly smaller than Vos Gillis. The banners of various Kazan clans fly from rooftops, their tiles painted in vibrant colors. In the distance, the masts of large sea vessels stripe the skyline.

When the river turns, exposing the open waters where the Xya River empties into the sea, I suck in my breath. Saengo's hand finds mine. Ships dot the horizon for as far as the eye can see. Every last one of them flies a pennant with the silver moon of Evewyn.

THIRTEEN

As soon as we dock, Kazan officits pull Theyen and Lady Ziha away.

I watch the Evewynian ships, marveling that such a fleet exists. The Evewynian navy remained docked somewhere between Vos Gillis and Needle Bay, so I've never seen them en masse before. I've heard the Empire's fleet triples Evewyn's, but it's hard to imagine.

The Kazan also have ships, as they often trade with countries across the sea. According to Theyen, the Silverbrows even have a navy. But not nearly on this scale.

With the Evewynian blockade, fishing boats swarm the docks, unable to leave port. Likewise, all trade up and down the river has been stalled.

The shadowblessed watch from afar, guarded and suspicious,

as the Nuvali make camp along the hills beyond Tamsimno. It must be unsettling for the shadowblessed to have Evewyn's ships blocking the sea to the south, and a Nuvali company camped in the north. As Saengo and I unpack our tent, a tall figure strides up alongside us. Saengo freezes, and I set down the canvas.

Juleyne doesn't speak, but she rests one hand on the hilt of her sword, which I recognize as Phaut's. Winimar followed through with his promise.

"Juleyne, right?" I say. Everything in Juleyne's stiff posture makes it clear she isn't here to exchange pleasantries. "I'm—"

"I know who you are," she snaps, scowling. "You're the one who got my sister killed."

Phaut's loss spears through me, but it's probably nothing compared to what her sister must feel.

She steps closer, lowering her voice to avoid drawing the attention of nearby soldiers. "You might have everyone here fooled into thinking you're some kind of savior, but I know the truth. You're not a hero. You're a murderer."

The hatred in her eyes would've been startling if I wasn't expecting it. There's nothing I can say to appease her anger, but I still say, "I'm sorry."

She spits at my feet, spins on her heel, and stalks away, nearly colliding with Theyen. She offers a half-hearted apology when she recognizes him, and then vanishes into the disarray of the settling camp.

"She looks familiar," Theyen says as he approaches. I open my mouth to explain, but he holds up a hand. "I don't care. Queen Meilyr has extended an invitation to board her ship. But only if you're in our party."

I tense at this. It's not surprising for the queen to assume I might arrive with Theyen and his Nuvali allies. "I see. And the other leaders will allow it?"

"They argued against it, but I convinced them otherwise. And, just in case you're unaware, should things go awry—and I've a feeling they might—we'll be surrounded by enemies without an immediate means of escape."

"I can take care of myself."

He looks me over with an unimpressed tilt of his brow. "Really? Because I recall having to rescue you not so long ago."

"Stop antagonizing me. When do we leave?"

"Immediately. The rest of the party is already waiting. The invitation is only open until sunset, which is in two hours."

"That seems unusual," Saengo says. "The queen specifically wants Sirscha present, and yet you've got a feeling that things will go wrong." She turns to me, hands outstretched and looking incredulous. "It's a trap. You can't possibly go along with this."

"We've been at a stalemate for nearly a week," Theyen says. "This is the first time the queen has agreed to speak with us since her ships arrived. I've no reason to trust she will adhere to the rules of war, but if there's even a small chance of avoiding bloodshed, we'll hear her out."

"And if she doesn't adhere to the rules?" Saengo asks, brows raised in a disturbingly perfect imitation of her father.

"We have a plan," he says, which doesn't appear to mollify her.

It's a blatant trap, but the last thing Theyen wants is his clan being drawn into a war, so he's willing to take this risk. I don't have a choice, either. I came here for information, and getting on that ship with Queen Meilyr seems the surest way to get it.

I apologize to Saengo for leaving her to set up our tent alone, but she waves me off and insists on accompanying us to the docks. I toss my cloak alongside our bags. I need only my swords, which are strapped to my back. Shamans and shadowblessed alike gather along the pier to watch our departure.

When I glimpse the rest of our party, I pause. Aside from Theyen and myself, there's a Silverbrows officit, his shadowblessed subordinate, Lady Ziha, and Juleyne. She must be Lady Ziha's guard.

She spots me and turns away with a sneer. I sigh. This should go well.

We board two narrow boats, and Juleyne and the shadowblessed soldier row us out. The waves slosh against the hull. A light spray dampens the backs of my hands as I grip the sides of the boat.

Behind me, Theyen leans forward so that his words are delivered only to my ears. "If you must speak, say as little as possible. Don't let her provoke you."

I nod. Ahead of us, the queen's ship grows larger. Flying high above the crow's nest, the silver moon of Evewyn catches in the late afternoon breeze. The briny air and the warm sea breeze remind me of Vos Talwyn, and I can't help feeling the sharp stab of homesickness.

As our boats pull up alongside the ship, sailors unfurl a rope ladder down the side. Excruciatingly aware of how exposed we are, we begin to climb.

Once we reach the main deck, a human woman in a stiff officit's uniform steps forward. Standing beside Nuvali shamans, I realize how easily the queen could use my presence to support her lie that I'm a traitor.

Queen Meilyr stands on the quarterdeck, wearing a flowing gown of brilliant green beneath a silver breastplate bearing the triple-horned stag of House Sancor. A velvet cape drapes down her back, and a sword rests at her hip. I wonder if she knows how to use it. I never thought to ask Prince Meilek or Kendara. Her hair is pulled back into an elegant braid that wraps around a glimmering crown that resembles long spears of broken glass. She's certainly dressed for the role of a conquering queen.

"I am Admiral Yang," the officit says with a bow. The queen

doesn't move from her place on the quarterdeck, allowing Admiral Yang to speak for her.

As they exchange introductions, I take a quick headcount. Two dozen soldiers stand in formation behind the admiral, and that's just on the main deck. Two officits remain with the queen on the quarterdeck, and my craft senses the pull of more below deck. I still can't separate them; every soul aboard this ship melds into a formless reverberation—all except one.

I draw a steadying breath, forcing away the tension gripping my limbs. One soul stands apart from the others, growing from awareness into a near physical presence. It weighs on my mind and senses like the air from the greenhouse in my dream. Or the hidden chambers in the Temple of Light.

It feels old. Earthen.

Somewhere aboard this ship hides a soul as ancient as the Soulless. My confusion transforms to dread, every muscle in my body seizing at the fear that the Soulless is here and that I've miscalculated his strength.

But then reason returns to disperse the panic. The soul I'm sensing is close, too close to be inside the belly of the ship. I scan the assembled faces, but the only shamans on deck are the Nuvali and me.

Queen Meilyr draws my gaze again. Her fitted green sleeves are edged with lace and cinched at her wrists with silver vambraces. She clasps her hands, fitted in dark gloves, at her waist, where two silk sashes form an elegant and elaborate knot.

Beneath the sashes, an ornament hangs from a thin silver chain. It's difficult to tell from across the deck, but it looks like a misshapen lump of rock, or an uncut gem, clutched within a cage of yellowing bone. My craft strains against my control, reaching for the soul that's all but bursting from within.

I swallow down the confusion closing around my throat. Why, in the name of the Sisters, is the queen wearing a soul around her waist like an accessory? The immensity of its presence and similarity to what I felt at Spinner's End, to what I feel in my dreams, can only mean it's tied to the Soulless somehow.

Kyshia had said that some Scholars believe the Soulless removed his soul and hid it away in a talisman. I'd scoffed at the notion, but now I'm not so sure.

"We are not here to negotiate," Lady Ziha says harshly, catching my attention. She's responding to something Admiral Yang said.

"Then we're agreed," Queen Meilyr says, voice sharp enough to cut across the deck. "But I will not entertain any suggestions to retreat until I've spoken with your soulguide." Her gaze finds mine, a challenge bright behind her eyes. "Alone."

I'm surprised she recognizes me. We've never officially met, although I suppose Kendara would've told her about me as her pupil.

Lady Ziha begins to object, but I cut her off. "I'll do it."

A muscle jumps in Theyen's jaw. "Can you not be impulsive for—"

"I'll do it," I repeat, lifting my chin. I want to hear what she has to say, and, more importantly, I need to know what she's wearing.

Theyen's eyes flash. I imagine he'd like nothing better than to throw me overboard.

"Out of the question," Lady Ziha says, stepping in front of me.

Theyen takes my arm and speaks in a harsh whisper, "Have you forgotten she wants to capture you?"

"I have to speak to her," I hiss back. "Besides, you said you have a backup plan."

His nostrils flare with a furious inhale, and he releases me. He nods at Lady Ziha, whose fingers twitch as if imagining reaching for her sword. Instead, she steps aside.

Queen Meilyr smirks and descends from the quarterdeck. That odd jewel rests against layers of green spidersilk, swinging lightly on its chain. The presence within presses around me, beckoning. Tempting. My magic burns at my fingertips.

An officit opens the door to the captain's cabin, but I don't move until Queen Meilyr enters. The officit looks at me, waiting.

Before I can follow, a second officit gestures for my swords. I smile, all teeth, and hand my sword belt to Theyen. His glare bores into me as I cross the desk and step into the cabin. The officit enters with us and shuts the door.

The cabin is comfortably large with maps pinned to the walls and a massive oak desk. Queen Meilyr sits behind the desk, perched at the edge of a high-backed chair carved to resemble the head of a giant squid. Two soldiers stand against the wall behind the chair. Her gloved hands are folded in her lap, almost cradling the strange talisman. Its power is like a vibration in the air, a hum that makes my teeth clench.

I begin to cross the room, but a hand falls on my shoulder. Fingers dig beneath the edge of my leather spaulders. "That's far enough," the officit says.

I resist the impulse to smash my elbow into his face and jerk my shoulder from his grip.

"Why am I here?" I demand. Once, I wouldn't have dared to raise my eyes above the queen's collar. Now, I meet her gaze as she takes my measure.

"Sirscha Ashwyn," she says, almost mockingly. "Kendara spoke well of you. You were very nearly my Shadow. It would have raised you far above your current station."

I don't speak, waiting for her to get to the point.

"I'd like to propose a trade."

"What sort of trade?" I ask.

"Bring me my brother, and you and your friend will receive a full pardon."

I nearly laugh. I'd be a fool to trust any promise from her lips. Even if I did, I would never help her against Prince Meilek.

"My brother is a traitor to his crown and country. After such a service, I might still reward you with the honor of being my Shadow. You've the resilience and resourcefulness necessary for the position, and you've already proven your skill above my previous Shadow's."

At the reminder that I killed Jonyah, I only raise one eyebrow. Given the chance, I'd do it again. He killed Phaut.

"You spent four years enduring Kendara's absurd tests, and for what? I'm offering you a chance at what you always wanted. All I ask is that you prove your loyalty to me by bringing me my traitor brother. Kendara said you had good instincts. What do they tell you now, Sirscha?"

"Not to trust you."

She smiles and cocks her head like I'm a child in need of guidance. "You trust the Nuvali over your own queen? I'm not what they say, you know." Her voice softens, and her eyes lower. "My brother is my only family. There is no one else. You know a little about what that's like, don't you? Can you imagine being betrayed by the one person you trusted above all others?"

I once trusted Kendara as I trusted no one save Saengo. She may not have betrayed me to an enemy, but her lies were a betrayal all the same, and her abandonment twice over is worse. Love is a painful emotion.

"I can imagine," I say. "But now you seek to punish him for following his conscience?"

"Why shouldn't I? I am his queen as much as I am his sister. More than that, I wish to speak to him—to understand. His actions are misguided, but we might be able to mend this rift."

Her words are a lie. I know it, and yet, I suddenly recall an evening long ago—the anniversary of the queen's coronation. There had been a party. As usual, Saengo and I had slipped from the barracks to hide in the palace gardens and watch the court mingle in their glittering jewels and flowing robes. As one, the assembled reiwyn quieted, moving toward the edges of the ballroom.

In the cleared space, Queen Meilyr stood in layers of wispy fabric, a crimson sash knotted into an extravagant bow at her back. Facing her, Prince Meilek grinned, all but glowing with affection.

The high, lilting notes of a flute floated through the hushed ballroom, and both siblings raised their arms to one side in elegant swan poses. Saengo and I shared a look of excitement at such a rare occurrence. The two danced in elegant, perfectly coordinated movements, silks sweeping around them. As the queen spun, arms extended and sleeves billowing through the air, I remember being struck by her expression. I'd never seen her eyes so gentle.

It was a little unsettling. She didn't look like someone who ordered the deaths and imprisonment of her own people. With a simple golden hairpiece, she didn't even look like a queen—just a lady dancing with a brother she adored.

The next morning, I conveyed the moment to Kendara, who scoffed and said I would do well to remember that Queen Meilyr was not to be misjudged. Gentle was not the queen's way, and whatever she willed, as her servants, we would submit.

But Prince Meilek is her brother. He knows her as no one else does. I can't help but wonder if he'd accept an offer to reconcile. When we last spoke, it was clear how dearly he still loves her.

"Last I heard, he'd gone with you into the Empire." She's still smiling, but her nose wrinkles slightly. "A poor choice for allies."

I frown. "Why are you so threatened by shamans?"

Her smile fades, all hint of softness vanishing as her lips thin into a hard line. She and Prince Meilek share the same mouth and the same tilt at the corner of their eyes. It's unsettling to see those familiar features twist into something bordering cruel.

"Magic is a perversion of nature. True power doesn't rely on tricks and sorcery. True power lies in the right to rule."

I'm taken aback by the venom in her voice. Prince Meilek said she always liked the idea of power, and I can't deny there's some truth to the notion. Any amount of power sounds intoxicating to a person who grew up with nothing.

"Magic is—" The words stick in my throat. I meant to say that magic is a gift, thinking of the Fall of Suryal. But what about *my* magic? My craft could never be a gift. "Magic is in our souls. Even in humans."

"A cute notion, but humans have never needed magic. Evewyn has endured as long as it has because of the strength of its rulers. We will not bend before those who manipulate nature and disgrace the gods."

She's clearly made up her mind, so I don't bother pointing out that, as much as I love my kingdom, Evewyn likely survived the Yalaeng Conquest and other conflicts between magical races due to its geographical location. Nestled at the western edge of the continent, it stands the farthest from the Empire.

Although it takes effort, I force my craft to shift its focus from the soul in the talisman to the others in the room. I can only just distinguish the queen's from the others. It doesn't have the weight and presence of the soul in the talisman, but it's strong and vibrant. And without even touching her, I could rip it loose.

But probably not without also taking her soldiers'. Would

ending Evewyn's part in this conflict be worth killing them along with her? It would delay the Soulless's plans and save Prince Meilek the moral dilemma of taking his sister's throne.

I should do it. I *want* to, which is maybe reason enough not to. I've killed, but I am not a murderer. I'm not the monster she wants me to be.

Besides, I made a promise to Prince Meilek. That, too, should be reason enough to hold myself in check.

And yet. Despite all this, my craft surges against my control, pulsing at my fingertips, demanding. Power is a heady thing, and since taking the throne, Queen Meilyr has grown drunk on it, corrupted by its allure as sure as the Soulless's power corrupted Ronin.

Just as it could corrupt me if I'm not careful.

"I don't make this offer lightly," the queen says, a threat underscoring her words. "And I won't make it again. Bring me my brother, and I will allow you and your friend to return to Evewyn. Don't you want to go home?"

Home. I do want it. My chest aches for wanting it. "I think I'll pass."

"A pity," she says, inflection draining from her voice. She stands, smoothing her gown with her palms. Her fingers brush along the talisman's golden chain. Behind me, the officit opens the door again. "I hoped you'd see reason."

The soldiers at her back move forward to escort me out.

Before they reach me, to test her response, I say, "Reason? You sent an assassin after me in Luam."

"Actually, that was for your familiar."

I stiffen. Anger pitches through my gut. My magic quickens beneath my skin, but her ready admission gives me pause.

"Not to kill her," she continues, like that should be obvious. "To capture her. Even you know that taking a shaman's familiar is the easiest way to defeat them."

When she says this, her finger traces the fragile-looking bone that clutches the lump of rock at her waist. And suddenly, I know what it is.

Priestess Mia said that the Empire conducted experiments to alter the relationship between shaman and familiar.

The soul inside the talisman is the Soulless's familiar. It must be. It would be invulnerable to attack or disease, and, clearly, he doesn't need to be near it to access his magic. But it's still his familiar, and a powerful one at that. This is why she's allied with him. This is the guarantee that he won't betray her.

Her soldiers take my arms, pulling me out the door, but I dig in my heels. "Where did you get that?" I ask, dropping my gaze to the talisman.

"I wondered if you would notice." Her fingers close around the yellowing bone. "It was a gift from my father, and a gift to him from his Shadow."

"Kendara," I say flatly to disguise the surprise rippling through me. Assuming Queen Meilyr is telling the truth, for Kendara to have had it, she would've stolen it from Ronin.

She wouldn't have stolen anything from the Spider King without knowing exactly what she had in her possession. If her loyalty was to the Empire, why would she give it to Evewyn?

Twenty years ago, Kendara would've been in competition to become the Shadow's apprentice. Ensuring her place as Shadow would've been integral to her success as a spy. I suppose robbing the Spider King of such a valuable relic would've done just that. I doubt she told King Senbyn what it was, given no one knew the Soulless was alive.

But had Kendara known?

Either way, that talisman is the key to defeating the Soulless. My blood rushes in my ears as my pulse quickens. I have to destroy that soul.

Magic sears my fingertips, keen to be let loose. Even as the soldiers push me back onto the deck, my craft stretches toward the soul in the talisman. But my control is a meager, feeble thing, and I feel the tether of other souls begin to unravel. I clench my jaw tight.

A moment later, the soldiers shove me toward Theyen and the queen emerges from the cabin. I catch my balance before Lady Ziha can reach out to steady me. The others glance warily between me and the queen.

Theyen scowls at me, as if I'm the villain, and hands me my swords. I mouth, "Later," and strap the weapons to my back.

"Evewyn and Kazahyn have little reason to quarrel," Queen Meilyr says. She pauses at the foot of the stairs to the quarter-deck, still too far for me to confidently grasp her soul without risk to others. "We only want access to the river. Allow us through, and we will pose no threat to the shadowblessed or their lands. Really, we ought to be allies."

Lady Ziha and Juleyne exchange a quick, guarded look. Clearly, they've considered the fact that they're the only two Nuvali on board, and even those of us within their party are barely allies.

Admiral Yang's hand slides to the hilt of her sword as Theyen steps toward the queen, and his lip curls with contempt. "You will not be granted access. This was never a negotiation. We came only as a courtesy to hear you out. Now that you've had your audience with the soulguide, you will turn your ships around and leave."

"Will I?" The queen says lightly. She makes a vague gesture to her navy and the massive catapults that crowd their decks.

Theyen raises one fist, high enough to be spotted from the docks. Admiral Yang's hand tightens on her sword hilt, uncertain. I'm not sure what he's doing either.

Then, from the city comes a low rumble. The air begins to stir. Every person onboard the ship turns as one toward Tamsimno.

From the hills beyond the town, dozens of the dark figures shoot into the sky. My mouth falls open. Chills race down my arms despite the warmth.

The figures are massive, even from a distance, with broad leathery wings and long, whiplash tails tipped in dark feathers. And perched on the backs of each is a shadowblessed rider. Awestruck, I'm unable to do much else than watch as the army of wyverns sweep through the clouds with stunning swiftness.

Within moments, they descend on the ships, circling and whipping the air with their mighty wings. They must be thrice the size of a drake, their wingspans enough to cast most of the main deck in shadow. I look to Theyen, who has not moved, and then to Queen Meilyr.

Her nostrils flare, but she keeps her composure. Her soldiers, though, turn in circles and rush to the railing to get a better view of those farther off. Some of them cower, peering fearfully at the sky as if afraid they'll be plucked from the deck by the wyverns' massive claws.

Every soldier in the Royal Navy would've gone through the Queen's Company. They would have worn the honor of a braid dressed in feathers to symbolize a wyvern's tail. Their faces reflect my own fear and reverence. Theyen was smart to exploit that knowledge.

"You may have your ships, but we have the sky," Theyen says. During the Yalaeng Conquest, the shadowblessed held off the Empire for over a decade. Even with all the crafts available to the shamans, they couldn't defeat the Kazan clans. With this show of strength, it's clear how formidable an enemy they would make. "We will warn you only once more. Turn your ships around and leave Kazahyn."

The queen does not speak. Her soldiers have scattered.

No one is looking at us. Or the queen.

Slowly, I make my way across the deck, trailing Juleyne, who has drifted from Lady Ziha's side to observe the sky.

A wyvern circles above every ship. Unlike the slick scales of a drake, the wyverns' scales are a matte black, allowing them to disappear into the crevices of their mountain aeries. Something falls from a wyvern onto the deck of the nearest ship. Turning, I see all of the wyvern riders dropping something onto each ship—a scroll of paper.

"What's happening?" Admiral Yang demands. She's noticed the same thing.

Theyen doesn't reply, but he pulls a similarly sealed slip of paper from his pocket. I edge closer to where the queen stands, but with her soldiers scattered across the deck, I don't have a clear path. Fortunately, Theyen commands the queen's attention as he hands the scroll to Admiral Yang.

"What is this?" She breaks the seal and unfurls it. Her eyes scan the brief message, widening in disbelief. "Is this a joke?"

She passes the message to Queen Meilyr, and I glimpse

only a familiar signature and the stamped seal of House Sancor.

Theyen doesn't dignify the question with an answer. Instead, he addresses the soldiers on board the ship. "Anyone who wishes to pledge their service to Prince Meilek of Evewyn will be awarded for their loyalty. He vows to serve Evewyn's people by ending this conflict and restoring peace."

FOURTEEN

So, this is the arrangement Prince Meilek and Theyen had come to in Luam. Despite myself, I'm impressed by the level of planning that must've gone into this.

At Theyen's announcement, a murmur spreads among the soldiers. They look to each other in surprise, distrust, confusion—and hope. I'm not ready to believe it might mean anything, though. Fear of the queen's reprisal will prevent anyone from acting on the prince's offer. But, if nothing else, it might further divide and weaken the queen's ranks. Every ship in the queen's fleet will have received the same message, signed by Prince Meilek himself.

Abruptly, Queen Meilyr laughs, a sweet tinkling sound, and says, "My brother is a traitor, and any who align with him will meet a traitor's fate."

Her eyes settle on me. I freeze, mere paces away. The power within the talisman begins to burn away the awe of the wyverns, demanding my attention.

"You should have accepted my offer," she says, her smile brittle.

Juleyne turns, suddenly noticing my presence beside her. Instead of sneering at me, she puts a hand to Phaut's sword and faces the soldiers that close in around us.

"Admiral Yang," the queen says.

The admiral shouts a command. Every soldier on the main deck draws their sword.

My pulse jumps as I draw my swords. Warily, Juleyne does the same, positioning herself so that we're back to back. Overhead, three wyverns hover above the ship, the steady beating of their wings vibrating across the deck.

"Would you wager the speed of your wyverns against the speed of a sword?" the queen asks Theyen. "Who will fall first? Should we test it?"

Fury claws through me. The only life she values on this ship is her own.

I slowly shift my weight, my left foot sliding backward as I lower my swords. "The queen," I murmur to Juleyne.

With Juleyne covering my back, I can reach Queen Meilyr in two strides. If we can take her hostage, her soldiers will back down. I might be standing with the Nuvali and the Kazan, but that doesn't mean I want to see my countrymen cut down.

Just as I'm about to lunge, Juleyne cuts in front of me, her blade thrusting into my path.

I jerk back, bringing up my swords to block. Juleyne's expression is of tightly wound fury. She twists her sword, forcing me to block again and back up a step.

"What are you doing?" I demand. I lower my weapons as she points her own—Phaut's sword—at my chest.

"You're going to get everyone killed," Juleyne spits. Her voice is hoarse with unabated grief. "But I'm not my sister. I'm not going to die for you."

Behind me, the queen's soldiers take advantage and close in. The tip of a blade presses at my lower back, and I go still. Whatever small advantage we might've had together is gone.

"Juleyne," Lady Ziha all but growls, her fists shaking at her sides.

"At least one of you is capable of making a smart choice," Queen Meilyr says, sounding bored. "Seeing as diplomacy is no longer an option, here are my terms, Hlau Theyen. I will take your soulguide, and you will allow my ships to pass. Once we're through, you can have her back."

"No," I say, as a soldier wrenches Juleyne's sword from her hand, tossing it onto the deck. Two more grab my arms as someone slams a boot into the back of my knee. My legs fold, and I grimace as my knees strike the deck. Pain shoots through me. Hands come down on my shoulders, their grips bruising as they hold me in place. Someone kicks the swords from my hands, splitting the skin over my knuckles.

Queen Meilyr closes the distance between us, and I find myself looking directly at the talisman dangling from her waist. Spindly bones clutch the lump of black rock enclosing the soul. Its presence drowns out everything around me, and my craft spills forward.

Magic rushes from me, engulfing the talisman and seizing at . . . nothing.

Confused, I try again, grasping for the soul trapped within. It's like the wind clutching at a mountain. Every one of my senses feels the weight of that ancient soul, and yet my magic does little more than thrash against its cage. A cold, sick feeling spills through my gut.

I can't destroy it.

No, I tell myself. The fingers gripping my shoulders dig into my skin. I can't destroy it *yet*. If I can get it from Queen Meilyr, then I can figure out a way. My craft probes at the barrier of the talisman, searching for a way inside.

The queen, oblivious to my intentions, says, "Admiral, send the Kazan and Nuvali back to shore and take this traitor below deck."

I twist my head back to try and see Theyen, but they're outnumbered unless he signals for the wyvern riders to attack.

I understand his hesitation. A battle means casualties. Not all of his riders will survive. But why doesn't he use his shadow magic? Swarming the deck with shadows might protect them long enough to reach the boats and buy me time to snatch the talisman.

As the soldiers haul me to my feet, I try to rein in my craft. My control falters and slips. There's too much to track—the low growl of the wyverns, eager to swoop down over our heads, the weapons all pointed in my direction, soldiers shoving Juleyne as she reaches desperately for Phaut's sword lying on the deck.

Annoyed, a soldier rams his knee into Juleyne's gut. She gasps, her face crumpling in pain as she doubles over. The soldier lifts the butt of his sword over the back of her head, and, for the span of a breath, all I can see is Jonyah driving his blade through Phaut's chest.

With a roar, I turn and smash my forehead into my nearest captor and tear free of the other one. Shouts ring out as I dive for the soldier, ramming into his legs, sending us both sprawling. His sword clatters to the deck. Just as I reach for it, I freeze.

Cupped in my palm is a single glowing orb. I stare at it, ice spilling down my spine.

The soldier I'd knocked over scrambles away. A hush falls over the ship. I turn, spying the body of a woman lying prone on the deck. Dead.

Horror rises in my throat, sharp and cloying. The woman's soul pulses warm against my fingers, a strange counterpoint to the undercurrent of terror swelling around me. Soldiers back away hastily, colliding with their companions. I look down at my hand, sick with disgust and guilt and regret, and then close my fist around the orb. It vanishes in a wisp of glowing white.

There's a collective silence. I look up, finding Theyen first. He watches me grimly, anger simmering behind his eyes. Lady Ziha looks as if she might pass out. Her face is flushed, her chest heaving with quick, deep breaths. Her sword arm shakes as she points her weapon at me. Juleyne, at least, has retreated to Lady Ziha's side, her sister's sword secured.

I lift my hands, eliciting a panicked shifting of feet. Slowly, I stand. My gaze falls on Queen Meilyr, who has returned to the quarterdeck, surrounded by her officits. She smiles viciously, satisfaction alight in her face.

Whether from Ronin or the Soulless, she already knows what I am. "I want her taken alive," she says.

For a moment, no one moves. Then, her soldiers muster their courage and charge.

There's no more time for remorse. I duck the first two blades swinging for me, jabbing my fists into their ribs. I roll, avoiding another swipe, just in time to recover my swords still lying on the deck.

A screech pierces the air, making me wince, and a massive shadow dives for the deck. Theyen must've given the signal because soldiers are shouting and scattering. A soldier screams as he's plucked from the deck by massive claws and then flung into the sea.

Even as they rush for cover below deck, more soldiers pour out carrying bows and quivers. Within moments, they have their arrows nocked and pointed at the sky. Without the chance to loosen more than a single volley, a wyvern swipes across the deck, its massive wings crashing into the entire line of archers. Archers scream as they're slammed against the ship railing. Some topple overboard.

A glance confirms that the chaos has erupted all across the naval fleet, with wyverns diving and tossing soldiers into the sea. Arrows fly, finding tough wyvern scales. It won't take long before the first catapults are readied. But farther out, sails unfurl on several ships as horns blare through the tumult, calling for a retreat.

The queen shouts something I don't hear. Swords in hand, I rush across the deck as her officits usher her back into the captain's cabin. Cursing, I crush my hilt into a soldier's collarbone and then shove aside another. But there arc too many in my way, even with the wyverns circling and diving overhead.

A rider falls from their wyvern, an arrow in their shoulder. The wyvern screams, diving after its rider. More soldiers stream onto the deck, and then instantly drop to their bellies as a wyvern shoots past, claws flashing.

Someone grabs my arm, and I whip around, swords raised.

"Sirscha!" Theyen says. He pulls me after him in the opposite direction of the captain's cabin.

"The queen," I say, wrenching free.

"It's too late!" He rushes to the taffrail and leans over. "Get back to shore!"

I peer over to see the others have made it to the boats. Theyen looks skyward and lets out a piercing whistle that cuts through the clamor.

I wince and sheathe my swords. "What are you—"

A shadow falls over us as a gigantic wyvern drops onto the deck with a resounding boom, shaking the entire ship. I gasp and shrink against the rail, my heart lurching. Its wings knock over soldiers and push others overboard. Others willingly jump ship as the wyvern raises its thorny head and roars.

Theyen doesn't cower. Instead, he pulls me over to the enormous creature and climbs up its forearm. I gape, torn between wonder and fear as I haltingly follow. He shoves me into the black leather saddle on the creature's back and settles in behind me.

"Oh Sisters," I say breathlessly, heart racing. Theyen's arm circles my waist, and I can do nothing but hold on as he leans forward and pats the wyvern's shoulder.

The wyvern's wings unfurl and give a mighty flap. I gasp as we shoot into the air, and my stomach drops. Soon, the ships and the sea and the screams become clouds, a darkening expanse of sky and salty air in my lungs.

"You're a soulrender," Theyen shouts over the wind, his voice thick with anger. With accusation. "Did you know?"

I nod, the exhilaration of flying warring with the horror of the battle below.

"That's how you defeated Ronin," he says, with grim understanding. "You absolute idiot. You've revealed yourself to everyone."

He's right. I breathe in the fresh sea air as we soar over the pier and Tamsimno, clearing the city within seconds. Far below, bodies are running across the hills to meet us. Although most are too small to make out, I instantly spot Saengo, the light of her candle flame like a beacon.

I wish I could marvel over the wonder of riding a wyvern and the impossibility of touching the clouds. After four years of being Kendara's apprentice, I didn't think I could feel such exhilaration and surprise again. But there's no time to feel any of that. The wyvern descends toward a clearing in the wooded hills, and its wings stir up a cloud of loose grass and dust.

I shield my eyes until the wyvern touches the ground and its wings fold. Theyen rises and climbs down the creature's shoulder. I follow, my thoughts racing. Once our feet touch the ground, the wyvern spreads its wings, and there's a deep, resonating *whumpf* as the creature again takes flight. I spare a moment to watch it go, part of me wishing I could escape with it.

But then I hear my name called, and I look away. Saengo collides into me, nearly knocking us both off our feet in a crushing hug.

"What happened?" she asks, breathless. "Are you injured?" She pulls back, looking me over.

I shake my head and grip her shoulders. "Ready our drakes. I'll grab our things. We need to leave."

Despite the questions building behind her eyes, she clamps her mouth shut and nods.

"I'll meet you back here," I say, squeezing her arm in reassurance. She hugs me again and then dashes away.

Theyen storms off ahead. When I make to follow him, he shouts over his shoulder, "Don't go anywhere. I'll be right back."

He doesn't check to see if I obey, so I ignore the order and head back to camp for our things. The shamans and shadowblessed will reach the docks any minute now, where they'll report what they saw me do. I can't be here when that happens.

Fortunately, Saengo didn't unpack anything but our tent. I duck past the canvas flap to retrieve our bags from the corner where she'd left them. I sling both over my shoulder. Outside, I spot smoke from a cooking fire nearby. I head over and, without a word, snatch a wicker basket filled with warm steamed rice. The lid is sealed, so I shove it into my bag.

"Hold on there!" the shadowblessed cook shouts, jumping to his feet and swinging his ladle like a sword.

"Hlau Theyen will reimburse you for everything, with interest," I say, which shuts him up. I grab a bag of soft apples and a tray of dried, salted fish, and secure them in my bag before brushing past the blustering cook.

I nearly make it to the edge of camp before someone shouts, "There she is!"

I start to run but come up short as a group of shadow-blessed emerge from the hills ahead of me, possibly having just landed their wyverns. Had they seen what I did as well? They would've had a great view from the sky.

Behind me, Lady Ziha, Juleyne, and others weave through the tents. I curse, eying the quickest path for escape.

"Arrest her!" Lady Ziha shouts. "She's a fraud! A soulrender!"

I dart between tents, keeping low, as shamans and shad-owblessed stream in from the camp to see what's happening. I drop to the ground behind a large black tent, scanning the hills now dotted with shadowblessed. They're heading past the camp, so I wait for them to thin out.

"You can't be serious," someone says, as everyone begins shouting.

I lose most of what they're saying in the commotion, but

I make out enough to know it's not good. Theyen's voice rises above the rest, and I wince. He's done so much to help me, and I've made a mess of everything.

"There's a battle going on. What is all this?" he demands.

"The shamans lied to us," someone calls in Kazan. "They tricked us into believing they have a soulguide. We never should've trusted them."

I hear the sound of swords being drawn. The alliance between the shamans and shadowblessed was already tenuous, animosity barely restrained. It wouldn't take much for them to turn against one another. Guilt fills my belly.

"Honorless, the lot of you," Lady Ziha hisses.

"Shamans know only deceit," someone spits back.

The Nuvali are outnumbered, but the air thickens with their magic. I don't understand why I haven't seen a single shadowblessed use magic, but it doesn't matter. I can still hear the sounds of screeching wyverns and ballistae smashing into the sea reverberate through the town. Unless their respective leaders can bring either side under control, a second battle is about to erupt right here outside Tamsimno.

I close my eyes. None of this turned out the way it should have. I didn't make the Nuvali and Kazan hate each other, but I certainly didn't help. All I can do now, though, is finish what I've started.

The sun has begun to set, and I'm glad for the dwindling

light. Clutching my bags, I race through the next row of tents.

Shouts echo behind me, voices calling for me to stop. But within seconds, I dash past the last few tents and make for the hills. The sounds of pursuit trail my heels. I glance over my shoulder as a drake and rider bear down on me.

I draw one sword just as an arrow whizzes past me, striking the rider's shoulder. He shouts and tumbles off his drake in a tangle of limbs and cursing.

"Sirscha!" Just ahead, Saengo is already mounted on a drake, her next arrow nocked. She releases it, and, somewhere behind me, a woman curses in Kazan. "Hurry!"

She smoothly nocks another arrow, releasing it in the same motion. Yandor waits beside her. I reach them in seconds and swing both bags onto Yandor's saddle before leaping onto his back. Saengo looses a third arrow, which strikes the flat of a sword, jarring the weapon from the shaman's hand. Then, she rests her bow, grips her reins, and kicks her heels into her drake's flanks.

We take off through the hills, unsure of where we're going.

Drakes and dragokin tear through the grass as the Nuvali pursue. We weave through the trees, an arrow narrowly missing Yandor's leg. The ground begins to shift beneath our feet, the earth rumbling and splitting open. Somewhere behind us is an earthwender. Saengo raises her bow again, loosing three arrows with lightning swiftness. Shouts ring out, followed by the sounds of bodies crashing to the ground.

Suddenly, a roar reverberates through the branches, and a shadow sweeps over us. Saengo aims her next arrow skyward, but the creature doesn't plunge to tear us from our drakes. Instead, it lands with a teeth-jarring thud between us and our pursuers, scattering them and their dragokin.

Maybe it's because I was recently on its back, but I recognize the creature as Theyen's wyvern. It roars again, extending its wings to its full length to stall the riders. I whisper a quick thank you and a prayer that I haven't demolished his alliance with House Yalaeng.

Then Saengo and I continue through the trees, leaving the others far behind.

FIFTEEN

We follow a stream westward, hoping it will wash away our tracks. When it grows too dark, we've no choice but to find shelter for the night.

Shadowblessed have excellent night vision. So we do our best to shelter from searching eyes and take turns keeping watch until dawn.

Our food lasts only a few days, so I take to hunting. Now that we're not at risk of anyone discovering my craft, I'm free to use it for the task.

The way I lost control on the ship haunts me, that soldier's soul a memory of heat and light against my fingertips. An entire being, snuffed out with the clenching of my fist. The thought shudders through me every time I rip the soul of an animal shuffling through the underbrush, or a bird alighting on a branch.

But if I'm to find some semblance of control, I must try. I didn't dare practice in Mirrim. Doing so within the shaman capital, even if I believed we were alone, would've been too risky.

During the day, we stop only to hunt and rest our drakes. We don't say it aloud, but we both know exactly where we're heading—to the one place our pursuers won't follow.

The Dead Wood.

I wrestled with the decision for days, talking myself round and round in circles. But the truth is we don't have any other option. I need to know how to destroy the Soulless's talisman. Spinner's End is our best source for information that hasn't been either tampered with or destroyed altogether. I wouldn't be surprised if Ronin kept a private archive apart from the main library.

I don't know how much time Theyen bought us, or how much distance we've managed to put between us and our pursuers. Either way, I would rather take my chances against one shaman, albeit a powerful one that terrifies me, versus the armies of the Nuvalyn Empire, Kazahyn, and Evewyn, all of whom wish me dead or captured.

I close my eyes, leaning forward in my saddle to rest my forehead on Yandor's smooth scales. Yandor snuffs, throwing his head back and nearly bashing my nose. He can sense my anxiety, and I give him a pat on the shoulder.

"You're right," I say, as we draw nearer to the black stretch on the horizon. "Focus on what lies ahead of us."

"Are you talking to Yandor again?" Saengo asks, drawing up beside me.

I smile weakly. "It's a habit from when I used to take him on my tasks for Kendara."

"I'm sure he's a perfect traveling companion."

"And an excellent listener." I rub his neck, and he gives a happy toss of his head.

"Dare I ask what you were talking about?"

I sigh. "Just about what lies ahead. But also . . . I can't stop thinking about why I couldn't reach the soul inside the talisman. How can that be possible?"

Our first night out here, I told her about Queen Meilyr possibly possessing the Soulless's familiar, and she'd agreed it made the most sense, given what we learned in Mirrim. From the start, we've known that cutting off the Soulless from his magic is the best means of defeating him. And now that we know what happened to his familiar, we need to learn how to destroy it. Actually acquiring the talisman will have to be a problem for another day.

Saengo watches the trees ahead as she considers my question. Her hand creeps over the troll-bone talisman around her wrist. "Talismans are fashioned from the bones of magical creatures. Whichever beast that talisman was made from must be protecting the soul inside."

"Well, whatever it is, it must've been powerful. Troll bones protect against magic because living trolls were *resistant* to magic. But what sort of abilities would lead to a creature's bones being able to cage magic?"

"Not just cage magic, but deflect against a soulrender's craft," Saengo says.

Her words send a jolt through me. "Sisters, I'd forgotten. Sunspears!"

Saengo angles me a puzzled look. "What's that?"

I explain the suits of armor on display in the Hall of Heroes. They were fashioned from the bones of sunspears as full-body talismans to protect their souls against the Soulless's craft. Evidently, the Soulless found other uses for their bones.

"I don't know much about talismans," Saengo says. In truth, I don't either. What little I know, I learned from Kendara's books. "Can't you just . . . break it? Smash it with your sword or toss it into a fire. It's just bone, right?"

"I doubt it'll be that easy. Why go to all that trouble for a vessel that could be so easily broken?"

"A fair point. How are talismans even made?"

The making of them matters less than the destroying of them. We could experiment with the troll-bone bracelet, but the talisman has proven useful. Besides, it was a gift from Kendara.

"Can you even imagine what the Empire must've put his familiar through?" Saengo asks, voice hushed. "And after that talk of sacred bonds."

The bond is meant to be one of mutual benefit. Trapping a familiar inside a talisman would protect it from attack and make the shaman less vulnerable, but it would also presumably change the nature of the bond and rob the familiar of their end of the agreement.

"He must have been terribly powerful to be able to . . . to rip his own familiar's soul and place it within a talisman."

"Do you think he did it himself?" Saengo asks.

"I suppose it could've been someone else, but only another soulrender could've done so."

Had he always been that powerful, or had the Empire made him so? The talisman only reveals what was done to his familiar. I haven't yet fully considered what was done to *him*.

As the hours pass, the Dead Wood grows from a dark stain into a looming shadow, and my unease grows with it. There's no telling how the trees will behave without the leash of Ronin's power, and the Soulless's awakening. At least I've some idea of where we are, which will be all we have to go on.

That night, we make camp near the border of the Dead Wood, agreeing that we should wait for dawn before entering the forest. We make do with eating a hare Saengo shot after I failed to focus my craft on a single creature. Then we put out the fire and sleep with our drakes for warmth. Neither of us is willing to risk a light to signal our location.

"You're certain you can make it through the Dead Wood?" Saengo says, voice quiet in the dark. We sleep facing one another, hands entwined, our drakes pressed to our backs.

The last time I tried, Saengo was dying, and I could barely summon my craft. Now, my magic is a constant hum beneath my skin, eager and willing. This doesn't change the fact that the Dead Wood terrifies me, but at least I've got a ready weapon.

"We'll make it," I say. Hopefully.

"The Soulless will be there."

"I know," I whisper. My eyes are closed, but my fingers tighten around hers.

"What's your plan?"

Despite the hour, the forest vibrates with sounds of life. Insects sing, hidden in the wild grass. Nocturnal birds hunt through the trees and something small leaps from branch to branch above our heads. The restless creatures are comforting, given we're to enter the oppressive silence of the Dead Wood in the morning.

"He's weak. He can't even leave Spinner's End yet. So we sneak in, search Ronin's archives for information, and then get out before he knows we're there."

"How do you know you'll find anything?"

"You said it yourself back at Spinner's End, remember?

Ronin kept meticulous records. The Empire altered information to suit the story House Yalaeng wants to tell. They've destroyed or hidden evidence of what they did during the conquest, including the truth about the Soulless. If anyone else still has records from that time, it would be Ronin. He lived it after all. And there has to be something in that library about how to destroy talismans."

The truth is that there are no good options here. This is the only path that will take us closest to our goal, and it'll hide us, at least temporarily, from the contingent hunting us.

"And after?"

I shrug one shoulder. "I haven't quite worked that out yet."

Saengo is silent, her breaths slow and even. I wonder if she's fallen asleep when she whispers, "I've been thinking. To defeat the Soulless, Ronin, and his familiar—"

"No," I say, my eyes flying open. I know what she's about to say because the thought has already crossed my mind.

"Sirscha—"

"*No*. Don't even think it. We're doing this to save you. Sacrificing yourself doesn't help."

"It does if it makes you strong enough," she says, sounding infuriatingly reasonable. Still, a tremor races through her. The idea scares her as much as it does me, yet she's still suggesting that we . . . I can't even think it. It's horrific—and likely desperate—what Ronin did to his familiar, and I refuse to entertain the idea.

"Nothing is worth that. Besides, Ronin didn't defeat him. It was only a respite."

"But you're a soulrender. Ronin wasn't. Theoretically, it could make you powerful enough to, well, to *kill* him. I've been avoiding that word in my head, but we might as well be clear about our intentions if we're considering all possible avenues."

"I've considered it, and my answer is no. Who's to say I would even survive the trauma? Ronin is the only known success. It's off the table, and we're sticking with the plan. We find out how to destroy the talisman, and then we retrieve it from the queen."

Saengo sighs, but doesn't argue. Slowly, I allow my body to relax against the hard ground. Our blankets make for a poor sleeping pallet.

Several minutes pass before Saengo says, "I don't think I should come with you."

My eyelids, which had begun to feel heavy, snap open again. "What?"

Her thumb sweeps along my knuckles in a soothing gesture. "To be honest, I've been considering this since we left Mirrim, but I think I need to return to Falcons Ridge."

I frown. "We don't know who's still behind us. We can't split up."

"It hurts, Sirscha." Her words are only a warm movement of air between us, but they fill my lungs like a gasp of icy breath.

I rise onto my elbow, trying to pull my hand from hers so I can reach for her collar. "Has it spread more quickly than usual?"

She tightens her grip and pushes me back. "It hasn't changed since you healed it last."

Panic flutters in my gut, but I lie down. Despite my exhaustion, I'm wide awake. "Tell me what you mean, then."

"I think it's the proximity to the Dead Wood. It hasn't hurt like this since the last time we were here, except, maybe worse. Sharper. Like it's trying to force its way into my heart."

Every word is a dagger in my chest. "Then I'll come with you. We'll make our way north and remain close enough to the trees to deter any Empire scouts—"

"No," Saengo says. Her voice is gentle but firm. "It's like you said. Spinner's End gives you the best chance to find what you need. But what *I* need is to go to my father and convince him to help Prince Meilek take the throne. I'm his heir. He'll listen to me. Then, when you've finished at Spinner's End, you'll have a safe place to find refuge. I'll make sure of it."

"Saengo—"

"This is what I can do to help. So let me help."

Drawing a deep breath, I shut my eyes and curl my body around our linked hands. *We used to be a team*, she said at Spinner's End. *Now all I am is a piece of you. A shadow tethered to your soles, looking at your back.*

But she isn't. She's my familiar, but she is also her own person, and she is free to make her own choices. She has to do what she believes she must, just as I do.

Besides, she isn't wrong. If Prince Meilek can get the support of House Phang, it could make all the difference when he challenges his sister for the throne.

"It'll be dangerous. The Empire—"

"Is looking for a lightwender. I'm just a human girl."

I hate the idea of not being there to protect her. She'll have to follow the border of the Dead Wood north, straddling Empire territory. Once she reaches the grasslands, she can cut west into Evewyn. The grasslands are the only direct land route left between the two kingdoms. At least she'll be close to Phang lands, and once she reaches Falcons Ridge, she'll have the protection of her House.

It's a dangerous journey, though, and at least a week's worth of travel if she keeps her pace. I wish I could go with her.

"I'll miss you," I say at last. "Promise me you'll take no chances and travel as swiftly as you can."

"Of course. You too. I'll miss having you at my back."

"You'll make it to Falcons Ridge," I tell her because saying the words out loud feels like a promise. "You've good instincts, and you're an accomplished rider." She's been riding drakes all her life, after all. I only learned at the Prince's Company. "You would've made an exceptional soldier."

"I would have," she agrees, and I laugh because it helps to ease the fear.

The next morning, when we've cleared evidence of our passing and stalled for as long as we dare, we've no choice but to part ways.

"Don't take longer than two weeks," Saengo says. Her bag is secured to Yandor's saddle, along with her bow, wrapped to protect against the elements, and her quiver of dwindling arrows.

I'd insisted she take Yandor. He's brave, fast, and I trust him not to leave her behind should they run into trouble. We've already set the other drake free.

"I'll be at Falcons Ridge well before then," I say, frowning at her collar and the small bundle of blue veins hidden beneath. Two weeks is as long as we dare be apart before the rot spreads too deeply, or our bond grows too weak.

I open my mouth to say something else, but the words elude me. A roiling knot of anxiety sits low in my belly, but not because I think Saengo can't take care of herself. The desire to protect her stems from my own guilt. Saengo has always been strong and solid, even now with the rot.

I pull her into a hug, fear lending urgency to our embrace. But there's hope, too, and it burns far brighter than any uncertainty.

"I'll see you soon," she says fiercely.

Nodding, I pull away. "May the Falcon Warrior protect you."

She cups my face, eyes bright. “May the Twins lend you favor.”

We press our foreheads together, breathing the shared air for a moment more. Then, as if by mutual agreement, we release one another. Saengo turns to mount Yandor, who bumps my shoulder with his head. I give him a firm pat and press my lips to his cool scales.

“Keep each other safe,” I tell her. “Travel quickly. Hopefully, Millie finds you before you reach the north. She’ll make a good scout.”

Saengo smiles one last time. Then, she jabs her heels into Yandor’s flanks, and within moments, they disappear into the green foliage.

SIXTEEN

The Dead Wood looks different. The branches still block out the sky, and the roots still twine into a tight thicket. But the trees seem . . . stretched, all in the same direction, as if the souls within have been pushing against their wooden prison, straining to get away from something.

Chills skitter across my skin. Once, the souls had warned me to run, to escape the presence I hadn't known was hiding within Spinner's End, something they're not capable of doing themselves.

I grip the strap of my bag and take a deep, steadying breath to summon my courage. My magic warms beneath my skin and skips across my fingertips. The trees are generally quiet, with only the crackling of a branch here or the shifting of a root there. They're always deceptively still until they're not.

I shake off my apprehension and step into the woods. The trees, if possible, seem more chaotic than before. They look less contained. Their trunks are twisted, spun in unnatural shapes as if torn apart from within. Branches dig angry claws into neighboring trees. Roots sprawl and tunnel, climbing over one another. Some trees bulge to the side, the imprint of faces screaming through the bark as if the souls trapped within are trying to escape.

I swallow with difficulty. The souls are just as afraid of the Soulless as I am, which, if I'm lucky, means they'll be too focused on his power to bother me. I'm not sure what that means for me when I reach Spinner's End.

I travel quickly, the sun a whisper of light over my head. My senses and craft remain alert, but my thoughts can't help returning to what might've happened in Tamsimno. Did the queen's navy retreat? Is Theyen's alliance with the Ember Princess in shambles?

I can't help the guilt, knowing I exposed the truth of my craft at the expense of an innocent life. The queen wasn't surprised, though. Ronin wouldn't have told her his suspicions, not if it meant ceding power to her. But then why would the Soulless tell her?

I suppose the disaster we'd left behind is answer enough. Even if he only intends to target House Yalaeng, sowing chaos across Thiy will benefit him. The kingdoms will be too focused on each other to pay him attention.

And when he recovers his full strength and rises from Spinner's End like the specter from my nightmare, the kingdoms will be so fractured that they won't be able to stand against him. The Empire will fall.

A quiet, wicked part of me whispers, *Why not let it?*

Thiy was once a continent of many kingdoms. Now, because of the shaman emperors' greed, only three remain. The Empire has conquered lands and destroyed lives and hidden secrets, all to expand its power. Wouldn't Thiy be better without it?

Maybe. But too many lives would be lost in its falling. Much as I hate to admit it, the Ember Princess genuinely seems to want peace for her people. With her at its helm, there might be a chance to avoid war. But not if the Soulless kills her and the rest of House Yalaeng.

Something moves in my periphery, and my magic leaps against my skin, like a water serpent scenting blood. When I allowed the Soulless's magic to channel through me, it was like a spark igniting oil, the immensity of it almost too much to contain in one person. It's possible that he saved my life, that I wouldn't have been able to defeat Ronin without his assistance.

Regardless, I lost control on board that ship and killed a soldier. Whether by ignorance or the Soulless's influence, my craft has grown wild, like the trees, and it must be brought under control.

By the time I spot the white drape of webbing that encircles Spinner's End, the slivers of sky beyond the branches have turned a deep plum. The Dead Wood is nearly too dark to see. The panic clawing up my ribs is kept at bay only by the reassurance of my craft.

Lifting the bottom of the drape, I eagerly duck beneath. The castle looms before me, and I've never been so relieved to see it. I've arrived somewhere near the back, close to whatever remains of the garden maze after I set the greenhouse on fire.

The barrier of webbing separating the grounds from the trees remains largely intact, but there are spots where the branches have pushed through, tearing holes in the material. Unease teases at my shoulders. Without Ronin, the barrier no longer provides the protection it once had. I can only pray that the troll-bone palisade is enough to keep safe the soldiers and staff still trapped here.

The grounds are quiet, which isn't unusual. But the torches, which the guards always kept lit through the night, are dark. By the looks of them, they haven't been used in some time.

The moment I pass the palisade, an awareness begins at the back of my mind—a whisper and a temptation, a blade wrapped in silk trying to wedge its way beneath my skin. I press my fist to my stomach. His presence is just as potent as it had been the last time I was here.

Still, he's as trapped by his recovering body as he was in

that cocoon. I'll be in and gone again as quickly as possible. Even with the dark to conceal me, there are no guards to avoid as I creep along the side of the castle. Candlelight flickers behind a few windows though—hope that those left behind are still alive.

When I spy a way into Ronin's study on the third floor, I use the stone of window traceries to climb. Fortunately, the window to his study is open. I push aside the heavy drapes and climb inside.

The sliver of moon provides little illumination, but I can make out an oversized desk set near the window. More tables and shelves line the walls. Weaving around furniture, I cross the room toward the door.

I listen at the door for a moment, but there's only silence. A small brass key rests inside the lock, left by a steward no longer concerned with their duties. I twist the key to lock it, and then return to the desk and the lantern sitting at its corner. Within seconds, warm, golden light fills the room.

Ronin's study is, as I expected, exceedingly neat. Paintings of snow-covered valleys, glaciers, and frozen mountain peaks hang from the walls. I realize with a strange sort of feeling that those must be what Ronin's homeland looks like. He came from the far north, where massive ice spiders build nests in the mountains and the earth never fully thaws.

Framed above the mantel is a map of ancient Thiy. Unlike

the one on the library ceiling, it's in excellent condition, considering how old it must be. I recognize none of the borders. Nuvalyn is but a minor kingdom to the east, centered around the shining capital of Mirrim. Evewyn appears as a sliver of country to the southeast, and the wilds of the north were not yet tamed by the Drake Queens.

A richly detailed forest covers the land where the Dead Wood now sprawls, cut through with rivers and streams and a smattering of villages. At its heart rests a single castle surrounded by a small town. No evidence remains of that town now, nor any of the villages taken by the Dead Wood. But the castle's bones were claimed by Ronin for Spinner's End.

Neat stacks of parchment, books, and other things sit on various bookshelves alongside dead plants left unattended after Ronin's death. The idea of Ronin keeping plants would seem strange if I wasn't aware he'd been a sower.

Saengo said he kept his ledgers in his desk, so I begin there. I'm not looking for his historical records just yet. While my main purpose for being here is to acquire information about the Soulless and how to destroy the talisman, there's something else I need to know too.

From his desk drawers, I withdraw stacks of books bound in aged leather. Opening the one on top, I note the neat penmanship and the carefully stitched pages. It's a list of monthly supplies, which isn't what I'm looking for. I need his guest logs.

Flipping quickly through the others, I find some potentially interesting financial records, but still not what I need. I open more drawers, rummaging through countless ledgers that go back decades. Tucked behind a pot, I find a thick book and lift the cover.

On the first page is a list of names and dates. My heart jumps against my ribs.

The first name listed is dated three decades ago, and when I skip to the back of the book, the last names precisely entered are mine and Saengo's along with the dates of our arrival and departure to the north. He even recorded the dates I left with him to Sab Hlee and returned from Vos Gillis after freeing the shamanborn. A meticulous man indeed.

I work backward, paging through dozens of names until I find the years when my mother might have been here. I don't know her name. I doubt Kendara would've told me, but I never even asked. Part of me hopes I'll recognize something—that it'll spark some long-buried memory, or . . . I don't know. Anything. But as I scan the names, none of them stand out. My heart sinks.

My eyes close in frustration. I was so young when Kendara left me at the orphanage. Any memories from before that time have corroded with age. What if the Soulless had been lying about another soulrender? What if it hadn't been my mother at all but some other soulrender running from the Empire's persecution?

But where else would Kendara have taken her? Spinner's End is remote and well protected. Ronin refused to take in the shamanborn who escaped from the Valley of Cranes, so he couldn't have known the truth about my mother's status as a fugitive and soulrender.

How Kendara even managed to gain his cooperation is a mystery, but she is a spymaster. Maybe she knew secrets that would ensure his aid and discretion. Or, whoever she'd been in her old life still held influence.

I lean over the pages, the lamplight flickering across the neat strokes of ink. Every passing second is a waste of precious time, but I can't stop. I have to know if she was here. It's the only tangible proof I'll ever have that my mother existed. With her family dead, and all knowledge of soulrenders erased by the Empire, all that lives of her now are Kendara's memories. And as much as I love Kendara, I no longer trust her to be truthful with me.

The oil in the lantern burns low as I skim through unfamiliar names, my hopelessness growing until—

"Kendara." There's no surname, but it must be her.

I find her name numerous more times over the next three years, with anywhere between weeks to months in between. She must've checked in often on my mother. I flip back to when Kendara's name first appears, and right below is the name 'Sewae.' No surname, either. She's only listed once, but the date of her arrival matches Kendara's first visit, and the date of her departure is marked three years later.

She was here for so long. My finger passes over her name, marveling at it. It might not even be her real name, but that doesn't matter. Here is proof that she existed, despite the Empire's efforts to erase her.

And proof that the Soulless told me the truth.

I glance again at the year she left, and something stirs at the back of my thoughts.

I don't know my birthdate. It wasn't information passed onto the orphanage. I know only the approximate year because I was young enough that I couldn't be older than two. The date of my mother's departure suggests she left at the end of the year before I was born.

I shove away the disquieting thoughts wriggling for purchase. It doesn't mean anything. The year the monks gave me could be wrong, and a year is a long time. Twelve full months, longer than the period of pregnancy.

Except Kendara said that the last time she came to check on her, she found "the fool girl pregnant." My pulse quickens as I skim her last year at Spinner's End. Numerous guests came and went, too many to mean anything. She could've taken a liking to any of them.

I close my thoughts to any other possibility.

It doesn't matter. What matters is, for the first time ever,

I can piece together a bit of my past.

Sometime after Kendara took my mother away from here, Ronin must've discovered that she was a soulrender and that she'd had a child. Knowing that soulrenders were hunted, he would've assumed my mother either left the continent altogether or hid in Evewyn where, at the time, humans and shamanborn lived peacefully. And to further keep me from notice, so long as I never bonded with a familiar, I could pass as human—once my ears were clipped. I touch the nearly invisible scars lining the tips of either ear.

It took Ronin a long time to find me. Kendara hid me well. But her mistake might've been in making me her apprentice. He would've remembered her connection to my mother, and he would've kept an eye on those around her.

It's all speculation, of course. But it matches what Kendara said in Mirrim. Once he learned the truth of what my mother had been—of what I might be—he conspired with the queen against us.

I set the guest log aside and begin a different search of his study. I flip through every book, every ledger, and every scrap of parchment. His ledgers go back decades, but I need the records that go back centuries. I explore the walls, feeling for seams to secret passageways. I tap the bottom of drawers and the backs of bookshelves for hidden compartments. I even scrutinize the ceiling and the floor for possible hidden nooks.

By the time I finish, the lantern has nearly burned out, and sunrise is only a couple hours away. Wherever Ronin is keeping his archives, it isn't in here. Exhausted, I settle onto the floor beneath the window. I remove my swords and set them beside me within easy reach, then pull the book with the guest logs into my lap. Opening the pages, I once again find my mother's and Kendara's names.

My fingertips rest over the old ink as I close my eyes and focus on the warm flame of Saengo's candle, assuring myself that she's safe. I stay there until the lantern burns out, and sleep finally overcomes me.

SEVENTEEN

Footsteps disturb the quiet. By the time someone rattles the doorknob to Ronin's study, I'm wide awake and strapping on my swords.

Light creeps in through the open drapes, so I haven't been asleep for long. I'm out the window and climbing above the frame just as the door slams open with the crack of splintering wood.

"She was here," someone says, as two pairs of boots rush into the room. I press my back to the wall, fingers clinging to the stone as one guard's head appears out the window. If he looked up, he would see me.

He doesn't, though. He scans the ground, shakes his head, and then disappears again.

"We have to find her," a second guard says. Her voice is high and thin with fear.

"How did she even get into Spinner's End?" There are muffled sounds, like the guards are rearranging all the things I moved in my search. "No one can do that without a gate except Lord Ronin."

"She almost made it the first time she was here, remember?" the second guard says. "Do you think . . . do you think she could get us out with her?"

The trembling hope in her words makes me wince with sympathy. Would it be possible? I wasn't even sure I could get here, but now that I have, could I help them escape?

There are too many still trapped here. I wouldn't be able to protect a party of that size in the Dead Wood. Not even Ronin traveled the woods with more than a handful of people at a time. It would take weeks to get everyone out, and that's only if the Soulless didn't catch wind of what was happening.

But do I owe it to them to try?

Maybe once I'm done here—if I can somehow get the word through to the castle staff.

There's a cry of pain, and then the heavy thud of a body hitting the floor. Moaning fills the room as the second soldier shouts, "We don't know where she is!"

Fury wells within me. They don't know, but likely the Soulless does. If he can sense my soul, then he knows where I am. My teeth clench as the guard screams again.

Cursing, I climb down, gripping the window frame, and

slide back into the room. Inside, one guard lies on her back on the floor, fingers clenched around the fabric at her chest. Her head is thrown back, neck muscles straining. The soldier kneeling over her looks up at my entrance. He startles back, reaching for his sword.

"Get back," I say as I sink to my knees beside the gasping woman. Although her eyes are squeezed shut, the point of her ears tells me she's a shaman.

The other guard hesitates a moment, uncertain, before backing away. Grabbing her shoulders, I loosen the leash on my craft, which surges forward. Her soul is held tight in the Soulless's grasp, and no matter how my magic tries to wrench her free, it's useless. The shaman cries again, her face flushed. Sweat beads at her temple.

With a growl of frustration, I shove to my feet. "Where is he?" I demand.

The other guard, a human by the looks of him, glances helplessly between us. His skin is waxy and pale, his cheeks hollow, and dark shadows bruise the skin beneath his dark eyes. He looks like he hasn't slept in days.

I push past him and out through the broken door. The Soulless's magic sharpens around me, the weight of all that power closing in like the threads of a tightening cocoon. With a jerk of my head, I force it away, my own magic hot and frenzied beneath my skin.

Following the lure of his magic, I rush down the corridor and descend a flight of stairs. Soon, I pass beneath an arched entrance leading into a closed garden. My feet slow on the cobbles, only for a heartbeat.

This garden isn't like the maze with its overgrown weeds and abandoned flower beds. This one was nurtured until not so long ago. Slim trees thick with leaves cluster in the corner and stand sentinel beside a cobbled path lined with sagging bushes. Swaths of ivy dressed in purple blooms cling to the brick walls. But like the plants in Ronin's study, the neglect is evident. The flower beds have wilted, weeds crowd the soil, and the path is littered with petals that have dried and curled.

It's a peculiar feeling to know Ronin surrounded himself in his private spaces with green growing things and paintings of his home in the north. What sort of man had Ronin been before the Soulless's magic corrupted him? What sort of man willingly sacrificed his humanity to save everyone else?

I wince as the shaman's faint screams quiver through the open air. I quicken my pace. The path curves around a grouping of trees that part to reveal a massive throne against the far wall. My stomach lurches at the familiarity.

Instead of from rotting trees, this throne was built from stone. Whoever created it sculpted creatures into the wide base and the arms, but the details have been lost with the centuries. Thick webbing stretches across the back and the brick wall, coating the ivy in ghostly white gauze.

I think of that little town surrounding a castle on the map in Ronin's study. This might have been a secondary throne room once, an open courtyard to receive guests for whoever once ruled here before Ronin. Before the Dead Wood. Before the Yalaeng Conquest.

I shuffle to a stop. The Soulless reclines on the throne, and part of me wonders if I'm dreaming. His skin has lost its green tint from when I first saw him in his cocoon, but it's ashen after long years sealed away from the sun.

His black hair isn't the matted tangle of roots and grave dirt like in my dream. Instead, it falls loose around his face and shoulders, slightly tousled as if recently slept on. He's dressed simply in dark gray robes, the rot-eaten clothing he was trapped in likely burned away with the flames that consumed his cocoon, the greenhouse, and Ronin's body.

He's thin, his dark hair framing the sharp bones of his face that only emphasize the slope of his nose and the angle of his cheeks. He's beautiful in an unearthly way, and for a man who survived a fire, he's remarkably unscathed. Proof that, despite how physically weak he might seem, he is far more than his appearance.

His power hangs over me, a wave of ice threatening to crush me beneath its depths. He watches me approach through bright crystalline eyes, narrowed like chips of amber.

Fear rises in my belly, but I hold tight to my fury as the

distant cry of the shaman guard trails faintly in the silence.

"Stop it," I hiss. "I'm right here."

"Sirscha." My name is a soft breath from his lips, like a long-held exhale. "I knew you would come to Spinner's End eventually."

"Why are you doing this to them?" I say. "They're useless to you as prisoners. The Dead Wood already does all the work of keeping away enemies." The shaman's distant wail has gone quiet, and I pray it's because he's let her go.

"Prisoners," he says, amused. "A castle cannot function with a single resident."

As he speaks, my craft flows from the tips of my fingers, seeking. I can't sense any other souls in the immediate gardens. There is only us.

Could I grasp his soul? Could I end it all, right now, if I dared to try?

"What is it you want?" I ask.

"I thought we'd covered this already," he says.

"If House Yalaeng is your target, then let these people go. Keep a skeleton staff if you must, but release the others."

My craft skirts around his magic, searching for a way in. If a soul is a flame, then his is a bonfire, blazing and present. As oppressive as the soul of his familiar had been on that ship, his own is a dozen times worse.

Even so, I will my craft to push against the force of his.

It's like wading through a fog of disembodied hands, fingers grasping and clawing at me. I grit my teeth and press on.

Suddenly, agony rips through me. I gasp, and my legs buckle. But instead of slamming to my knees, I'm frozen in place, my soul gripped tight. The Soulless doesn't move from his recline. He watches me, expression blank, as if his magic isn't a vise around my soul, as if he couldn't tear it free and claim it for the Dead Wood with nothing but a thought.

I want to scream, but I can't. His craft is a thousand razor blades cutting me open. Sisters, is this what others feel when I use my craft? It's worse than anything Kendara has ever subjected me to. It's like I'm being torn inside out, everything that I am on the verge of being ripped away with scorching hooks.

Despair washes through me. How could anyone hope to defeat him when, even weakened by centuries of imprisonment, he's still so powerful?

"You wield your craft like a club, swinging it gracelessly," he says, sounding disappointed.

The claws grasping my soul loosen enough for the pain to lift. I suck in a hoarse, shuddering breath.

"Have you ever missed the sounds of life, Sirscha?" he continues. "Footsteps on stone. The murmur of voices. The blade of an ax splitting wood. The warmth of a hearth. The scent of cooking fires. I should know these things, yet they're like memories I can't quite recall."

If I could sneer, I would. With painstaking slowness, I grit through my teeth, "You expect me to believe you torture the people here because you're, what, lonely?"

He laughs, a quiet sound like leaves rustling. "What do you hope to find here?"

"Information."

"For what purpose?"

To kill you. As Saengo said, I should be clear about my intentions, at least to myself. But to him, I say, "To go home."

It isn't a lie. It's just not the whole truth. Over the last two months, how often have I yearned for the streets of Vos Talwyn and its familiar faces, aching for the simplicity of what had been? I'm so tired of being afraid.

He watches me, expression impossible to read. Fear suffocates me. The pain builds, making my jaw ache with the need to scream. But I don't. Kendara taught me better than that.

"You're not going to kill me," I say, infusing my voice with disgust.

Why come to me in my dreams otherwise? Why tell me he wants to know me? He spoke of fate and meetings. He spoke of a brother as well, which means, somewhere inside him, he remembers what it is to be human and to crave what he lost.

Suddenly, it doesn't seem quite so ludicrous that he might be lonely. The realization floods me with new determination.

Although he's recovering from what Ronin did to him,

maybe that isn't his true weakness. The most powerful evils can only be driven by something equally powerful.

Maybe what drives the Soulless is a fear of being alone.

Abruptly, he releases me. I gasp and stumble. The pain of my knees striking stone barely registers after the agony of the Soulless's craft. My fingertips scrape over stone and bead with blood.

Neither of us speaks, but I am acutely aware that I'm alive only by his whim. I push to my feet, willing my knees to hold me up.

The silence takes on a presence of its own, steeped in the wordless threat of the Dead Wood. Surrounded by haunted trees, there is no birdsong, no creatures snuffling through the underbrush. Despite those who remain prisoners here, even the castle is quiet.

Since he hasn't contradicted my assertion about not killing me, I dare to ask, "Why Queen Meilyr? Evewyn isn't strong enough to stand against both Nuvalyn and Kazahyn."

I doubt he'll admit she has his familiar, and presumably, their alliance includes his intention to reclaim it.

"Worried you won't have a home to return to if the other kingdoms raze it?" he asks, head tilting. "The queen has her uses." He doesn't elaborate. A moment later, his gaze slides past me.

The human guard from earlier comes up the path, somehow

summoned without a word. I wonder what the Soulless is doing to him, to his soul, and I wince in sympathy. He doesn't look at me. He only bows once as the Soulless orders him to escort me to a room.

The relief to escape his presence is slow to come. His magic burns through me, a poison I can't expel.

I follow the guard, and to my surprise, he leads me to the rooms I'd shared with Saengo the last time I was here. It feels wrong returning to them without Phaut shadowing my steps or guarding the door, glowering at me. Guilt stabs at my back, along with the memory of Juleyne's hatred.

Before I can close the door, the guard stutters, "Thank you. Thank you for going to him. To save my friend."

I shake my head. "I didn't have a choice. And I can't . . . I wish I could help you escape. But I don't know—"

"It's impossible," he says, looking down. "He'll know, and he'll kill us. The last one who came to help us, the shadow-blessed gate . . ." He closes his eyes as a tremor races through his entire body. "We didn't know that he was here yet. He surprised us."

The anger helps to focus me. "We're going to beat him. And then we'll come back for all of you. Do what you must to survive until then. Okay?"

He doesn't look like he believes it, but he nods all the same. I don't know what to say. I don't know how to offer hope when

I can barely muster any for myself.

Once the door is shut, I slump against it, the back of my head thudding against the wood. My things, which I'd left in Ronin's study, are now sitting just inside. On the table, a maid has left me a modest meal of rice and boiled greens in bone broth. Anger heats my chest at the idea of anyone being forced to serve me when we're all trapped here together.

What does he mean by treating me like a guest rather than the prisoner I am? What's the point of this farce?

I don't have much of an appetite, but I eat to keep my strength and to thank whoever made this meal in such circumstances. Afterward, cleaning up in the attached washroom feels strangely routine, as if Saengo and I were here mere days ago rather than weeks.

Our beds are exactly as we left them, the blankets neatly tucked. But the truth is in the light layer of dust that coats everything. No one's been in here since Ronin died.

Without him, Spinner's End will return to what it was before—a ruins to be devoured by the Dead Wood as if he'd never been here at all. It's sad, I suppose.

Even the legacy of Ronin the Spider King, who lived for centuries as one of the most powerful shamans in all of Thiy, can be easily erased.

Dust and ash.

EIGHTEEN

I spend the first two days combing through the castle, even the parts Ronin had left undisturbed, but the crumbling floors and collapsed ceilings are enough to convince me that the ruins are too treacherous to be useful as a means for hiding a secret archive.

When my search turns up nothing, I change tactic. Maybe I'm thinking about this too hard. Ronin would've needed a large storage space. The library seemed too obvious, but now I wonder if it's actually the perfect place to hide such records. It's also the largest room in the castle.

I take a lantern and walk the entire perimeter of the library. The last time I was here, the servants kept at least some sconces lit for the castle's guests. Now, aside from a few windows, the vast space is largely shrouded in darkness.

Saengo and I spent countless hours in here. My worry for her is a constant pit in my gut. With so much distance between us, I can't sense her emotions anymore, but our connection remains strong, her candle flame undimmed. If she's kept her pace, she should reach the grasslands within the next couple of days. After that, it's only a few days more westward to Falcons Ridge.

I continue onto parts of the library I haven't explored before. Several minutes pass before my lantern illuminates a plain door, tucked between two wall shelves and easily overlooked, especially in the dark. It's small enough to be mistaken for a cupboard.

When I yank on the door, I'm unsurprised to find it locked. I can't find a keyhole, though. Seeing as no one is left in the castle to care about whether I break anything, I return to my rooms to retrieve my swords. Then, with less elegance than I would like, I wedge the blades between the door frame until the hinges snap.

It's a messy job, and it would never pass any of Kendara's tests, but I succeed in opening the door. I have to bend over to pass through the entrance, but once inside, I lift my lantern to reveal what could almost be an entirely separate library.

The room isn't nearly as large, of course, but it's filled to the brim with books, scrolls, and stacks of parchment. My heart thunders as triumph soars through me.

Holding the lantern high, I cross the length of the room, taking quick stock of its contents. Most of the shelves are covered in dust. Pulling a book off one such shelf, I brush away a thick layer of gray before opening the cover. My pulse races in anticipation.

All at once, my excitement turns to frustration. The handwriting is Ronin's, but it's written in a language I don't recognize. It isn't Nuval, which I can't read anyway, but something else entirely. If I had to hazard a guess, I'd say it was from Ronin's home in the north—a language that's likely gone out of use after centuries of assimilation into the Empire.

I check several more books and stacks of parchment, my frustration growing as they all reveal the same. It shouldn't surprise me, yet I feel like an idiot for not anticipating this. It's no wonder these records are so poorly protected with a single lock. Should someone find their way in here, no one but Ronin would be able to read the contents.

Damn him. I slam the lantern onto a desk against the wall and sink into the accompanying chair. My craft rushes through my veins, making my fingers twitch restlessly as I rub my temples. I can't give up so easily. Not until I've gone through this entire room.

It's already been a few days, and I don't have much time left before I need to escape and return to Saengo. I constantly worry about how much her infection has spread.

I begin my sweep of Ronin's documents, starting from one end of the room to the other. Although it takes the better part of a day, I finally discover scrolls in Evewynian, a bound manuscript written in Nuval, and several stacks of correspondence in Kazan.

The Evewynian scrolls date back centuries and appear to be letters exchanged between Ronin and a former Evewynian queen about a marriage with a Nuvali royal. They're not relevant to what I'm searching for, but I tuck them away with my things. I imagine Prince Meilek would be interested in such historical documents.

I can't read the Nuval manuscript, but it might be useful in teaching myself the language, so I hold on to that as well. I briefly entertain the idea of seeking out a shaman guard or maid to help translate, but since I don't know what the manuscript is about, I can't trust sharing it with just anyone.

As for the Kazan correspondence, Ronin has jotted notes in his language along the margins, but the original messages are intact.

It's an old dialect, and I can't understand everything, but I can pick out enough words to understand their meaning. Each piece is dedicated to one of the temples in Mirrim, detailing things like who the High Priest or Priestess was at the time, the hierarchy, methods of training, and each craft's strength and weakness. With a jolt of surprise, I realize these must've been written by Kazan spies.

Pulse racing, I shuffle through the pages to find the Temple of Light. There's mention of a High Priest, an exhaustive list of subordinates, a description of the Light Temple grounds, and then the various lightwender crafts. My breath catches when I see "soulrender" among those listed. This was written before the conquest, before soulrenders were hunted and stricken from training at the Temple of Light.

The paragraph on soulrenders is tragically short, and I almost laugh at a remark about how the craft is generally useless given it can only be used against game and small animals. History would make fools of everyone who ever believed that.

The most interesting part, though, is an observation of a soulrender teacher *sharing* her magic with a student to help her learn how to summon her craft. I linger over the word, wondering if I'm mistranslating it. But even as I consider the word choice, the Soulless's magic stirs within me, uncomfortably close ever since he held my soul in his grip.

I can almost feel his magic slithering beneath my skin, a snake in the high grass coiled to strike. I've been avoiding him and ignoring the pull of his magic trying to lure me back to him.

When I fought Ronin and allowed the Soulless's magic to fuel my own, I thought I was using his power as one might a talisman. But maybe I'm wrong. Maybe this sharing is why our crafts can bridge our consciousness in dreams—why my magic has felt unruly and unpredictable since allowing his magic to mingle with mine.

I skim the letters for further mention of soulrenders, but there's nothing—no mention of the Yalaeng Conquest, or the Soulless, or how to defeat him.

I should begin searching the library for mention of talismans, but the question of soulrenders and sharing magic remains like a pebble wedged in my boot.

For all my frustration, there is one source of information in this castle I've not yet tried. It seems I will have to face the Soulless again.

There are no guards. He needs none.

This time, I don't find him reclining on a stone throne like an ancient king reawakened. Instead, he has relocated to a chaise at the center of what might have once been a reading room. Overhead is a domed glass ceiling that would fit right in at the Temple of Light.

Sunlight filters through the glass, bathing him in a soft glow. His skin is so pale that I can make out the faint impression of veins just beneath. His dark hair spills over the side of the chaise in a black tangle. A line of silver buttons runs from his high collar down the center of his tunic to his waist, where his long fingers are loosely laced.

He is completely still as I enter the room. Only his eyes

move, his gaze shifting from the glass ceiling where the sunset has drenched the sky the color of persimmons, to me.

I wonder if he watches the sky because he was kept from it for so long. I shake away the thought. I may pity him, but that's not the same as sympathy.

He watches me approach, his expression neutral. His stillness is disturbingly unnatural.

This isn't a social visit, so I don't bother greeting him. Instead, I ask, "What does it mean that soulrenders can share magic?"

His gaze shifts away, back to the sky laced in wispy pink clouds. The shadows beneath his eyes have deepened as if he's had trouble sleeping. Or perhaps he doesn't wish to sleep, having had enough of it.

"You've kept yourself busy, I see."

Although I remain near the door, it still feels too close. There can never be enough space between us and his poisonous magic. "Is it true?" I prod.

"All soulrenders have the ability, but as with most things, some possess a talent for it, and others do not."

"But we do." It's a statement, not a question.

"It's not quite so simple. Even those with a talent for it have to find a receptive match. All souls are unique, after all."

I mentally cringe at the idea of being a match with him in any capacity.

"Depending on the soulrender, our magic can function like

a current," he continues quietly. "Why do you think the mere awakening of your craft resonated with all lightwenders? That is a rare thing, but only possible because the nature of our craft allows our magic to touch other souls."

Frowning, I ask, "But what about Ronin? He could use your magic, but he wasn't a soulrender."

He sounds almost amused when he replies. "Ronin was an exception to much of shaman magic. He consumed his familiar. It changed his soul, and his craft, in ways we can never truly know. He was not quite a man, not quite a familiar."

"Familiar," I murmur, thinking of Saengo. I wonder how her soul has changed. She died that night at Talon's Teahouse. It was only the awakening of my craft that brought her back, transforming her into what she is now.

"I understand she was your friend before she was your familiar," he says, which makes me stiffen. "You want to keep her safe. I respect that. But it's an illusion. So long as she is your familiar, she will never be safe."

I sink onto a padded bench against the wall and swallow back the bitterness of that truth. Saengo's life is tied to mine. If I die, then she loses the only tether keeping her alive.

"I can sense your despair," he says. "But what if I told you that you could restore her to life?"

NINETEEN

My stomach processes the words of the Soulless before my head does, flipping against my spine. But then reality catches up, and I sneer. "You're lying. That's not possible."

His lips twitch into a smile. He looks exhausted, but his eyes remain determined, watching the sky deepen to a vibrant plum. "What do you know of possible? You've been a shaman for a matter of weeks. When I was trapped in Ronin's cocoon, although I slept, I was aware. The spirits here, and my connection to them, allowed part of my consciousness to perceive the world around the trees, and learn from the souls claimed by the Dead Wood."

If he was aware inside that cocoon—even if only partially—how could he remain sane after so long in confinement? Maybe the spirits in the Dead Wood helped to carry that burden.

Maybe all their rage and vengeance and violence aren't their own. Maybe it's the Soulless's.

"Then how?" I ask, humoring him. "Soulrenders only destroy."

"Look around us. The Dead Wood is proof that magic can bend however we wish, so long as we're strong enough. And together? You and I could have the power to restore life if we dared to."

His power and his words are a spell, ensnaring my hopes. I hate myself for wanting to believe them. But in the end, I'm too much of a realist, and I don't trust him. There's much I don't understand about our craft, but I do know this—we wreak too much pain to give life.

I remember thinking not so long ago that the Soulless's legacy isn't mine. But if soulrenders only destroy, then what does that make me? I killed that soldier in Tamsimno. People have a right to fear me—even *I'm* afraid of what I can do.

If only I'd shown Ronin mercy, then none of this would have happened. What's wrong with me that I hadn't?

"I know what it is to lose someone, Sirscha."

I scowl, wondering what my expression gave away in my silence. "Your brother. House Yalaeng creating an army of soulrenders during the conquest. Is that what you wanted me to learn?"

At last, a reaction. For a moment, his mask fractures, and

I glimpse the bright vein of fury buried beneath the surface. Then his expression smooths over, and he's once again an illusion of calm.

"The Empire says I went mad with power during a battle against the shadowblessed and killed both friend and foe. As far as their lies go, it isn't so far from the truth. But do they say why?"

The abandoned barrack at the Temple of Light flashes in my memory, along with the echo of long-ago pain. "No. Only that your magic became too much for your mind."

His laugh is a dry, uncomfortable sound. "I had no particular love for the Empire. They conquered my city before I was born, though there were some who remembered a time before the Empire's control. But my little brother wanted more than what our city could give him. He wanted glory and recognition from what he claimed would be the greatest empire in the world."

"So when the Empire came looking for soulrenders for their army . . ." By becoming Kendara's pupil, didn't I want something similar? After too long being discarded and dismissed, I wanted not glory but the acknowledgment of my value.

"He jumped at the chance. Except he would only go to Mirrim if I went with him, and how could I tell him no? So off we went, two fools in search of our own destruction."

My heart sinks. I don't want to feel anything for him other

than hatred. Tragedy doesn't excuse atrocity. But if I mean to kill him, then I ought to do him the small favor of knowing his story.

"The Temple of Light taught us to channel one another's magic, but in ways that defied natural boundaries. None of our souls were truly receptive to one another, so we had to fight to push our craft beyond our abilities."

"So that you could use your craft against other people, instead of beasts. Did they make you practice on . . ." It feels wrong to say it.

"Yes. But every shaman has their limitations, and some were simply not meant to wield more power than their own, or to use their craft against another human soul."

"What happened to them?" I ask.

"It was like a fire burning too fast and too hot. It was too much. Their souls burned out. We were nearly depleted. I wanted to leave, but my brother saw it as a challenge to prove himself. When we were at last ordered to battle against the shadowblessed . . ."

He trails off, and I wait, the back of my head against the wall as the light gradually dims.

"Maybe the strain finally became too much," he says. "Maybe his soul finally fractured beneath the weight of all the souls he'd ripped. But he began killing everyone around him, even our own soldiers. I could see it in his eyes—he was undone. Something inside him had broken, and wherever my brother had gone, he was no longer in control.

"But he was still a powerful soulrender. In the chaos, our armies scattered and the shadowblessed were gaining ground."

Because the last conversation I had with Saengo has been haunting me for days, I suspect I know what he did. A weight settles in my chest.

"You killed him," I whisper.

His eyes harden, amber chips faintly glowing in the last dregs of sunlight. "I tore his soul from his body. And it broke me."

I ball my fists at my sides, knuckles digging into the bench cushion. I think about what it felt like on that ship with so many souls crowding around me as my control crumbled. It would have been easy to rip every single one of them from their moorings.

If I'd been in the Soulless's position—if I'd just killed the one person I loved most—then I might have done it without remorse. If I was already a monster, what would it matter anymore?

Saengo would be disappointed in me for having that thought. Saengo always thought the best of me. Even when no one else believed in me, she did.

"When my grief had run its course, the battlefield was empty of the living. But in my bitterness, I refused to release the souls still gripped within my craft." His gaze slides to mine. The fury bleeds from his voice like a wound run dry.

"The Empire paints me as a madman because that absolves them of their part in my creation."

The Empire committed a terrible crime against their own people, and House Yalaeng doesn't deserve the power they built by taking from others. Their secrets should be exposed. Even so, allowing the Soulless his revenge isn't an option.

"Why not let them go now?" I ask, head tilted. "Is it like channeling another soulrender's magic? Do the souls make you stronger?"

He takes his time contemplating a response before saying, "I couldn't release them even if I wanted to. They've been a part of me for too long. While I was imprisoned, every soul taken by the Dead Wood allowed me to glimpse how the world has changed. I learned what the Empire had done to all soulrenders because of me." A line appears between his brows. "And then I felt your craft awaken. I have not felt such power in a long time. It's not every soulrender whose magic resonates with other lightwenders. That was rare even before the conquest. Now, I imagine few people understood the truth of it."

Ronin must have, though. He'd known a time before the Soulless and the Dead Wood. How ironic that the Empire's own efforts to eliminate knowledge of soulrenders played in my favor.

Although he doesn't move, the Soulless's magic is a constant, sinuous presence. It wraps around my shoulders, my neck, looping ever tighter. "We will right the wrongs that began with House Yalaeng. If the world will not allow us to exist, then we will forge a new one."

I continue watching the sky, feeling the weight of his gaze—his certainty.

"You see. We are not so different," he says. "We both wish to know a home again."

I shiver. His magic is a siren luring me to sea. I focus on Saengo's candle flame, letting her light guide me instead.

Strangely, I don't hate him. Not in the way I loathe the queen for how easily she discards the lives of her people. The Soulless lost his brother in the worst way imaginable, but I am at risk of losing Saengo if I don't stop him. So long as he exists, so long as his magic infects the Dead Wood, Saengo will never be safe.

I stand, uncomfortable with doubting my goal, even for the span of a heartbeat. "I'll think on your words."

He watches me leave, and I don't relax until I'm well away from his rooms. Then I slump against the wall, my fingers digging into fibrous patches of spiderweb. I need fresh air.

I make my way toward the courtyard where Theyen tried to invoke my craft. I'm grateful now that I failed, or else I might have killed him. I suppose that's what Ronin wanted. Irrefutable proof of what I am, and a dead Kazan prince to start a war between the kingdoms.

When I reach the balcony overlooking the courtyard, movement from above catches my attention. My gaze snaps to the figure of a small brown falcon sweeping into the tower aviary. At once, I turn on my heel, my legs already in motion. Unless the Soulless has other secret allies, only one person could have sent that falcon.

I rush through empty hallways and take the stairs two or three at a time until I reach the tower. The aviary door, usually kept latched, is wide open, and it's immediately clear why. Aside from the arriving falcon, the aviary is empty. A servant steps into view with a scrap of parchment in hand. Sweat slicks his forehead. Seeing me, he startles so violently that he drops the message.

I scoop it up, tucking it against my palm. "Hello. If it's all right with you, I'd be glad to deliver this to him for you."

He blinks as if my words make no sense. His mouth opens and closes soundlessly before he, at last, manages to say, "Please do."

"I had a feeling you wouldn't mind," I say, offering him a kind smile. He wipes his forehead, looking like a man spared from execution.

Once I'm out of sight, I unfurl the parchment. It isn't signed, but the message is clearly from Queen Meilyr. She is awaiting the arrival of her northern ships before returning to Kazahyn. She doesn't anticipate much resistance this time, given the Kazan clans have shifted most of their attention to their northern borders and the Empire.

I crumple the parchment, my thoughts racing. If she's waiting for more ships, then that means one of two things. Either she's taking an even larger navy than before to claim the Xya River, or her ships were so heavily damaged in the battle against the Kazan that she needs reinforcements while the ships are repaired. Either way, this means she's back in Evewyn.

But not for much longer.

Once she's on a ship again, she'll be nearly impossible to reach undetected. I have to get to her—and to the Soulless's talisman—before she leaves Vos Talwyn.

I came here looking for information on how to defeat a monster. Instead, I found glimpses of the man buried beneath.

Time is running out. I skim volumes on the history of talismans, when shamans first discovered bones could be fashioned into weapons and wards. I page through crudely bound books about famous talismans such as the Inferni's Rib, which could render the wearer impervious to fire crafts, and the Weaver's Crown, which amplified magic and was, allegedly, lost at sea.

The sun has begun to set when I, at last, stumble on a

passage in a stack of loose parchment. It's an essay of some sort written by a shaman Scholar, arguing the theory that magic is an exhaustible resource.

Every shaman and shadowblessed carries within them a remnant of the fallen sun god and the power gifted to them when she fell. As those possessed of magic grow in number, those remnants are not duplicated for successive generations. They are divided, diminishing the strength of our crafts.

In the earliest ages of Thiy, the Callings of magic held sway over the very foundations of the continent, awakening the ancient spirits of the elements. Crafts were more potent. Even the talismans created during this time were more effective. Most have either been lost to the centuries or collected by Scholars for research, as none can be destroyed. Only magic equal to that which created them can destroy them, and such wells of power are long dry.

I skim the rest of the essay, but there is no other mention of talismans. It doesn't matter, though. I have my answer, and my heart sinks at the simple and inescapable truth—I can't destroy the talisman because I'm not powerful enough.

But maybe I could be. I abandon the dusty bookshelves, retrieve my swords from my room, and then make my way outside to the courtyard.

As I approach the bone palisade, it's eerily quiet. I miss Saengo. Except during breaks at the Company, we were rarely apart for more than a few days.

Up ahead, a section of the webbing hangs in shreds. The roots have gained ground past the barrier, but so far, the troll bones have held fast, warding off the trees. My footsteps are silent as I pass through the gates.

The Soulless's magic rears within me, sinking hooks into my gut. He's trying to latch onto my soul, but maybe, as a soulrender as well, I can resist his craft so long as I'm not standing before him. Perhaps he knows that, which is why he tortured his guard to force me to go to him.

He must be worried I'm leaving, knowing that I could do so at any time. The way he spoke of what we could do together, the temptation of giving Saengo back her life, the past he hadn't needed to share to gain my sympathy—he doesn't want to keep me here with threats and forced promises. He wants me to stay by choice.

But I won't. Saengo needs me, and I have to get to Vos Talwyn before Queen Meilyr's northern ships arrive. Still, how can I become strong enough to destroy the talisman when I can barely control my magic?

The trees groan as I push back the tattered remnants of the white drape, and I remind myself not to let my thoughts wander in their presence. My pulse quickens, fear searing in my veins. If I can master my fear, I could learn from the trees, just as I tried the last time I was at Spinner's End.

Then, I had Phaut to watch my back. That familiar pain strums within me. This time, I'm alone with the souls, their anguish and rage palpable even without my craft. Magic rushes hot and eager to my fingertips, even as the hooks of the Soulless's power continue to wrench me backward. I grit my teeth, letting my own magic course through me, building in gradual waves until I feel like I'll burst from it.

For the first time in weeks, I'm completely alone without the risk of ripping any living souls. If I relaxed my control, just a little, what might happen?

The Soulless's strength isn't tempting for the power alone. The allure is in forcibly carving myself a space where I've never before been welcomed. And in my desire to heal Saengo and right the wrong I did her.

If I embrace my craft rather than leash it, would it change anything?

I glance over my shoulder at the silhouette of the castle, just visible in the descending dark. It's already halfway to becoming a ruins again.

Then, blood rushing in my ears, I step deeper into the

trees, glaring at the roots whenever they threaten to snag my ankles. The branches twitch, mimicking my trembling hands. Impressions of faces shift in and out of the bark, there and gone again before I can focus on them.

I shake out my fingers and roll my shoulders. Then I close my eyes. Unlike last time, when I could barely stir the embers of my craft into flame, the moment I will it, my magic blazes to scorching life. It burns hot in my belly, a cauldron on the brink of boiling over. The souls surrounding me shiver into clarity, spots of light that press against all my senses, making my lungs constrict in my chest.

With a slow, controlled exhale, I let it loose.

My magic escapes from me like a current. The souls shrink away. The trees shriek, lashing out. A branch stings my cheek. Another rakes the back of my hand. I don't flinch, ignoring it all as I will my magic to spread through the trees like a spider building a web, ensnaring every soul within my grasp.

Then, with only a thought, my craft shears through the tether that binds them to the Dead Wood. I don't open my eyes, but their relief shudders through me like a collective gasp.

I don't release them yet, though. The Soulless said the souls here were a part of him. They're connected to him. And although he didn't answer my question, I suspect some of his strength comes from the sheer number of souls he's bound to the trees.

The Soulless, who seems to have realized I'm not escaping, has loosened his hooks. But then his magic slithers to my shoulder, dripping poisonous temptation in my ears. If the souls make him stronger, then they could make me stronger as well. I could become powerful enough to heal Saengo. Maybe even to restore her life—to give back what I took from her.

But the steady flame of Saengo's candle illuminates the truth: using these souls means embracing the monster lurking within.

Even so, I hesitate. Ronin said that I'm destroying the souls when I free them from the Dead Wood, but maybe he was wrong. Maybe releasing them will allow them a true death so that they might find their way back to the Sisters. There's no way to be certain.

The longer I grip their souls, the more I realize I can feel them—their emotions, like how I can sense Saengo's. Anger and sorrow filter through my magic and my defenses, making my breath catch. Is this the danger of being connected to other souls for too long? How does the Soulless manage it?

The world begins to compress. All my senses narrow down to the rising flood of their agony. I grit my teeth as their rage tunnels deep, dragging my own from the depths of my mind, all-consuming. The ground falls away. I can no longer feel the earth beneath me or the air in my lungs or the wind against my skin.

Another soul brightens before me, familiar somehow, but

I don't know why. My thoughts are a chaos of confusion. All I can focus on, all I can feel, is their anger—to tear the souls from others, to make them suffer as they have suffered, to share their despair.

Do it, a voice whispers within me, silken and dark. *Take his soul.*

Then another voice, barely audible, hisses, "Sirscha!"

My eyes fly open. The souls remain, orbs of light caught within the glimmering web of my magic. But standing before me, just as tightly snared, is Theyen.

With a gasp, I release all the souls at once. I stumble away, heart pounding, head spinning, as Theyen collapses to his knees. The souls wink out of existence, their emotions fading into murmurs and then whispers and then blessed silence.

All around us where the souls had been, there is only a large swath of bare earth, the trees containing them having disintegrated into ash.

My hands shake as the realization of what I'd nearly done crashes around me. "Theyen," I begin.

His head snaps up, eyes flashing. He lunges for me. His body slams into mine, and all the air rushes from my chest. We both fall backward. I brace for impact, but it doesn't come.

Instead, the edges of the shadow gate close around us as the Soulless's magic is ripped from me, like claws torn from flesh.

TWENTY

My back arches as I scream. But in the utter silence of the gate, with my other senses muffled, all I feel is the pain.

My fingers gouge into Theyen's back. My soul feels like it's being torn in two. Nausea roils in my stomach. Through it all, Theyen's arm remains firm around my waist. After what feels like an eternity, my back slams into something hard and wet as the shadow gate spits us out.

I gasp at the impact. The discomfort is minuscule, compared to the ache deep in my bones after being torn from the Soulless's reach. My shoulder blades throb dully as I attempt to regain my breath. My stomach lurches again, and I'm glad I haven't eaten anything since lunch.

Above me, Theyen groans in discomfort. He landed with one arm around my waist, and the other braced beside my head to keep from crushing me. Grimacing, he rolls to the side so that we're lying next to one another. For a moment, all we can do is pant up at the black sky that, judging by the puddle I'm lying in, is currently pouring. I blink rain from my eyes and open my mouth to allow the cool droplets to dampen my tongue and aching throat.

Theyen stands first, cursing as he swipes a hand over his soaked clothes. His circlet sits slightly askew over his damp hair. I try to focus on his silhouette, but the rain blurs my vision.

Sisters, I think, fresh horror rising within me. In the Dead Wood, I'd lost all sense of myself. I hadn't even noticed Theyen's arrival. All I knew was the unrestrained fury raging within those souls. Is that what it's like for them, trapped in those trees? A tremor races through me.

I swallow again, my heart pounding in my ears, nearly drowning out the rain. "You came for me."

"I'm already regretting it," he says, extending his hand.

I squint against the rain and accept his assistance. He pulls me to my feet but doesn't let go. Instead, he tugs me close enough that I can see the raindrops collect on his ivory lashes. He glares, his gray skin creating the illusion that he's been chiseled from stone. There's something in the intensity of his gaze that I haven't seen since the first time we met: uncertainty. As if he doesn't quite know me.

His fingers tighten around mine, coming just shy of

painful. I clench my teeth, my hackles rising. "Let me go. Or I will make you."

He eases his grip but doesn't release me. "You didn't seem to know what you were doing, and since I took you by surprise, I will overlook it this once. But the next time you lose control like that, don't think I won't stop you."

We share a taut moment of silence, the threat hanging between us sharp as a blade.

I'd like to see you try. The words hover behind the cage of my teeth, the memory of rage fighting to gain ground.

But with effort, I push it back. He's right. I nearly killed him. If I lose control like that again, I would want him to stop me.

"I'm sorry," I say quietly. I try to relax my muscles, but every part of me is still wound too tightly. "Thank you for coming after me."

His lips tighten, nostrils flaring on a sharp inhale. Rainwater slides over the angles of his cheeks and nose, settling into the crevice of his lips. His fingers are firm around mine. His grip, the ground beneath my feet, and Saengo's flame burning steadily within me help calm the chaos of my thoughts. I am here; I am still myself, and, wherever we are, the Soulless can't reach me.

At last, Theyen releases me and steps back. He turns without a word, his boots squelching through mud and wet grass. I have no idea where we are, the darkness and the rain blotting details into amorphous shadows. Eventually, my eyes adjust, and I can make out the shapes of evergreens, their needles speckled with water droplets.

Abruptly, my stomach heaves. I double over, gagging. My head spins, and my heart drums against my ribs. I brace my palms against my thighs, drawing deep, long breaths as the rain pelts the back of my head.

Is this a side effect of gripping all those souls? When the hammering in my temples dims, I straighten slowly, groaning.

"It's from the shadow gate," Theyen says.

I press my palm to my stomach. "That's never happened before."

"Because I was careful not to take you over too great a distance. The farther we travel, the longer you spend within the gate. For those born without the craft, it can put a strain on their bodies. Spend too long within the gate, and eventually, you lose all comprehension."

My fingers rub my forehead. "Well, that's good to know. Where are we?"

"Somewhere safe," he says, and proceeds ahead.

I follow, hugging myself. The rain is warm, given we're still in the summer months, but my back is soaked and the rest of me is following. "How did you know I was at Spinner's End?"

"I caught up with Saengo in the grasslands."

My hand shoots out, grabbing his sleeve. "Where is she?"

He stills, his head turning just enough to tell me, "En route to her father. I left two of my soldiers with her. She'll send her falcon when they arrive to confirm her safety."

Relief rushes through me, and I release him. "Thank the Sisters."

With a wyvern and his ability to open shadow gates, few people can cross the continent as swiftly as Theyen can. I wonder how common the craft is. Do those with the ability visit strategic locations across the continent just to be able to travel there by gate? It's brilliant, really. It would also be a dangerous, useful skill for any assassin or spy.

The shadowblessed would have people believe they're content inside their mountains, but Theyen is always well informed about the goings-on of other kingdoms. That's no coincidence.

"Have you been to Vos Talwyn?" I ask, curious.

"No."

I'm not certain he's being truthful, but I've also never heard of Kazan diplomats entering the city. The queen has always received them in Vos Gillis.

Ahead of us, the trees part to unveil a small cabin. The cloud cover doesn't reveal much, but I can make out shuttered windows and the slope of a roof, slick with rainwater. A sconce hangs beside the front door. Its light doesn't extend far in the downpour, only a dim, golden glow, like diffused starlight.

A safe house, I assume. It's well hidden, and if we're on top of a mountain somewhere in Fireborn Queens territory, which I assume we are, then no one will find me. The only question is: Am I being kept here to protect me, or to protect others from me?

He unlocks the door and pushes it open on silent hinges. It's dark inside, but my craft doesn't sense any other souls aside from forest creatures sheltering from the downpour, nor do my other senses pick up on anything amiss. So I follow Theyen inside, glad to be out of the rain.

"I'm keeping count, Sirscha Ashwyn." He shuts the door. The sound of the rain diminishes to a quiet patter against the roof. "You owe me your life, several times over. It is a debt that you will repay me someday."

I slowly take in the darkened house. I'm uncomfortable with the idea of owing anyone a life debt, but he isn't wrong. "I thought that first time was out of friendship."

"I suspect friendship isn't meant to involve so much threat of painful death."

"Saengo would disagree," I mutter. "Why are we here?" I spot a hearth with a heaping pile of wood stacked beside it. I feel around on the mantle, rewarded when my hands find a tinderbox.

There's a shuffling sound as he removes his boots. "Because no one can know I saved you. This place is warded against shadow gates, and no one knows it exists save for my family."

"Am I a prisoner?" I ask. This place isn't exactly difficult to escape from.

He scoffs. "If you wish to leave, then by all means, but I can't guarantee anyone you come across won't try to kill you on sight. House Yalaeng has issued a warrant for your capture, wanted alive if that's any consolation."

I frown, but I focus on my task until a healthy fire illuminates the cabin's interior. The simple space is more modest than what I'd expect from such a distinguished clan. It's furnished with a bed and dresser in one corner, a small kitchen and pantry in the opposite corner, and a square table with four seats at its center.

Satisfied, I stand to remove my boots and line them up against the wall beside Theyen's. "Why are you risking your alliance for me?"

"I don't do it for you," he says curtly. He removes his sodden jacket and drapes it over the back of the nearest chair. "It's in my clan's best interests not to allow the only two soulrenders on the continent to conspire with each other. We've enough of a threat from just the one."

"I wasn't conspiring with him." I give him a summary of what I realized on board the queen's ship—that she possesses a talisman that contains his familiar—and then of my discovery at Spinner's End. In order to destroy the talisman, I must find a way to strengthen my craft.

He regards me with a skeptical tilt of his brow. If Theyen is genuinely acting in his clan's best interests, why wouldn't he turn me over to his mother, the High Queen? Theyen is annoying at best and insufferable at worst, but he is, in my limited experience, an honorable man. Even if he makes me want to punch him.

"Why didn't you use shadow magic on the ship? You could've easily secured me enough time to acquire the talisman." In fact, I don't recall any of the shadowblessed using shadow magic in Tamsimno.

"Don't be so dense, Sirscha. Haven't you figured it out yet? Why would Queen Meilyr's offer to meet expire at sunset?"

I tilt my head. "I've only ever seen you use your craft at night. Shadowblessed can't use magic during the day?"

"Shamanic magic rests on having a familiar. Shadow magic rests on the sun. Rather, the absence of it. Every dawn renders us as powerless as any human."

"Not completely," I say, remembering soaring above clouds on the back of a wyvern. "And who says humans are powerless? They thrive without any magic at all, day or night."

Theyen's lashes flutter, like he's resisting the urge to roll his eyes. "In any case, my alliance with House Yalaeng is in question now that you so grandly and publicly exposed yourself to all three kingdoms in one fell swoop."

My shoulders bunch around my ears as I settle down before

the fireplace. The reminder doesn't help the sick feeling in my stomach. I feed another log to the growing flames, letting the dry heat warm my fingers.

Theyen moves into the kitchen. Rummaging through the cabinet pantry, he begins unearthing hidden caches of salted meat and root vegetables that look like they haven't been here all that long. How often is this place in use that it should be regularly stocked?

I watch him, turning my soaked back to the heat to hopefully dry more quickly. "Queen Meilyr has returned to Vos Talwyn. I hope this means your allies didn't suffer too greatly."

He locates two plates, looking mildly resentful at having to serve me. "There will always be a cost on either side. When the queen's ship was spotted passing Vos Gillis, it was accompanied by only a handful of other ships. It seems the bulk of her navy is missing."

"Sank?" I ask, my heart wrenching. So many Evewynian lives, most of them simply following the queen's orders.

"Not confirmed," he says, his tone indifferent. It sets my nerves on edge, but when he hands me a plate, I take it without a word. To my surprise, he settles on the ground beside me before the fire.

His crown is still crooked, his damp hair dripping down his neck and into his collar. "Maybe their ships were too heavily damaged by the wyverns and their own ballista, and they sank in a storm. Maybe they're marooned somewhere in the middle of the sea. What matters is that people are dead because of Queen Meilyr. And now, thanks to you, the Nuvali and Kazan are gathering forces to fortify the borders between our kingdoms. Princess Kyshia won't be able to hold her father back from open war much longer."

Although I chew the food in my mouth, I can't taste much of it past my anxiety. "Queen Meilyr is awaiting reinforcements from her ships in the north. She will try to take the river again once they arrive in Vos Talwyn."

"Did *he* tell you this?" he asks, contempt dripping from his words. "If the Fireborn Queens and our allies are focused on the Empire at our northern borders, there will be fewer to stand against the queen in the south when she returns. We cannot fight on multiple fronts. Kazahyn is already a fractured kingdom. There are too many clans and too many long-held grudges. There will never be a true alliance."

"But it's happened before." The Yalaeng Conquest is recorded as the only time in Kazahyn's history when the clans united against a single purpose—to protect their lands against the shamans.

"That was a very long time ago. Now, just getting certain clans into the same room with one another without bloodshed would be a miracle. As it is, the Fireborn Queens are already being pressed to decide between our alliances with other

Kazan clans and my marriage alliance with House Yalaeng."

"You will pick Kazahyn." I can't imagine Theyen would ever prioritize a marriage he never wanted with a shaman princess over the shadowblessed clans.

"I will," he says simply.

"What have you heard from the Ember Princess?" I ask.

He gives me an annoyed look. "I've said enough. My clan's business is not yours."

"Fair enough," I say, shoving the last of the food into my mouth. Having something in my stomach helps to settle it a bit. His lip curls, but given our circumstances, the last thing I care about is how I eat. "I don't know much about politics. My only goal is to stop the Soulless."

"Spoken with the kind of ignorance I'd expect from someone unused to responsibility or the consequences of their actions." He stands to return his empty plate to the kitchen sink.

I glare at his back. "The kingdoms have hated each other for nearly as long as they've existed. You can't pin that on me."

Theyen turns from the sink to face me, and although his movements are slow, his expression is tight with anger. "But you made it worse by lying."

"What should I have done, Theyen?" I ask, my voice rising. "Told everyone what I am so that they could kill me sooner rather than later? I had to enter the Empire to learn about the

Soulless, which would've been difficult if the whole continent was hunting me."

"You should have had some foresight when you decided to kill Ronin."

I draw a furious breath. I killed Ronin because I didn't think I had another choice. He'd become corrupted, believing the only way to find peace would be to destroy the kingdoms altogether. Not to mention, he'd been trying to kill me and nearly succeeded.

And yet. I count my heartbeats, breathing slowly through my nose until my pulse calms. Hadn't I had a similar thought? If only I'd shown Ronin mercy, if only I'd struck to injure, not to kill.

I force myself to say, "I should not have killed Ronin. At least not then."

"Little good that does us now."

"If you're so angry with me, then why are you helping me?"

"Because like it or not, Sirscha, you are an asset in this war, and I would rather have you on my side."

"Well, you're doing a piss poor job of winning me over."

We glower at one another, the silence threaded with frustration. If Saengo were here, she would know how to soothe the tension. Sisters, I miss her.

"I have been in contact with Prince Meilek," he says abruptly, evidently just as eager as I am to move on. He retrieves his jacket from the back of the chair and drapes it over his arm since it's still damp. "I will deliver you to him in two days' time. He's hiding in Evewyn, so we'll have to wait for him to reach the rendezvous point."

I stand, setting my plate on the mantle. In truth, I'd like his help retrieving the talisman from Queen Meilyr. The task would be easier with Theyen's abilities, even if he's never been to Vos Talwyn. But he's already risked too much by helping me escape Spinner's End. The Fireborn Queens are suffering because of me. I can't ask any more of him, not when I already owe him a life debt.

"Are you leaving now?" I ask.

"I've been gone too long as it is." He doesn't say goodbye or anything else as he opens the front door. The scent of fresh rain and wet grass sweeps inside, making the fire jump in the hearth. Then he's gone, the door clicking shut behind him.

I ensure the door is locked and the windows tightly shuttered. Then I strip out of my wet clothing and lay them out near the fire to dry. I spend the next hour pacing, thinking of all the things that need doing once we're in Evewyn. I didn't have enough time at Spinner's End, but part of me is relieved. The experience in the Dead Wood left me shaken, and there's no telling what might've happened had I stayed within the Soulless's influence.

His magic corrupted even Ronin, who sacrificed so much

to defeat him. The longer I'm around him, the deeper his magic would twine with mine, and the more afraid I am that it would turn me into something I'm not.

Or, if I'm being honest, turn me into a version of myself that I know lurks within me, but has always been suppressed. By Saengo, by my own fears and moralities.

But Kendara knew it was there. She must have. She wanted me to be callous and to put myself first. To escape all of this. If only I could.

TWENTY-ONE

"You're very much like me when I was young," says the Soulless.

I'm in the Dead Wood, I think. In this bizarre dreamscape, the trees are spider thin. The roots sprawl through the earth like spindly legs, and the branches stretch high into a vast darkness, devoid of stars. Mist swirls around me, faces hidden within the gray plumes. Ghostly fingers trail along my arms, sending ice across the back of my neck.

I endure the phantom touches with my fists clenched at my sides. The Soulless is trying to unsettle me, but there's no need to play to his game.

His figure is indistinct through the mist and the skeleton trees, shifting in and out of view. But he is on his feet, strolling almost leisurely, and I'm not sure what that means—whether it's an illusion, or if he's getting stronger.

"You're much like me *before* I lost everything," he clarifies. Although he's walking some distance away, his voice flits around me, without direction. "You are running full speed toward the same future. You should break your ties before they betray you."

"You said there was a chance we could restore Saengo to life."

"And maybe we can if we try. But is that what you want? To give her back the ability to walk away from you forever?"

His words lodge in my chest, clawing out a fear I've long held inside and refused to expose to the light—that one day, Saengo would realize the mistake she'd made in befriending me and leave, just like everyone else.

"No one will ever accept people like us. The fact that there are only two of us left is proof enough."

His silhouette appears to my left, and I spin to face him only for him to vanish again into the mist and shadows.

"We hurt everyone who isn't strong enough to match our power. You've already hurt Saengo. Maybe not today, maybe not tomorrow, maybe not even a year from now, but someday, she will leave you."

I'm not like you, I think fiercely. *I will never be like you.*

"Make no mistake, Sirscha. Your friend's love will turn to hate. When you begin to age, and she does not. When she must watch her family and all she loves die, and she lingers as a part of you, unchanging. When the world moves on around her, her existence forgotten, she will hate you for it."

My stomach clenches tight, my chest aching. His words flay open the heart of me, laying bare the blood and bone of my fears.

Although his figure is a flickering shape amid the trees, his voice is clear and close, as if perched at my shoulder. "I am the only one who will remain. I am all you have."

My fingers dig into my thighs through the coarse fabric of my pants. He may be right. Someday, Saengo will hate me for what I did to her. And who can blame her? I would do anything for her, but that hardly matters if I can't do the one thing she needs most—give back her life.

I'm not even real. But she is. She hurts and loves and *feels*, and she's still with me, despite everything. Even if I have no one else, even were she not tied to me as my familiar, I can trust in knowing that Saengo will stand by my side.

"You're wrong," I say softly. The hiss of souls echoes from the trees and lashes out from the mist.

I won't end up like the Soulless. He's a monster, but even after all this time, he's still a man with human fears. I understand his desire to not be alone, much as I wish I didn't.

Before Saengo and Kendara, I never understood what it meant to hold another person close to your heart—to have a family, which I've always been hesitant to call them because, as much as I wanted it, I wasn't sure they felt the same.

The Soulless broke his magic and his heart in service to the Empire, and to stop his brother. That his actions continue to haunt him, centuries later, means some part of who he'd been is still there. If I can defeat him and release his soul, would that save him?

Would that save me from becoming like him, hoarding souls without regard?

"We're not alone," I say, searching out his form through the mist. He becomes clearer, a vague shape sharpening into lines and curves and shadows. "We don't *have* to be alone."

The hissing rises into snarls as half-rotted faces thrash within the mist, teeth gnashing. Disembodied hands reach for my sleeves, my hair, my shoulders, trailing damp cold. Patches of frost bloom against my skin as I turn in circles, fending off their chilling touch. My fist slams into the nearest tree.

I awake with a gasp, blinking up at the arched ceiling of Theyen's safe house, my knuckles stinging.

While I wait for Theyen to return, I formulate a plan.

I need to recover the Soulless's talisman while the queen is still in Vos Talwyn. As Kendara's pupil, I know how to get in and out of the city through hidden passages. Getting into the Grand Palace might be trickier, but I've an idea. I don't, however, know how to reach the queen's rooms. Prince Meilek should be able to help with that. Getting her alone, without her guards, will make taking the talisman less complicated.

I miss Saengo dearly, and I'm impatient to get this done, but I also miss this solitude. The only times I was ever truly alone was when I was on missions for Kendara, completing whatever impossibility she'd concocted to prove myself. My goals hadn't been simple even then, but they'd been straight forward. The only stakes were mine.

Midway through the second day of waiting, I can't help but wonder if Theyen actually intends to return. I've been certain that focusing on the Soulless's talisman is vital to removing him from the equation.

What if, by leaving me here, he's removing *me* from the equation?

I have to be on lands belonging to the Fireborn Queens. Last night, I studied the position of the stars and concluded I must be somewhere east of the Xya River. I need only to head west to reach the river or south to reach the coast. Although picking my way over unfamiliar mountains, on foot and without a map, would prove long and arduous. I would never make it back to Saengo before the rot took her.

Theyen will keep his word, I assure myself. Annoyed, I finish my food and wash and dry the plate. I used my craft to hunt. It's easy when I don't have to worry about hurting anyone else.

Since he's meant to come back for me tonight, I climb into bed to get some sleep before he arrives.

I dream of the Soulless again, but this time, he doesn't speak. He simply watches me, perched on this throne of twisted trees and trapped souls, picking at wisps of spiderweb clinging to his arms.

"What do you want?" I ask.

He only smiles, bright eyes cunning. His pale fingers pick, pick, pick at the webbing that never seems to thin. He seems to be waiting for something.

It's wholly unnerving.

Hours later, I awaken unsettled, certain that time is running out. What is the Soulless planning? He had an expectant air about him, as if he knows something is about to happen. My skin prickles, and I grow impatient for Theyen to arrive.

Other than my swords, I don't have anything I took with me to Spinner's End, so I've nothing to pack. I wait, pacing to the frenzied tune of crackling flames. The sky grows dark, and darker still.

At last, sometime after midnight, there's a sound at the front door—a key pushed into a keyhole. I dart behind the door and wait until it opens to reveal Theyen. Then I relax, easing my swords to my sides.

Theyen's eyebrow raises in a mocking look. "Have you gone feral in my absence?"

"I was being cautious. Besides, I wasn't entirely sure you'd come back."

"I did consider leaving you here."

"You're an ass."

"You're welcome."

I douse the fire, and since I've already tidied up, there's nothing left to do except leave. Seeing as I had two days to familiarize myself with the surrounding terrain, I lead the way, heading west, which is where we first arrived.

Preferring to avoid what happened last time, we take two shorter trips through the gate to reach our destination. I still need a minute to compose myself in between, though.

When we emerge from the second gate, we're in another forest. This one seems familiar, as if I've walked through these exact trees before, although I can't recall when or where. Even the way one tree leans against the one beside it, branches entwined, seems familiar. It's not until we reach a creek, and the small cottage nestled at its edge, that I recognize it.

We're on Phang lands. Once, years ago, Saengo took me to Falcons Ridge. We'd just graduated from the Prince's Company, and she'd yet to tell her parents about her decision to join the Queen's Company with me. Afraid of their reactions, she asked me to come with her, hoping my presence would deter them from doing anything too harsh.

Her parents received me as any highbrow reiwyn couple would a child with no means, no family, and no connections. They offered me a stiff greeting and then took Saengo aside to loudly inform her that, knowing of their disapproval of our friendship, how could she possibly think they'd welcome this social climber into their home? Was Saengo really so easily duped?

Just as loud, Saengo told them that she had enrolled in the Queen's Company, and there was no backing out, not without shaming the name of Phang. Then she took my hand and stormed out of the keep. We rode our drakes for hours and hours, well into the night, following a creek that ran from the main property over sloping hills and through wooded lands until we reached a small cottage at the water's edge.

It had been her grandmother's once, she'd said. We only stayed there a single night before her father's soldiers found us. I was carted back to Vos Talwyn, and Saengo was forced back to Falcons Ridge for the duration of our break. It had been a very long month.

The sight of that cottage and the warm light flickering behind the windows makes my heart leap. I rush down the slope. But then I pause, Saengo's candle flame a distant warmth in my chest. She isn't here.

TWENTY-TWO

I step up to the entrance with caution. Before I can knock, the door opens. Kou peers through the dark to ensure it's just Theyen and me, and then steps aside so I can enter.

The interior of the cottage is just as I remember. It's cozy and warm, with a curious collection of wooden figurines piled atop the windowsill. Thick, mismatched rugs cover the wood floors. Portraits of various Phang heirs hang on the wall, and the Phang crest—a falcon in mid-dive—has been painted above the mantel.

"Sirscha." Prince Meilek grins, rising from a table where a map is spread. I'm glad to see him, safe and whole. I begin to bow, but he stops me, grasping my hand between his. "I heard about what happened in Kazahyn. I'm glad you're safe."

"Did he know?" Theyen asks, arching one eyebrow. "That you're a soulrender."

When I don't immediately respond, Prince Meilek nods. Theyen's other eyebrow rises to join the first.

"Anyway," I say, turning back to Prince Meilek. "Have you been traveling this entire time?"

"Just about. We could all do with a rest," he says, indicating his Blades. Kou and two others either sit at the table or recline in overstuffed chairs, as if not quite sure how to occupy such a quaint space.

"How were you able to bring us here?" I ask Theyen. "You've been here before?"

"Only yesterday. My soldiers who escorted Saengo were able to show me the way."

I smile. She must have succeeded in convincing her father to hear out Prince Meilek. How else would he be here? "Will she be coming?"

"They sent a falcon. They'll be late," Prince Meilek says.

"They," I repeat, mentally cringing. Of course, Lord Phang would need to be here as well.

"We are on his land, something he's only allowed because of Saengo. And we need him if we're to win the north to our cause."

I still don't like him, but he is important. And he loves Saengo, which is his best quality.

"Saengo said she would arrange for our safety here," I say. "If Lord Phang supports you against your sister, it'll be because of her influence."

Prince Meilek nods in agreement. We wait for them to arrive, but when an hour has passed without a sign of them, we can't delay any longer. Their absence makes me uneasy, but Saengo is safe on Phang lands. It's probably the safest place she could be. But the longer we're apart, the worse her infection will become. Worry gnaws at me.

I relay my plan for how to get inside Vos Talwyn and the Grand Palace. When I ask Prince Meilek for details on how to reach the queen's rooms, though, he surprises me by insisting on coming.

"There's no need for you to do this alone," he says.

I'd planned to do it alone. Not because I have to or even because I want to, but because I simply assumed I would be on my own.

"My scouts have confirmed the queen's ship is docked in Needle Bay, and she has holed up within the Grand Palace," Theyen says. "Falcons have been spotted arriving, but only one has gone out, I assume to keep in contact with the Soulless."

My dream of the Soulless and the creeping certainty that something is about to happen prickles within me. I shake off the nerves and address Prince Meilek, "So you'll be able to get us into her rooms?"

He nods. "There's a passageway that connects my room to hers so that I could reach her quickly in the event of an attack. It'll be easier to get to my rooms first, and then access hers that way. Yen was able to acquire a position in the Grand Palace. She's been keeping an eye on things for me. She can help us if necessary."

I remember Yen, the cheerful, somewhat clumsy girl who Prince Meilek sent back to Evewyn weeks ago. "I don't think we should share our plan with anyone outside this room."

"I've known Yen for years. I trust her," he says.

Frowning, I look to Theyen, who meets my gaze. I haven't forgotten that the assassin in Luam knew about Prince Meilek's room rotation. It's possible there'd been a spy among the group. Yen would be one of the last people I'd suspect, which makes me all the warier of her. I know the advantages of being underestimated better than most.

Reluctantly, I nod and make a mental note to keep an eye on Yen should we run into her. I may not trust her, but I trust Prince Meilek.

"One more thing," I say, steeling myself for his reaction. "We leave tonight."

Prince Meilek frowns as his Blades glance uneasily at one another.

"This must be properly planned, Sirscha," Prince Meilek begins.

"There's no time," I say, impatience making my words harder than I intend. The memory of the Soulless and his small knowing smile makes my skin itch with restlessness. Besides, we don't know when the queen's ships will arrive. It could be any day now. "We can't delay. If we leave now, we should reach Vos Talwyn tomorrow night. We'll buy supplies on the way."

Kou steps up and leans close to murmur in Prince Meilek's ear. They exchange words I can't hear as I wait impatiently for his verdict. Theyen only watches, his expression revealing none of his thoughts.

After a moment, Kou steps away, and Prince Meilek crosses his arms, looking resolute. "This is a dangerous plan," Prince Meilek says. "The fewer people involved, the better. We'll travel faster as a pair. My Blades will remain here to continue working with Lord Phang."

I can tell by the expressions on his Blades' faces that they're not pleased with the decision. But I understand why he's leaving them behind. If this fails and we're caught, then they will be far from the queen's reach and her wrath.

My jaw tightens. We can't be caught. Not just for our sakes, but for Saengo's. As soon as we're finished, I have to find her. Retrieving the talisman can't wait, but neither can her rot.

"Then let's go," I say.

Kou lends me his drake, and we gather what supplies are immediately available. We don't need much. As we'll be traveling through the night, I'm glad I chose to find a few hours of sleep before Theyen returned for me.

Once we're gathered outside, drakes readied, Theyen

summons a gate, preparing to leave as well.

"Thank you," I say. "I know you're angry with me, but I hope we can be friends again someday."

Theyen gives me a withering look. "You're an idiot if you think I offer my help to just anyone. Didn't I tell you once that you'll have to be less dim-witted if you mean to keep my company?"

Then, without waiting for my reply, he vanishes into the gate, and it closes behind him.

I look at the empty place where he'd been, and then to Kou who's standing next to me, saddling his drake. "Did he just . . . say we're friends?"

"He did," Kou confirms, amusement pulling at his mouth.

Theyen is a strange, contradictory man.

Since Prince Meilek is more familiar with Phang lands than I am, he leads us. His Blades are reluctant to see us off, but they dutifully obey their prince.

We ride quickly, our sure-footed drakes guiding us through the night.

"Did you have to make promises to Lord Phang to earn his cooperation?" I ask, as we travel along a narrow path between fields of rice. I know little about Saengo's father, only that he's a proud man and very much a reiwyn lord. He commands power with the surety of someone who has never known otherwise.

"Some," he admits. "But none that I couldn't keep if I'm made king, and none that would weaken the crown. If I'm to lead them, they must know I won't be easily controlled."

"It's possible some allies might only be interested in positioning themselves closer to the crown. Do you think Lord Phang wants to be king?" I recall Saengo saying that there were those within the kingdoms who tired of Ronin reining in their ambitions. With him gone, and Evewyn in upheaval, maybe Lord Phang sees his opportunity.

House Phang has always been a prominent northern family, their origins going back to the court of the first Drake Queen. While they've never ruled, they've always had close ties with Evewyn's kings and queens.

But Prince Meilek says, "I doubt it. Lord Phang isn't a fool. Evewyn's people would never accept a usurper. It must be someone next in line to rule. Besides, he wouldn't have agreed to hear me out without Saengo's influence. He is loyal, which is a good quality in one's allies."

"It sounds like you've decided what to do," I say. When we spoke in Luam, he hadn't yet been certain about removing his sister from the throne.

He frowns as we push our drakes faster through open fields. It might be dark, but we're still exposed. "Mei is . . . lost right now."

I nearly scoff but restrain myself. Prince Meilek loves her.

How can he not? She's his sister, which still means something to him despite everything she's done. Queen Meilyr isn't lost, though. She has chosen her path, and she will walk it no matter who she has to step on.

Shortly before dawn, we pass from Lord Phang's lands onto a neighboring reiwyn lady's. To the west, the Coral Mountains transform with the sunrise from hulking slashes across the night sky into hazy green peaks. The orchards are past blooming, the boughs beginning to sag from heavy clusters of plums.

At the Company, I woke to the sight of those mountains each morning, and still, I am left breathless by the ragged peaks and the orchards that shroud them in clouds of vibrant color. In the spring, whole mountainsides transform into a fuchsia sea, their scent sweeping through Vos Talwyn to mingle with the salt from the bay.

We continue on, stopping only to rest and water our drakes. For once, the trees are our allies, Evewyn's thick forests keeping us well hidden. We circle around roads and the wooded paths more commonly used by farmers.

It's nearing sunset again, a gloom descending through the forest, when something disturbs the quiet.

"Wait," I whisper, drawing my drake to a stop. Prince Meilek follows suit, listening. I tilt my head, closing my eyes to better focus on the sound.

"Drakes," Prince Meilek says a moment before I do.

There are several of them, and they're moving quickly. I jam my heels into my drake's side, urging us into motion.

"Soldiers?" I ask Prince Meilek, but he only shakes his head. He doesn't know either.

I lean low over my drake's neck, letting it pick up speed. Its claws tear through the undergrowth, leaving a clear path for our pursuers to follow, but there's no helping it. From behind comes the sound of a bowstring releasing an arrow.

"Get down!" I shout as the arrow slams into a tree trunk ahead of me.

As my drake thunders past, I glimpse the arrow shaft and fletching. My stomach flips, and I jerk on the reins. Prince Meilek shouts my name as I wheel around to face our pursuers.

Within moments, a familiar drake breaks through the trees bearing an even more familiar rider. I yank on the reins and then leap from my drake. Saengo dismounts, and then she's there, her arms around me, squeezing me as I gasp my relief into the blunt ends of her hair.

My heart pounds. I breathe her in, turning my face into her neck. Theyen said she was safe, but only now does the ache of worry inside me finally ease. Part of me had wondered if she would leave Falcons Ridge at all—if, having returned to her family, she would choose to stay. I wouldn't have argued. The opposite, in fact. But she's here, and all of me leans into her embrace.

She's stood with me for so long that I can no longer imagine looking at my side and not seeing her there.

At last, we pull away, grinning like fools. I press my forehead to hers and thank the Sisters that she's safe.

Saengo clasps my hands, her eyes shining with every agonizing moment she'd spent wondering what had happened after we parted ways. "You're okay," she says.

"We're okay," I repeat. She's pale, though, and her hair is thoroughly windblown.

Behind her, three soldiers in Evewynian green and silver watch in tense silence. The smile slips from my face. They're wearing brooches with the falcon of House Phang pinned to their collars, and I also spot Prince Meilek's Blades. To have caught up with us, they must've followed soon after we left and not stopped to rest. Like Saengo, they look exhausted.

"What's happened?" Prince Meilek asks, urging his drake forward.

"It's the queen," Saengo says. "She's clearing out the Valley of Cranes in the morning."

TWENTY-THREE

"How do you know this?" Prince Meilek asks. Disbelief and anger tighten the lines of his face.

"Northern soldiers keep my father apprised of the queen's orders regarding the camp. They have family and friends there. The queen has commanded that the prison be shut down and the prisoners . . ." She can't say it, but her meaning is clear.

The atrocity is unimaginable. Is this what the Soulless had planned? The sense of dread grows into an ache behind my ribs.

"It's likely a trap," I say, looking between Saengo and Prince Meilek. "The queen must know that by ordering this, it will draw you out of hiding."

He swears beneath his breath. Then he sets his jaw and turns to his Blades, his mouth compressed into a grim line.

"Trap or not, I have to go to the Valley of Cranes. I have to stop her and release the shamanborn."

Each of them nods resolutely. Kou says, "We will follow wherever you lead."

"My father is sending more soldiers to support us. They'll meet us on the road." Saengo turns to mount Yandor, but I grip her wrist.

"I want to come. You know I do." I look at Prince Meilek, the impossible decision tearing me in two. "But I can't. This might be a trap, but it's also a delaying tactic. The Soulless knows what I'm after, and the longer he can keep me from it, the stronger he becomes. If the Soulless leaves Spinner's End before I have his familiar, then there's no stopping him."

While the queen is in Vos Talwyn is our best chance to get that talisman. Who knows when we'll get another.

"I understand," Prince Meilek says. "Do what you must. I'm sorry I can't continue with you."

"I sent a falcon ahead," Kou says. "Yen will meet you inside and guide you to His Highness's rooms and the passageway."

Annoyance pinches at the nape of my neck. For Prince Meilek's sake, I hope my suspicions are misplaced. Yen could be an important ally, but do I risk trusting her to pass quickly through the palace, or do I avoid her and linger about the grounds in search of the passageway?

"I'm coming with you," Saengo says to me.

"You can't."

"You're not going in there alone, Sirscha, and you can't force me to stay behind. You promised that we would do this together."

I curse myself for making that promise, but she's right. I can't decide for her. Reluctantly, I say, "You watch my back."

A smile blooms on her face. "And you watch mine."

"The talisman," Prince Meilek says, drawing our attention. "If she isn't sleeping with it on her person, then she will likely be keeping it in the lockbox on her bedside table. It's silver and crusted with gems. It won't be hard to miss. She keeps her most valuable things in there."

Saengo addresses her father's soldiers, ordering them to accompany and protect Prince Meilek. If he is walking into a trap, then he'll need every extra hand. Saengo has always seemed hesitant of her leadership, as if taking control will prove her father right and lead her back to the ancestral lands she's meant to manage someday.

Her success in reaching Falcons Ridge and gaining her father's support for Prince Meilek only proves she's meant for so much more than what I've saddled her with.

Prince Meilek bows without a goodbye, and I return the gesture, sending prayers to the Sisters to protect him and the others. He flicks his reins, and within seconds, he disappears into the rapidly growing shadows with his Blades following close behind.

Saengo's soldiers pause just long enough to bow in respect. Even if she isn't going with them, she's still a lady leading her soldiers, as it should be—as it will be once this is all over.

"Here," Saengo says, handing me Yandor's reins. "He'll be glad to have you back."

I smile, taking his reins and leaning into his neck. My fingers trail down his cool, green scales. His warm breaths puff against my hair. "I missed you too, my friend. Thank you for keeping Saengo safe."

"He was excellent company," Saengo says.

Before we leave, I treat her infection. When Saengo unfastens the buttons of her high collar and tugs down the fabric, my stomach lurches. The infection has spread up her neck in vicious blue lines, nearly reaching her jaw. My gaze flies to her face, seeing her exhaustion anew. She shrugs one shoulder as if it's nothing.

But it isn't. The pallor of her skin, the shadows beneath her eyes, the faint tremor in her lips as she smiles—she's clearly in pain, and yet she rode without rest for a day and night to catch up to us.

"Saengo," I whisper.

"Don't look so stricken," she says softly. "I wasn't going to let the rot stop me from reaching Falcons Ridge. Or you."

"You are a marvel, Lady Phang."

She snorts, and I bite back any more words. I attend to the

infection, a renewed sense of urgency swirling through me. We have to get that talisman and end this.

Once we're both mounted, we continue in the opposite direction Prince Meilek had gone.

I let the silence settle before asking, "What did you promise your father?"

Her shoulders stiffen, then slump in defeat. There's little chance her father would've agreed to let her ride off to impending battle after she'd so recently returned home. Prince Meilek's Blades could've delivered the news on their own, but they hadn't. While Saengo might have escaped—I've learned never to underestimate her—that seems unlikely given her arrival with an escort of soldiers.

"I told him that once this is all over, if Prince Meilek sits on the throne, then I will return and become the heir he wants. At least until I can train another to replace me since . . ." She trails off with a light shrug.

Saengo cannot have children. Not anymore. The Soulless's words taunt me: *When the world moves on around her, her existence forgotten, she will hate you for it.*

"Is that what you want?" I ask. Even if it means leaving me, as long as it's what she wants, I would never stand in her way.

Her lips twist into a melancholy smile. "I don't know what I want anymore. I didn't mention the Soulless. I'm not sure we'll even survive him."

I consider telling her about what he said, about how there might be a way to give back her life. But I can't speak false hopes without knowing for sure that it isn't a lie.

Vos Talwyn is only a few hours southwest of us, so we continue through the night. After years of sneaking in and out of the city to do Kendara's bidding, I'm familiar with where the sentinels will be at the wall and the patrol routes through the surrounding forest.

When we're close enough to see the shining dome of the Sanctuary of the Sisters through the branches, we dismount and let loose our drakes. Yandor doesn't object. He's familiar with the area, and this isn't the first time I've let him run around Vos Talwyn.

The forest is kept culled well away from the wall. We crouch beneath the shadowy cover of the trees, watching the distant figures of sentinels between the crenellations. The golden spears of the Grand Palace thrust skyward, rising above the walls. Out of habit, my eyes seek out Kendara's tower.

It's abandoned now, of course, and I can't help feeling a stab of mourning for all of Kendara's things. It's stupid—they're only objects. But like my own possessions, which the queen had likely destroyed, they are the physical collection of my time here.

Kendara's weapons, her books, her odds and ends collected from all over Thiy—what did the queen do with them? I think it might hurt to walk through her door with its half dozen locks and find her room empty, everything I'd done there, every lesson I'd taken with her on that balcony, cleared away.

That's the kind of sentimentality Kendara wanted to rid me of. Nothing should ever be irreplaceable, not objects, and not people. It was a necessary mindset for a Shadow, and even more so for a double agent. But it seems an awfully solitary way to live. I suddenly understand how she can repeatedly walk away from me despite claiming to love me. She's had a lot of practice in letting go.

Somehow, the realization doesn't make me angry with her anymore. It just makes me sad at the life she must have led. She's always been so steady, so certain. But even Kendara must have doubted herself at times, and all at once I'm glad she left. She chose a new path, and I hope she's happy about it, even if that path leads away from me.

We wait just long enough for Saengo to string her bow, and then we follow the tree line south.

I step slowly and quietly. Saengo is less careful, although I know she's trying. Still, every crackle of a leaf and shifting of dirt beneath her boots makes me cringe and glance warily at the wall. The ground begins to slope downward, and the smell of the sea grows sharper.

The wall turns westward along the rocky coast, the earth dropping sharply away at its base. Saengo and I wait at the edge of the forest, watching the sentinels. The moon is high against the stars but shrouded in wisps of gray clouds. I'm prepared to be patient and wait for the right moment to step into the open when a low roar rumbles through the forest north of us. I grin. It's Yandor, likely chasing some poor nocturnal creature through the underbrush.

The sentinels all shift away, peering northward. I glance at Saengo. "Now."

We sprint the distance, miraculously unseen as we reach the wall. We're out of the immediate view of the sentinels high above, but we move slowly, keeping our spines plastered to the smooth stone. Beneath our feet, the ground transforms into loose gravel and then sheer, jagged rock.

"There's a hidden doorway at the base of the wall. We just have to reach it," I say quietly. The rocks are dangerous even during the day. They're slick with sea spray, and the fall alone would kill us. I don't tell her this, though. I just grip her wrist and tell her to follow closely. "It'll be fine. I've done this hundreds of times."

I step over a well of trapped water, thick with algae. Even in the dark, muscle memory wins out. My feet know when to step. My legs know when to shift my weight, and how far from the wall to stray. Saengo keeps close, stepping precisely where I do.

"Sisters, Sirscha," she says, her voice high and breathy. "You did this every time Kendara sent you out?"

"Not every time. Only during the late hours when the gates were closed."

"That was almost always," Saengo points out. "You could've died."

"But I didn't. Which was the point."

After a moment, a hidden set of stairs comes into view. They're not stairs in the traditional sense—they look more like broadly stacked rock slates leading downward. The rush of the sea and the wind cover up any sounds we might make, so we continue steadily for long, tense minutes.

Needle Bay is braced in the east by low mountains, but to the west is a narrow strip of land called the Thread where the queen's ships are docked. At the tip of the Thread is the southern watchtower, which doubles as a lighthouse. I used to sneak away from the Company and sit at the lip of the roof, watching ships pass beyond the bay. This is not the return to Vos Talwyn that I'd hoped for. But even so, the rhythmic sweep of the lighthouse always felt like a beacon, calling me home.

TWENTY-FOUR

The hidden door is small and cramped, and impossible to see unless you know it's there. I usher Saengo inside first before following.

I squeeze between the rocks into the narrow space beyond. We have to crouch to keep from bashing our heads on the ceiling. This feels a bit like another wild challenge Kendara has set for me, which helps to ease my nerves.

"What is this place?" Saengo asks, her voice muffled by the rush of the sea just outside.

I nudge her forward into the dark tunnel. "Every Shadow has to create their own entrance into the city, because when the Shadow before them leaves the queen's service, they destroy whatever secret entrances they used. At least, according to Kendara. I'm sure she has a dozen means of getting into Vos

Talwyn, but this is the one she showed me."

"Wouldn't the queen know to keep this guarded? Or to collapse it?" she asks.

The meager moonlight quickly fades, and we're pitched into complete darkness. Since I know where I'm going, Saengo takes my hand and lets me lead.

"I'm not sure she knows about this one," I say. "Kendara was a double agent, and she'd been the Shadow before Queen Meilyr took the throne. She served King Senbyn for years. I imagine there are many secrets she kept to herself."

Just as she kept so many from me.

The tunnel lets out at the back of an empty drake stall. The exit is so small that we have to crawl on our knees. I pause at the threshold, listening for any late-night stable workers, but there's only the steady breathing of sleeping drakes. At least in this immediate area, there are no other human souls.

Once we're out of the tunnel, we pass quickly through the stables and into the open. Shops line the street, their windows dark. Lanterns illuminate small spheres of night. We turn left at a corner bakery with a noodles stand out front where Saengo and I used to eat.

Most of the souls around us feel far away, doubtlessly tucked inside their homes and their beds. My fingertips grow warm with anticipation, and I quickly shove my magic back down.

Unfortunately, I'm not aware of any hidden entrances into the Grand Palace. There was a specific entrance for Company students, and the guards there knew me, so I never had any trouble coming and going. We're going to need a more creative means of entry.

We take two more turns until we enter the gilded district. Here, every window overflows with golden light. Dozens of lanterns string across the streets, and roofs and walls have been painted in bold shades of purple, orange, and pink. Colored glass globes cast fragments of blue and green prisms across the road.

The sound of various instruments blends with the din of raised voices, which spill from open doorways. People move from building to building, their robes draped off bare shoulders and heels clacking over the road. Laughter drifts from a window somewhere, and the air smells of salt and sweat.

"This way," I say, leading us toward a building that's painted a garish red with flaking gold trim. Cylindrical red- and-brass lanterns hang all along the eaves, tracing the entire roof in lights. It's a gaming hall and teahouse. Their dancers perform some of the most exceptional shows in Vos Talwyn.

We follow an alley along the side of the building toward the back, where the bright lights don't quite reach. Tucked behind the establishment is a stable and a row of modestly-sized conveyances. Among them is a beautiful carriage of dark wood, hitched to two waiting drakes. Although it lacks an identifying House crest, with its polished black lacquer and buffed silver finish, it clearly belongs to someone of means. A woman is slumped in the driver's seat, snoring softly.

Movement from within the stables steals my attention. Stable workers would surely be awake here, awaiting new arrivals and ready to return a drake to a departing patron.

It only takes me a moment to catch them unawares and knock them out. There are only two as far as I can tell.

When I return, Saengo has a pinched look on her face. "Why are we dawdling here, assaulting stable workers?"

"Once, Kendara tasked me with stealing something valuable from a reiwyn lady's room at the Grand Palace. I followed her around for a few days to learn her routine. She spent nearly every evening at this gaming hall and remained until dawn." I climb up into the seat beside the dozing driver.

The woman startles as the carriage rocks, waking up with a snort and a muttered, "So sorry, my lady."

I don't allow her time to notice I'm not her lady as my fist lands squarely on her jaw. Her head lolls to the side, and she's once again unconscious.

"Really?" Saengo says, sounding horrified. Still, she helps me haul the driver down from the seat.

We get her on the ground, and then I strip the woman of her finely made cloak and black tunic. As with the carriage, the tunic's lack of livery colors is intentionally ambiguous.

I hand Saengo my swords so that I can pull the tunic over my head.

"You don't think anyone will notice?" she asks.

"Not before we're gone." I belt the sash over the tunic, settle the cloak over my shoulders, and then open the carriage door with a flourish.

Saengo doesn't look certain, but she adjusts her quiver over her shoulder, tucks her bow against her side, and climbs inside with my swords. Despite weeks of travel and the various weapons on her person, she carries herself like reiwyn with her head back and her annoyingly perfect posture. If anyone were to peer through the windows of the darkened carriage and catch sight of Saengo's profile, there would be no doubt that a reiwyn lady sat within.

Once I'm settled in the driver's seat, Saengo slides open the partition behind me.

"You're sure this will work?" she asks.

"No reason it won't," I say. The carriage will be recognizable to the guards.

I guide the drakes out of the alley and onto the street. Most of the people milling about are on foot, traveling in groups as they pass between establishments. I keep my head down, the hood of the cloak low over my face as we weave around them. Soon, we leave the gilt and glitz behind for the darkened shops and homes lining the main road. Here, the only lights are lamp posts, burning slowly through the night.

Patrolling guards are scarce, but I force myself to relax and politely nod as we pass a pair. They barely glance in my direction as they nod back. We turn onto a road that winds around the wall of the Grand Palace. The main gates are used only during the day. Besides, anyone coming and going at this hour would use the more discrete entrance.

The guards posted at the side gate see us coming. One steps forward. My fingers tighten around the reins. Although the hood conceals my face, I tilt my head so that my hair, which has come loose from my braid, falls forward, shielding my face.

From inside the carriage, Saengo whispers, "Why aren't they opening the gates?"

I shush her, slowing the drakes as we approach. With the torchlight at their backs, the soldiers' faces are cast in shadow. One of them turns away, reaching for a torch hanging from the wall.

"My sword," I whisper, sliding my hand through the open partition. But Saengo doesn't place the weapon against my palm.

Instead, she calls out, voice pitched low and words slurred. "What's the delay?"

I freeze. The guards glance at one another. Even pretending

to be drunk, there's no mistaking her tone. She sounds like an impatient reiwyn lady who's had too much fun too quickly.

The guard abandons retrieving the torch and instead moves to open the gate. I slowly release my breath. As I nudge the drakes forward, one of the soldiers calls out, "Apologies, my lady."

Saengo harrumphs from within the carriage. I could kick her for taking the risk and kiss her for embracing the pompous reiwyn lady I've always known she could be.

We continue down a narrow lane that leads through the garden. If we follow the lane to its end, we'll reach the stables, but we don't need to go that far. Once we're out of sight of the gates, I stop the carriage and hop down.

The door opens, and Saengo steps out, shoving my swords at me. I secure them to my back as Saengo slings her quiver over her shoulder, her bow in hand. I lead us through the gardens where it's dark enough that we don't need to worry about being seen. Once we enter the palace, we move more slowly, wary of patrolling guards.

The royal family resides in the uppermost floors of the west wing, but I've never even been near that part of the palace. Saengo and I slip from shadow to shadow, darting past lit sconces and ducking into alcoves when we hear the approach of guards. It's a slow process, but one I'm familiar with after years of sneaking up to Kendara's tower at all hours of the night.

After a time, we reach the corridor where a grand staircase leads up to the royal apartments. Two guards stand at the bottom of the stairs. Saengo and I could take them easily, but I'm not sure we'd be fast enough to prevent them from calling out.

"What do we do?" Saengo whispers at my shoulder.

There is one way we could get past them, but I immediately regret the thought. Grasping their souls would leave them immobile long enough for Saengo to knock them out. But there are other souls nearby, patrolling guards and servants moving about the palace on late-night errands. It's too risky with my lack of control.

Not to mention, what happened in the Dead Wood. A shiver races down my spine as phantom screams echo through my skull. I'm wary of handling any human soul again.

I shake my head and reach for my swords. "We don't have a choice."

Footsteps echo through the corridor. I pause, and Saengo grips my wrist.

"Good evening," a girl's voice calls to the guards, uncomfortably loud for the hour. Yen.

I glance at Saengo. I shared my suspicions with her, but neither of us had concluded what to do.

"Late night, Yen?" one of the guards says. Clearly, they're acquainted.

"Always," she says with a sigh. "I don't mean to alarm you,

but I just saw two figures sneaking about the western garden."

"Are you certain they weren't patrols?"

"It's possible. But given the queen's concerns about security lately, I thought it best to report it."

The other guard says, "We should check it out, just to be safe. Thanks, Yen."

They grumble unhappily as they both march off, away from our hiding place. I watch them go. Yen waits, hands clasped at her back, fingers twitching restlessly. She's dressed in a servant's uniform, her hair still split into two black braids.

Once they're out of sight, she spins on her heel and rushes in our direction. Saengo and I duck behind a statue. As Yen passes, my hand shoots out, muffling her cry of alarm. It isn't until she spots my face that she relaxes, slumping against me.

When I release her, she grins and whispers loudly, "Sirscha! It's so good to see you again!" She looks around, confusion creeping into her face. "Where's Prince Meilek?"

She appears genuine enough. I'm probably being paranoid. Even so, I draw one sword.

Yen eyes the sword uneasily. "Um, Sirscha?"

"Prince Meilek couldn't make it. What did he tell you about why we're here?"

She hesitates, uncertain, but then says, "You need access to the prince's rooms and the hidden passage."

"Can you show us?"

She nods and gestures the way we came. "There's a more direct route this way. We'll be able to avoid any more guards."

As she turns to lead the way, I glance at Saengo and then again at Yen's back. Saengo nods, gripping her bow.

We follow Yen through dim corridors and sparse rooms likely only used by servants. She pauses before a set of glass doors with gold rivets in the design of blooming plum blossoms. After first peering through the glass into the empty garden path just beyond, she pushes the doors open.

She takes two halting steps and turns, fingers wringing at her waist. "Is Prince Meilek all right? He's not hurt, is he? Is that why he couldn't come?"

"He's fine," I say. "He needed to be somewhere else." Her lips twist in disappointment.

She crosses the small garden, stopping at a bare brick wall. She counts the bricks, her lips moving silently. When she's satisfied, she gives one a firm push, and a small section of the wall depresses enough for a person to slip through. With a quick gesture to follow, she ducks inside, disappearing from view.

With little other choice, we follow. Inside, we find a narrow corridor much like the one we used to enter the city. This one is noticeably less dusty, though, and a dim sconce shines in the distance. Clearly, the tunnel is often in use.

"This way," she says softly, urging us to continue.

"How do you know about this passageway?" I ask. Although I speak quietly, our voices carry.

"I grew up in the palace. The staff uses these passages to move about the grounds without disturbing the queen or her guests. Other passages are less known, though, like the one connecting the prince's rooms to the queen's."

"And how do you know about that one?" I ask.

Yen flashes a grin over her shoulder. "My mother. She was a lady's maid to Queen Pae. I was in training for the position once Queen Meilyr took the throne, so my mother showed me the passages for moving quickly between the royal chambers."

I glance at her uniform again. She's wearing the generic tunic worn by palace staff, not the elaborate clothing required for those working directly with the royal family.

"That's a high position for a servant," I say. "How'd you end up serving the Queen's Guard instead?"

Her shoulders tense. My eyes narrow at the reaction. After a moment, she replies, "My mother was shamanborn. She died in the Valley of Cranes. I wasn't taken because I didn't inherit any magic, but I was removed from my position."

My gaze lowers. Back in Luam, Kou mentioned something about her having shamanborn family, so she must be telling the truth in that regard. So many Evewynians have been lost to the camp and the queen's vengeance.

At my lack of response, she looks over her shoulder at me.

"You don't trust me, do you?"

"Prince Meilek trusts you," I say, in case she needs a reminder of her duty.

She smiles, the words seeming to fill her with purpose, then nods and faces forward again. I'm not sure what to make of her.

Behind me, Saengo says softly, "I'm sorry about your mother."

She shrugs. "It was a long time ago. Here we are."

She nudges a panel in the wall, and it slides open a fraction. She goes out first and then curses as she smacks her temple against the edge.

Embarrassed, she rubs her head and says, "Catastrophe, remember?"

"Careful," I say, as she eases the rest of the way through the gap.

On the other side is a dark, empty sitting room. Subtle stripes paper the walls, but there are no furnishings. The windows have been stripped of curtains, allowing the moonlight to cast a silvery halo across a bare floor.

"The queen cleared out her brother's rooms after she returned from the north," Yen says, twisting the fabric of her tunic around her fingers. "I don't know what she did with everything, but she wanted no trace of him left."

Suddenly, I'm glad Prince Meilek isn't here. He'd stood

at her side from the moment she took the throne. He'd shared her grief and helped a young queen guide a kingdom in mourning. He'd remained loyal through the execution and imprisonment of Evewyn's shamanborn. Even after the prison break at the Valley of Cranes when she'd ordered the escapees killed, he'd done what he could to help them without outright opposing her. Despite his efforts to gather allies, I know part of him has refused to give up on the only family he has left.

Seeing her attempts to erase him would break his heart. While he struggles to have faith in his sister and the person she'd been—the girl who once helped him sneak into a drake race and escape their parents to watch ships make port—she's done all she could to forget she ever had a brother.

"The passageway is here." Yen crosses the room to where a massive stone fireplace dominates the space. "You see the crest of House Sancor?"

I join her beside the mantel. Chiseled into the stone is the relief of a forest, with trees coming out of winter, their branches budding with spring leaves. At its center stands the likeness of a triple-horned stag. Yen runs her finger over the stag's third horn and pushes. There's a slight click, and then the wall beside the fireplace swings inward, revealing the entryway.

"Thank you," I tell her.

She grins broadly. "There's another stag at the end of this corridor. Come on."

I glance at Saengo as Yen steps inside first. Fingers twitching with the heat of my craft, I follow her into the dark. The path turns twice before we reach a dead end. Once Yen finds the other stag, we all back up as the wall swings inward.

Like in Prince Meilek's rooms, the hidden entrance opens beside the fireplace into the queen's sitting room. Unlike his rooms, hers are fully furnished. From a large window framed by sheer drapes, moonlight slants across plush sofas, thick rugs, and vases brimming with fragrant peonies.

My craft stirs, sensing the proximity of souls. One of them must be the queen's, but there are others nearby, probably her guards outside. More important, though, my magic presses against the boundaries of my control, urging me toward a presence that eclipses all the rest. It's like a shroud draped over my senses, muffling all else. The Soulless's talisman is near.

"Stay here. Keep an eye out," I whisper to Saengo before my gaze flicks to Yen. Saengo nods in understanding and removes an arrow from her quiver.

There are two doors in the sitting room. One of them is open, revealing a long corridor with additional rooms. It ends at a curtain of glimmering spidersilk, partially drawn with a golden cord to expose a moonlit balcony just beyond. But my craft pulls me toward the other door, which must be the queen's bedchamber.

With a glance at Saengo, who gives me an encouraging smile, I slowly turn the knob and push. The hinges are well oiled, and the door swings open soundlessly. Despite the late hour, the room is perfectly visible. Arched glass windows accented with curling, symmetrical traceries take up the entire back wall. They frame the massive bed at its center, where a gauzy canopy of sheer silks cascade over four thick posts, shrouding the figure sleeping beneath.

The queen lies on her side, half-buried beneath feather-stuffed pillows and heavy brocade blankets. The soul isn't there, though, it's to her left. Nestled atop the dark wood of her bedside table is a small golden container. It looks like a jewelry box sitting on four claw-foot pedestals. The sides are etched gold, and glimmering sapphires construct a snowflake pattern across the lid.

From within the box, the certainty of the talisman draws me nearer, its power calling to mine with the same mesmerizing impulse as the Soulless's magic at Spinner's End. It overwhelms all my other senses, compelling my craft to the fore. I think the soul *wants* to be released.

You were always meant to free me, the Soulless had said. Maybe he's right. Maybe this is how I do it.

I remove a pair of pins from my pocket. I've kept them on my person ever since finding the hidden doorway at the

Temple of Light. Then I lean over to inspect the keyhole. It's smaller than the lock on a door, but doable. The soul's power compresses around me, urging me on, its presence like a soundless scream vibrating in my ears and throat.

"Sirsch—"

I freeze, a chill seizing me. Saengo. All reason flies from my thoughts as I drop the pins and draw my swords. Before I reach the door, it swings open, startling me back.

Saengo enters first, her eyes fierce with anger and her arms held out at her sides. Behind her is Yen. She fists Saengo's hair with one hand and holds a knife to her back with the other. Saengo's bow and quiver are hooked over Yen's shoulder.

Yen moves with a smooth grace. Her feet glide soundlessly over the floor, and there's a hard edge to the way she watches me, which is new. A quick glance over her shoulder reveals three Blades, members of the Queen's Guard, all waiting with their weapons drawn.

"Drop your swords, Sirscha," Yen says.

TWENTY-FIVE

My eyes narrow, examining her in a new light—the predatory shift of her stance, the way she handles the knife, and her relentless but precise grip on Saengo.

I sneer in disgust. "I knew there was something about you I couldn't trust. You didn't know Kendara just from your work with the Queen's Guard, did you? You were one of her pupils."

She gives me a lopsided smile, an echo of the girl she'd been mere moments ago. "I was. Now I'm the queen's Shadow."

"I was in need of a new one," says a voice from behind her.

Queen Meilyr steps into view. My gaze shoots to the bed, where the woman I'd thought was the queen has risen from the blankets. She hurriedly pulls on a robe to cover her nightgown, her black hair tumbling around her shoulders, and scurries from the room on bare feet. She's beautiful but a stranger. A decoy.

I curse myself for a fool as I fix my gaze back on Queen Meilyr. Her thick green night robe fans around her feet in a pool of lush velvet and golden embroidery, and her hair is pulled back into a thick plait, a gleaming crown resting on her head. Even in the middle of the night, planning an ambush, she looks immaculate.

"Drop your swords," Yen repeats. Saengo sucks in her breath, back arching away from the blade no doubt digging into her spine.

My fingers tighten around my weapons. I'm not sure if she knows that Saengo is my familiar, as we never shared the knowledge during those weeks on the road together. But she knows what Saengo means to me. I glare at her, my craft aching to be let loose. But I drop my swords, which hit the rug with a hard thud.

They shouldn't have been able to ambush us. While I lack control, I can still sense the presence of souls. Except, that is, in the presence of the talisman, which the Soulless knows. Its power would overwhelm me—*is* overwhelming. I should've expected this. I should've known he and the queen would set a second trap, in case I didn't follow their bait to the Valley of Cranes.

"You're a fool to trust my brother," Queen Meilyr says. Yen drags Saengo aside to allow the queen to enter. "He's too open with his emotions and too eager to please. He doesn't have the stomach for ruling. He would be a weak king."

She approaches me, fearless even though I don't need a weapon to hurt her. But she knows I won't do anything. I could never risk Saengo's life. Not again.

In a flash, her fingers strike out, forcibly gripping my chin. I fight the urge to spit in her face.

When she speaks, her voice is so soft I barely hear her. "But he was a good brother, and my only family. He was the one person I trusted most." Her nails dig painfully into my skin. "And you turned him against me."

"Your lack of honor turned him against you," I say through my teeth. "You are not the sister he knew."

She slaps me hard enough to turn my cheek. With my face averted, something on the floor catches my eye—a shadow slithering in increments across the rug. I give nothing away as I return my gaze to the queen.

"You think you know him?" she asks, mocking. "No one knows him but me. He's easily manipulated by every bleeding heart who comes begging."

It almost saddens me how little she thinks of Prince Meilek. I may not know him as well as she does, but I know that his kindness does not equal weakness. If anything, that is his most enduring strength. Besides, he was trained by Kendara, who has never allowed weakness.

My eyes find Yen's. "If I were you, I would consider whether it's wise to serve a queen who's already gone through two Shadows in a swift amount of time."

Yen grins. "But you're not me. I understand you wanted to be, though."

The words don't sting the way they once might have. Would I have assisted the queen in her plot to murder the leaders in the north? Would I have watched from afar as she executed the shamanborn in the Valley of Cranes? I'd like to believe that even though I'd been afraid and desperate to prove myself, I would have drawn a line. It isn't easy to hold fast to one's moral obligation under threat of retribution. But one way or another, I hope I would have come to understand that loyalty to a person or people means placing their safety above one's self.

"How long have you been her Shadow? Did you know she offered me the position a week ago?"

Yen's eyebrows twitch, and her gaze flickers to the queen, uncertain.

"Don't listen to her," the queen says, sounding bored.

At my back, the soul within the talisman burns bright as a bonfire, demanding my attention. But when I probe at it, once again, my craft fractures against the talisman like sunlight against water.

"Did *he* tell you how to trap me?" I ask, just to keep the

queen talking. The sliver of shadow climbs up Saengo's leg, then her side.

The queen says something, but I'm not paying attention. The muscles in my body tense. Yen's eyes narrow, noticing the minute changes in my body language. The shadow circles Saengo's ribs to her back and wraps around the blade.

Yen's gaze flies to her hand as her knife abruptly pulls away from Saengo. The moment the blade leaves her skin, Saengo smashes the back of her head into Yen's nose. Yen gasps, both her hands wrapping around the knife that's trying to wrench itself from her grip. As the queen shouts for the soldiers, Saengo drops to the floor, kicking out her foot to slam the door shut. Then she flings herself against it, turning the lock as shadows explode through the room.

The queen screams. The door hinges rattle, and the wood groans as the Blades attempt to break it down. I turn, scrambling through the dark for the lockbox on the dresser.

Just as suddenly, the shadows fragment, moonlight splintering through. The smell of blood thickens the air. At once, my eyes find Yen, who has Theyen pressed against the wall, her knife driven through his shoulder. His jaw is tight with pain.

"Theyen," I begin, but his shadows are already moving.

They swarm around Yen. She falls back, stabbing blindly as the shadows snare her legs and then her arms. With a cry, she drops the knife. The shadows wind around her like ropes, squeezing until she screams.

Theyen pushes away from the wall, one hand pressed to his shoulder. Blood slides through his fingers, dripping over his knuckles. His eyes are dark with anger, teeth bared.

The queen puts her massive bed between us, shouting furiously for her guards to break through. Saengo is pressed to the door, adding her weight to help barricade it. Her bow and quiver lie near the foot of the bed, where Yen must have tossed them.

"A gate. Hurry," I say, going for the lockbox.

Before I can reach it, Theyen wavers on his feet. His eyes widen with furious realization. He staggers, blinking rapidly, before sliding to the floor. His shadows abruptly disperse, releasing Yen, who stumbles, groaning with pain.

My pulse races as I look between Theyen's slumped body and the knife at Yen's feet. "Poison," I hiss.

Abandoning the lockbox, I lunge for Yen. She manages to dodge, her leg rising in a kick. I throw up my hands to block and then jam my elbow against her ribs. Her heel smashes against the back of my leg, forcing me to one knee, but I flip backward in time to avoid her fist. At once, she twists away, reaching for her knife. I kick it out of reach.

She dives for it again, but I ram my shoulder into her side, and we both hit the wall. She's light and fast, her style reminiscent of Kendara's. Every blow feels like a blow from Kendara—every lie, every secret, every person she trained too well to stand in my path. Kendara might have left, but her legacy seems impossible to escape.

There's a shattering crack as the door begins to splinter. It won't hold for long. Movement draws my attention to the queen, who sweeps the lockbox into her arms before retreating to the other side of the bed again, screaming at Yen to stop me.

Yen twists out from between me and the wall. I dodge a jab of her elbow and hook her ankle. She trips, falls, and rolls smoothly back to her feet, knife in hand again. I leap for my swords, halfway across the room, as Yen flips the blade in her nimble hands.

Abruptly, she cries out as an arrow pierces her palm, blood spattering her servant's uniform. The knife slips from her fingers.

She recovers quickly, catching the knife neatly with her other hand before it even hits the rug. Despite myself, I'm impressed.

Saengo already has a second arrow nocked and aimed, loosing it as Yen flings the knife.

Every part of me screams as the memory of another weapon hurtling toward my best friend flashes through my mind.

Saengo's arrow pierces Yen's shoulder as Yen's knife sails across the room, slashing cleanly through the string of Saengo's bow.

Saengo curses, dropping her bow, but she's unharmed. Relief and fury surge within me.

"Secure the queen and the talisman," I tell Saengo, who retrieves the knife. If we can use her as a hostage, we might get out of here. I've no idea what we're going to do with an unconscious Kazan prince, though. The fool man keeps showing up to play the hero when I least expect it. He's still breathing so at least he isn't dead.

"Yen," the queen says. She clutches the lockbox to her chest. Her usual poise is gone. Her voice vibrates with outrage.

Yen growls her frustration as blood wells around the arrow shafts in her hand and shoulder. Her complexion has gone pale, her eyes bright with pain. I retrieve both my swords, twirling them as I close the distance between us. This won't take long.

The door bursts open. Wood splinters through the air, a stray fragment stinging my cheek. With a shout, I abandon Yen and run for Saengo as Blades and soldiers pour through the wreckage of the entryway. We press together, standing in front of Theyen's prone form. Dark-gray blood soaks his tunic.

Within seconds, we're surrounded, over a dozen drawn swords gleaming in the moonlight. More soldiers press into the room to secure the queen and Yen. My stomach drops as the lockbox disappears from view.

My heart pounds in my ears, panic fluttering into fear as

my craft flares within me. Their souls taunt me. My magic reaches for them, wanting to close around each spot of light and revel in the life at my fingertips. I raise my swords in front of me, blocking Saengo and Theyen with my body. Magic burns beneath my skin, hot enough to be painful.

Ripping human souls fractures your own; but to save Saengo, I'm willing to pay that price.

"Don't," Saengo says, grasping my arm. She knows. Her reason laps against the inferno building inside me, slowly dousing it.

These soldiers are innocent. They're only protecting their queen.

Even as my senses scream to fight, even as I glare into the cold triumph in the queen's face, I slowly lower my swords. The soldiers swell around us, and it takes all my willpower to do nothing as they drag Saengo and me apart.

TWENTY-SIX

I've seen the inside of more cells in the last few months than I have in my entire seventeen years. That is if I choose not to view the orphanage as a prison. But even so, the dungeons beneath the Grand Palace are the worst of the lot.

The darkness is nearly absolute. I can barely see my own hands in front of my face. Something rancid drips from the walls, and the ground is perpetually damp. The air leaves a bitter taste in the back of my throat. As far as I can tell, my prison is only a few paces in length and contains nothing but the tattered remains of what might have been a blanket, now a matted pile of mold. I sit against the driest part of the cell I could find, but the cold and wet still seeps through my clothes to bite at my skin. I keep my arms tight around my waist against the chill.

I'm not hungry, but I imagine I won't be seeing a meal for a while. Rations at the orphanage were never much, and withholding dinner was a common punishment, so I'm used to it. Still, I'm a long way from the child I'd been, alone and hungry in the dark, wondering what lay beyond the walls of the orphanage—if I had a place out there or if I would forever be a flake of ash at the mercy of a harsh wind.

I seem to be the sole person here, which is a small comfort. The shamanborn were imprisoned in these dungeons before they were relocated to the Valley of Cranes. The thought of whole families shoved into this dank, dark place makes me sick.

I close my eyes, my focus narrowing to the steady flame of Saengo's candle. Wherever the queen is keeping her, hopefully, her conditions are better. The important thing is that she's alive. But as she is the Phang heir, and the queen's leverage against the north, any lingering hope of finding an ally in Lord Phang is lost.

As for Theyen—I wish he'd stayed away. Unless the Fireborn Queens abandon him, his status as a political prisoner all but guarantees Evewyn's access to the Xya River.

That is if he's still alive. The uncertainty tears at me. If he's dead, it'll be my fault. Again. I can't lose more friends. I've tried to search for his soul in the palace, but it's impossible. The souls of the castle's inhabitants are too far away, and I can't distinguish one from the other.

Then there's Prince Meilek and those who went with him to the Valley of Cranes. Are they dead? Captured? He'd known it was a trap. *I'd* known it was a trap, and I let him go.

The cooperation of the north, access to the Xya River, and myself; everything the queen and the Soulless needed, I hand delivered to them.

I cover my face, my breaths warm against my chilled hands. I did this. I failed them all after they'd stood by me and risked their lives for mine. The ghosts of past fears emerge from where I'd buried them, wearing the voices of monks, officits, students—all who have looked me in the eye and then looked away again, seeing nothing there worth their time or attention.

"I am not nothing," I whisper to the dark, with no one to hear but me. "I am going to fix this. Somehow. I am going to fix this."

My eyes fly open at the sound of footsteps. I don't move as the glow of a torch grows nearer. When the light reaches my cell, I raise my head to find a woman standing beyond the bars, lifting her torch to illuminate me. Her shoulder is heavily bandaged, her arm in a sling, and her right hand wrapped in thick gauze that smells faintly of medicinal herbs.

When Yen speaks, there is no reproach or disgust in her voice. No victory either. "Sirscha Ashwyn. We weren't in the same year, but I remember you from the Prince's Company. I'm good with faces."

"Where is Saengo?" I ask.

"She's well," Yen says.

While I don't trust her to be truthful, Queen Meilyr would be a fool to mistreat Saengo and risk House Phang rising against her. She can't keep us apart for long, though, not while she has the rot. Using Saengo means walking a fine line between ensuring Lord Phang's cooperation and inciting his vengeance.

"At the queen's discretion, you will be escorted to the Dead Wood and given to the Soulless."

I expected this, but the idea of returning to Spinner's End and the poisonous magic of the Soulless still makes my stomach drop. "You approve of your queen's choice of allies?"

"It's not my place to approve or disapprove of Her Majesty's actions. My job is to obey orders."

"Must be nice not to have a conscience."

She laughs, the bright sound jarring in the torchlight. "Her Majesty says you were Kendara's favorite. I can see why."

"You must truly hate the shamanborn as much as the queen does."

Her smile wilts, and a placid mask slides smoothly over her features. "Of course I don't. My mother was shamanborn. I told you that. She was lady's maid to Queen Pae and a flame eater." She closes her eyes, something brief and pained creasing her forehead. "When she transformed into flame, it was like watching a phoenix rise from its ashes. She was magnificent."

I'd assumed it was a lie she told to gain Prince Meilek's trust. He said he'd known her for years. "But you serve the woman who imprisoned and killed her."

Her eyes open, that hard edge returning. She lowers her torch to her side, casting the angles of her face into deeper shadow. "My father died shortly after she did. I was twelve years old with two siblings to support and no means. We only survived because the queen allowed me a different position. Should I have chosen my pride and allowed my siblings to starve instead?"

I shake my head because I honestly don't know. The world isn't divided into good and evil, right and wrong. Who am I to judge her when I also sought to become Shadow, knowing what the queen had done to the shamanborn? I was afraid. Always so afraid. I did what I needed to survive in a world pitted against me, just as Yen is doing now.

When I don't reply, Yen says, "I only wanted to see how you're doing and let you know the Soulless awaits you. Stay alive, Sirscha Ashwyn. I hear you're good at that."

I frown, uncertain why she'd care. She doesn't say more and turns to leave. Confused, I watch until the light from her torch fades and decide not to dwell on her words.

Sometime later, a guard delivers a meal of thin bone broth in a shallow bowl. Chunks of something I'm not entirely sure are meat float in the liquid, along with a meager helping of stale rice. It's so thin that it's more water than broth. Still, I finish it. I don't know when I'll be fed again.

The first couple of nights, my dreams are of days past—times at the orphanage, times at the Company. Dreams wrought from my thoughts and memories.

When I dream of Spinner's End, I know my respite has ended.

In the dream, the Dead Wood has devoured the castle. Stones bulge beneath the earth, imprisoned by the roots. Gray branches swathe what remains of the towers, tree trunks bloated on their gluttony.

The Soulless walks among the ruins. His steps are slow and precise, but even in a dream, I can tell that his strength is returning. Slowly, perhaps, but growing.

"What now, Sirscha?" His voice resonates across the distance, echoing about my shoulders. I hate the sensation. "All your allies are gone."

"If anything happens to them—"

"By your own actions, you have lost them all. The Nuvali princess, the Kazan hlau, the Evewynian prince, even your best friend." His voice softens to a whisper. "Who will you turn to now?"

The truth is a knife in my gut, and I fall silent, unable to find any words. The Soulless's gray robes trail behind him, the frayed hem collecting earth and brambles. His feet are bare, blackened by dirt and tree rot, threads of spiderweb still clinging to his heels. He hasn't yet shaken off his time in that cocoon.

"You remind me of him. My brother. He was never comfortable with his magic either. He always felt a bit cowed by it."

I turn away from him, searching for an escape, but there's nowhere to go in this dreamscape. There's only destruction and decay.

"Fighting for the Empire helped him to focus his magic. It gave purpose to his ambitions." His voice grows hard with the taint of bitterness. "For all the good that did him in the end. It had been a false purpose. They taught him how to push his magic beyond its natural boundaries, without thought of what it would do to him or what it had done to others. And why would they care, when there were others to take his place? Tell me, Sirscha. Would you have sacrificed all that you are for your queen? Or your prince?"

Maybe. But now, I would be willing to give of myself, not for a single king or queen, but for Evewyn and its people. For the only home I've ever known, a home that a part of me still hopes to belong to again. And for Saengo, and all of the unexpected friends I've come to care for.

His lips stretch into a feral grin as if he can see my every thought playing out in my eyes. "Make all the world your home, Sirscha, and you will never feel adrift again."

A guard feeds me twice daily, assuming my internal clock is correct, which means I've only been here for a handful of days. But in the dark, with only the silence, the cold, and my own thoughts for company, it feels like far longer.

I waste a few hours feeling around my cell, searching every cleft of fractured stone, every moldering stretch of floor, and every rusty patch on the iron bars, but there is nothing that might be of use. Afterward, I curl tight against the wall, trying to find a position that will ease the damp chill burrowed beneath my skin. My jaw aches from the chatter of my teeth. My craft burns, but there's no true heat. It's only a sensation, which does nothing to relieve the cold.

Since Yen's visit, the only person who comes to my cell is the guard who delivers my meals. He doesn't carry any keys on him, so it's useless to attack him. The only other souls are too far away for my paltry control to reach.

But with each passing day, my resolve weakens. Each time the guard returns, his soul beckons like a candle in the dark, asking to be taken in hand. His tether is weak, and if I just reach out and nudge it loose, I could make myself stronger.

The urge scares me enough that I begin to murmur the old prayer of the Five Sisters, hoping it will drown out the eager rush of my magic.

On the fourth day, I dream of a memory. Saengo and I are children again at the Prince's Company. We lie in my bed, facing one another with our fingers laced between us. The soft breathing and occasional snores of our roommates fill the quiet.

"I miss Falcons Ridge," Saengo confesses in a whisper. We've only just begun our second year, and she's recently returned from spending her break on Phang lands. "I try not to. I should be used to it by now, but the Company is just so different."

I don't know what to say. I don't know what it feels like to miss home. I hated the orphanage and the monks, and I'm glad to never have to set foot there again. I suppose I miss some of the younger children, although I may see them again when it's their turn to join the Company.

"What do you miss most about it?" I ask, hoping to understand.

Saengo's voice wavers. "My family."

At this, something inside me aches, like a fist squeezing around my stomach. For the first time in my life, I'd begun to feel like maybe I'd found a family in Saengo. We're not real sisters, but could this be what it feels like? Saengo's words cut into me. She wants to leave me for her real family. My fingers tighten around hers, unwilling to let go just yet.

"My mother keeps a garden thick with flowering trees. I used to hide there while she and my father took their afternoon tea." She releases a quiet sigh. "I miss that too."

"Tomorrow," I say like I'm making a proclamation. "Tomorrow, we'll sneak into the gardens after dinner. We'll hide beneath the bushes so we won't be able to see anything but flowers and earth, and you can pretend you're back home in your mother's garden."

Saengo laughs, low and warm, and her hand squeezes back.

The dream fades away, lost to the ocean of my mind, and then I'm standing once again in the ruins of Spinner's End. The Dead Wood presses all around, the scent of decay and things long-buried thick in my lungs.

"You're sad," the Soulless says from behind me.

I spin on my heel to find him mere feet away. His dark hair is tucked behind the sharp taper of his ears, and his luminous eyes watch me with intense curiosity. A spider wanders from the folds of his gray tunic, leaving a trail of sticky thread.

I lift my chin. "It's none of your business what I am."

"There's no need to worry. The queen wants you weakened and malnourished, but I won't stand for it. Your imprisonment at the Grand Palace will end soon, and then we can discuss what must be done in person."

If it were up to the queen, she would either execute me or leave me in her dungeon to die of starvation, as other shaman-born have before me. That the Soulless should be the one to speak for me is bizarre, but not something I'll protest if it gets me out of this cell sooner.

"But that's not it, is it?" He crosses his arms, fingers tapping against his sleeves. "If your concern isn't for yourself, then it must be . . ." A small smile pulls at his lips. "Your friend. The familiar. How does a nameless orphan become friends with the heir to an ancient House? Or is it *former* heir now?"

As he walks, his gait is slow but sure. They're not the quivering steps of our first dream together.

"Saengo's father will come for her," I say, infusing my voice with false confidence. "By taking her prisoner, all the queen has done is start a civil war."

He looks amused by this. "The beloved heir to House Phang. You must have felt so inadequate. She could've been friends with anyone, but she chose you."

I resist the urge to shrink beneath his words. I won't be made small by a single truth.

"Could it be that you needed her far more than she needed you?" he muses softly.

I wonder what would happen if I punched him. Would it hurt him, or would he vanish into shadows and vapor?

"And now she's a lowly familiar tied to the life of a shaman.

Quite a fall from grace. Maybe in the deepest parts of your heart, you're glad of it? Now she needs you just as much as you need her."

The suggestion stuns me. Then white-hot rage fills me. I stalk across the dry earth and grab fistfuls of his ragged robes. The course fibers prick my skin, and the remnants of webbing lace my fingers.

"How dare you suggest such a thing," I hiss. "You don't chain the people you love to you."

"Oh, Sirscha," he says softly. Heat pushes up my neck at the pitying way his brows pinch together. "People like us—we can't help it. It is the nature of our magic. With every soul we touch, we either tether it to us or we destroy them. There is no middle ground."

"You're wrong." Maybe I don't know what I want or where I belong, and maybe all I can do with the magic within me is fumble along and hope, but I do know this—he is wrong.

All his pretty lies, all his poisonous whispers, and ugly temptations fall away. After drowning for so long in uncertainty, the sudden clarity is staggering.

Saengo is my family. Not one bound to me by blood or obligation. She chose me of her own free will. I would never tie her to me, and I will never be glad for what I took from her.

If only I could stop being so afraid. Afraid of hurting others, of becoming the monster the Soulless wants me to be.

I would gladly trade my soul for Saengo's if I could, but I can't, and my craft is the next best thing to helping us both out of this situation.

I am a soulrender. And I can either keep running from it or embrace it. If choosing to save my best friend means risking the monster within me, then I can live with that.

TWENTY-SEVEN

The pounding of boots against stone pulls my mind out of that restless place between sleep and waking.

My senses are instantly alert. This isn't the guard with my meal. There are too many souls. My craft quickens beneath my skin, but I don't move from against the wall. The flickering light of a torch brightens the corridor, along with the frantic shadows of soldiers.

As the soldiers reach my cell, their torchlight warms the backs of my lids. When I hear the jangling of keys, I open my eyes fully. There are eight of them in all. The one opening my cell looks anxious, his movements quick and clumsy. He nearly drops the keys. The others wait, some glowering, some glancing over their shoulders.

I don't stand. I want to see what they do. The soldier finally swings open my cell door and makes a sharp gesture at his companions. Two others hurry inside and grasp my arms, hauling me upright. The sense of urgency is puzzling.

Is Queen Meilyr eager to see me gone? Has the Soulless threatened her over the delay in handing me off? Or are these soldiers impatient to be rid of me? I doubt they even know what I am, other than a shamanborn prisoner. The queen keeps her people ignorant, offering no explanations and expecting absolute obedience without question.

The soldiers push me down the corridor. They don't even bother to secure my hands. If I'm to escape, now is the time, before we reach the queen. But as my craft stirs, fear creeps along my shoulders. I swallow down the sick feeling trying to climb up my throat. For Saengo's sake, I can't tolerate uncertainty. Either I do this, or I don't.

I inhale a steadying breath, my control a frayed, quivering thing. Then my magic unfolds around me, like a hand cupping water, closing around every soul within reach.

At once, the soldiers freeze in place. Slowly, I draw two swords from either soldier ahead and behind me.

They watch me with wide eyes, their pupils wild and frightened. I move past them, one careful step at a time. Sweat slides down a soldier's temple, her face turning red with the effort of trying to escape my grip.

Their souls feel like leaves in autumn, easily shaken loose

with the gentlest of nudges.

Afraid to grip too tightly, I relax my magic. My control wavers and some souls slip through. Two soldiers gasp, stumbling, as their hands fly to their chests to soothe the pain.

With a curse, I turn and run, releasing the others. As they collapse, groaning, the first two draw their swords, tripping over their companions to reach me. I dodge a blade swiping at my back. After days of imprisonment, my body feels weak and unsteady, but the sudden rush of energy gives me the strength I need to ram my elbow into the soldier's jaw.

A couple of them cower behind the others, shuffling between attacking and fleeing into the dark. But most of them recover quickly, charging down the narrow corridor.

I use the small space to my advantage. They can't surround me, and they can't all attack at once. I disarm one, snapping his nose, before pivoting to avoid a punch and plowing my knee into the face of another. The flat of my sword finds the skull of yet another, whose eyes roll back as she crumples. Her companion catches her just before her head can hit the stone.

I gather my breath as the remaining four soldiers hesitate. They know they're outskilled. Still, they edge closer, weapons held out cautiously.

I raise my swords. The blades are longer than what I'm used to, but I take comfort in their weight as if I can draw the strength of their steel into my tired bones.

When I glance over my shoulder to check the distance between myself and the exit, the nearest soldier surges at me. I disarm her, twisting her arm back and ramming my knee into her spine. She gasps and falls, arching in pain.

"You won't make it out of the palace alive," says a soldier hiding behind his companions. I'd stolen his sword.

"I'll take my chances," I say.

From behind me, my craft flares to the approach of more souls before I can detect the rumbling of hurried feet. Every ache in my weakened limbs protests the coming fight, but I grit my teeth and flatten myself against the bars of the nearest cell, one sword raised to the soldiers and the other sword at the door, which bursts open.

Prince Meilek storms through. At the sight of me, something dark and savage flashes in his eyes. His Blades follow close behind him. Movement catches in my periphery, and I react on reflex. My sword meets a steel blade as the hilt in my other hand smashes into a soldier's temple. She collapses into the bars with a grunt.

"Sirscha!"

"Saengo!" I turn my back on the remaining soldiers, leaving them for Prince Meilek and his Blades. Saengo hurtles down the narrow corridor and flings her arms around me. Weakened as I am, I nearly fold beneath our combined weight.

"Are you injured?" she asks, drawing back to get a proper

look at me. The torchlight doesn't offer much, but my condition must be plain because her face tightens with a rare fury.

"I'll be fine," I tell her. Now that the surge of energy from the fight is leaving me, my legs shake with the effort of remaining upright, and my head spins slightly. "What about you?"

"Nothing like this," she assures me. She takes one of my swords and then props my arm over her shoulder. I'm glad for the assistance.

"What's happening?" I ask.

"Well, we're certainly setting a record for rallying at the last minute," Prince Meilek says, coming up behind us. Somehow, I find it in me to smile. "The capital is under siege."

The smile instantly fades. "What?"

"More of a blockade, really, but it's incredible, Sirscha," Saengo says, a note of awe underlining her voice. "The ships that disappeared from the queen's navy. They didn't sink. They abandoned the fleet and pledged themselves to Prince Meilek."

My feet stall. Prince Meilek pauses behind me, the corridor too narrow for him to go around. He doesn't look like a prince who's just made a major stride toward dethroning his sister. He simply looks tired. Shadows bruise his eyes, his jaw is in need of a shave, and he smells faintly of smoke.

"How did they find you?" I ask.

"They returned to Tamsimno under a flag of peace. Hlau

Theyen was able to put us in contact. The ships remained hidden along the Kazan coast until I called them to Vos Talwyn." He frowns a little as if he still can't believe Evewynians had placed their trust in him and forsaken their queen.

In truth, when his message to the naval fleet was revealed, I didn't believe it would work as anything but a distraction. After what she did to the shamanborn, fear of the queen's reprisal is deep-rooted. I hadn't trusted my fellow Evewynians to oppose her.

"What about the Valley of Cranes?" I ask, bewildered.

"A trap, as expected. But Lord Phang sent as many soldiers as were willing to support me in defense of the camp. The rescued shamanborn are aboard the ships in Needle Bay."

Saengo adds, "The siege is to distract the queen's forces so Prince Meilek could get into the city to rescue us."

Thank you feels inadequate for what he's risking, for what everyone aboard those ships is risking. I've always had to rely only on myself because no one besides Saengo ever cared. I'm not used to this.

If a family can be chosen, then would it be too brazen to hope that I could choose mine? I'm still not sure, but the thought warms through me.

When we reach the door to the dungeons, we find Theyen waiting impatiently beyond. His arm is in a sling. He gestures for us to get on with it, and then catches sight of me. Although his expression doesn't change, he hesitates long enough that I imagine he wants to say something rude.

"At least I wasn't strangled this time," I say, saving him the trouble.

Theyen's eyebrow hitches. "No, only half-starved. That's an improvement, I suppose."

"Stop it," Saengo says, glaring between us. "Don't make light of this. We need to get you both to a healer."

"No," I say, withdrawing my arm from around her shoulder. My stomach protests the loss of support, but I steady myself. "I have to get that talisman, or all of this was for nothing. Theyen, can you get us back in the queen's rooms now that you've seen it?"

"Only long enough to be stabbed," he says dryly. "But it's possible."

I turn to Saengo, who grasps my hand tight. "Meet us in the vegetable gardens. You know the one. Where you used to pick me up after I left Kendara's tower."

She nods and hands back my second sword. "Please hurry."

A shadow gate opens behind Theyen. I give Saengo another hug and then hook my arm around Theyen's.

Passing through the gate makes my empty stomach roil and my head spin. Even after my feet touch solid ground again, my vision remains dark, and it takes a long second for my eyes to focus. Theyen's hand tightens around my wrist in warning. I grit my teeth, blinking quickly as my other senses attempt to gauge the danger. *Get it together*, I think fiercely. Kendara taught me better than this. She prepared me for this.

My success might not mean anything to her anymore, but it does to me. Whether I like it or not, she's one of the most important people in my life, one member of the family of my heart, and that means something.

The door to the queen's bedchamber is ajar, but the talisman isn't there. The lockbox on her dresser is open, its edges glinting in the light from the windows. Dawn is approaching, which means Theyen's magic will soon be gone. We need to hurry.

I can still sense the talisman nearby. Turning, I follow its lure toward the door leading out to the balcony. I edge forward, motioning for Theyen to remain where he is as I peer down the corridor. The spidersilk curtains are tied back, revealing Queen Meilyr at her balcony. It overlooks Vos Talwyn and Needle Bay. She must be watching the ships below, but I can't see anything beyond the slowly brightening sky.

Standing a few paces behind the queen is Yen. Her head is bowed, and her shoulder and hand are still bandaged, although the dressings are thinner than when she visited me in my cell. The queen's soft, clipped instructions carry in the quiet.

". . . stalling. Look at them. Cowards. As soon as the other ships arrive, they'll be outnumbered."

"Should I check on the prisoners, Your Majesty?"

"I've already sent soldiers to have them secured. See if you can find out which ship my brother is on. I want him taken alive." Subtle anger punctuates her command. She must view Prince Meilek's actions as a grievous betrayal. The irony would be funny if there weren't so many lives on the line.

Although the chain around her waist isn't visible beneath vibrant saffron-colored sashes, the talisman's presence is undeniable. I grip my weapons tight, send a prayer to the Sisters for strength, and then tap one blade against the door in a quick knock.

Silence falls at once. Theyen remains out of sight as I wait, my back pressed to the wall. My heartbeat quickens. I close my eyes, wishing for the battle calm. My magic wraps around my shoulders, still but alert.

The tip of Yen's sword appears through the door, and I strike.

She blocks neatly with only one hand and then blocks again when I swing the second sword. Teeth clenched, I summon every ounce of strength I can spare and slam her against the wall, my swords at her neck.

She cranes her head back and shouts, "Run!"

My gaze darts to Theyen, but he's already shot past us, his shadows leaping ahead of him. The queen screams as her escape into a separate compartment behind the balcony is cut off. Shadowy figures wind around her, their movements boneless and unnerving.

Yen's knee collides with my gut. I grunt as she grips my wrists and shoves my swords away from her neck. She groans through her teeth at the strain against her wounds, but they must be mostly healed by now. Kendara would have taught her the herbs and medicinal pastes to hasten healing.

I back away, rolling my shoulders and twirling my swords. I might be weak, but I know better than to let her see. She hesitates, taking my measure, calculating her odds.

"Come with us," I say suddenly, unsure where the words come from. Even though Yen betrayed Prince Meilek's trust, part of me can't stand the injustice of her protecting the woman responsible for her mother's death. I know what it is to have no options—to be certain that only one path exists, no matter who I must become to walk it.

My offer catches her by surprise. Then she sneers and attacks. I parry easily, twisting around the cut of her blade to ram the pommel of my sword into her back. She stumbles but only for a second before lashing out again.

"I'm serious," I say, avoiding another slash only to find Yen's foot planted into my gut. My back hits the wall, bruising my shoulder blades. I hiss a curse, then block a quick attack before reversing our positions, jamming my elbow beneath her chin.

Her teeth are bared and her eyes wild. It's a far cry from

the bright, grinning girl I met so many weeks ago. "And then what?" she spits. "Abandon my siblings? The queen will take out her fury on them. I'm not some nameless orphan with no family. I have people who depend on me."

Anger crystalizes inside me, disgust with her tired insults drowning out what sympathy I'd had.

I smash the hilt of my sword into her knee. She cries out as I hook her ankle and drag her leg out from beneath her. She falls hard, kicking up her other leg to take me down with her. I dodge, pinning her sword hand with one knee as my blades close once again around her neck.

Yen is a fearsome fighter and a talented actress. But there's a reason she wasn't first choice for Shadow, and we both know well enough that even injured, my skills outmatch hers. She scowls up at me, breathing hard, sweat beading at her temples.

"I do have a family," I tell her, hearing the words spoken out loud for the first time. "And she's depending on me too."

TWENTY-EIGHT

Before Yen can reply, shadows lash her to the ground. I back away as she struggles, kicking and snarling.

I turn to see Theyen's shadow creatures tear the talisman from around the queen's waist. As Theyen takes it from them, he tenses. A shudder races through him, fingers convulsing around the talisman's bone cage.

"Theyen?" I ask. He can't feel the soul within, not the way I can, but I wonder what he can sense of the talisman's magic.

His gaze snaps to mine. As he strolls toward me, he adjusts his grip so that he's holding the chain, not the talisman. "Let's go."

On the balcony, the queen kneels in layers of spidersilk. Her face is flushed with anger, her chest heaving, as she claws against the stone and shouts for reinforcements.

The doors to her apartments tremble as her Queen's Guard

attempts to break through. I take Theyen's arm, glad to be gone as his shadow gate opens.

He doesn't take us far, and we emerge in the gardens. As I suck in a lungful of air, Theyen tugs me into the bushes. The call of soldiers sounds somewhere nearby. Once my nausea passes, Theyen passes me the talisman as if eager to be rid of it. The soul within pulses against my palms. So much power compressed into so small a thing. Unnerved, I shove it into my pocket.

We cut through the garden, staying close to the ground. It doesn't take long to reach the servants' paths that lead into the vegetable gardens. Saengo, Prince Meilek, Kou, and five other Blades are waiting for us.

"I can only get us out one at a time," Theyen says, noting the diminishing night, "but it'll be faster than trying to escape through the city."

Prince Meilek opens his mouth just as a horn blasts through the palace grounds. We crouch against the garden wall, hidden behind rows of tall, hanging tomato plants. The horn blasts again, followed by shouting and dozens of booted feet.

"My sister knows I'm here," Prince Meilek says. "She's ordered the entire palace locked down."

Through the bushes, soldiers rush past to reach their posts. We're too exposed here. Prince Meilek begins to stand, but I grab his arm and pull him down beside me before he can do something stupid.

"Theyen, get everyone out. Start with Prince Meilek. Hurry." I turn to run and nearly collide with Saengo.

She grabs my shoulders, looking like she'd prefer to strangle me. "You can't do this. You'll be captured again."

"It should be one of us," Kou says.

I shake my head. "The queen wants most of you dead. She won't be able to hurt me. She needs me alive." I stab my swords into the earth and push Saengo back, gripping her wrists. "Get to your family, you understand me? They'll protect you."

"Sirscha," she says, anger and pain bridging our connection, leaving an ache in my chest.

"Have faith. I won't let her catch me again. I've got a talisman to destroy, remember?" I press the hilt of one of my swords into her hands and then nudge her back toward Theyen.

Before anyone else can protest, I retrieve my other sword and dart from the bushes, leaping over a row of cabbages. I'd told Saengo that I was her friend, not her keeper. But sometimes being a friend means forcing her out of danger's way, especially when she's too stubborn to do it herself.

Shouting erupts behind me. Soldiers crash through the carefully cultivated rows, crushing plants and tearing up supports wrapped in beanstalks. I vault the low wall surrounding the vegetable gardens and dash into the maze of the flower gardens. Here, the bushes grow thicker and higher, flowering trees clustered at every turn.

Saengo and I used to sneak back here through the enclosed paths that connect the palace grounds to the two Companies. The guard assigned to those gates was a relative of House Phang. I likely know these routes better than the soldiers chasing me. I veer left, rushing between two plum trees and onto a separate path that will lead me toward the Prince's Company.

The passage is usually guarded, but with everything going on, I might have luck on my side. Crouching, I slip behind a neatly trimmed line of shoulder-high hedges and run right into Prince Meilek.

He puts up a hand to stall my instinctual attack, and my heart leaps into my throat.

"What are you doing here?" Theyen was supposed to take him first. "And how in the Sisters did you beat me?" I'm too anxious to bother tempering my tone.

He shrugs one shoulder. "I've been playing in these gardens since I was a boy. I know all its secrets. There's a spot along the wall where we can get out into the city. Come on."

I follow him, dropping to my stomach beneath a thick patch of hydrangea just as my pursuers reach us. Their boots trample the surrounding flowers, destroying what took royal gardeners weeks or months to cultivate. Although they pass quickly, I can hear more coming.

Prince Meilek gestures with his head, and we crawl on knees and elbows until we reach another path. When it's clear, we rise and dart into a copse of magnolia trees.

"Saengo?" I ask quietly.

"Theyen took her."

Relief rushes through me. "You should have gone with them."

"I promised her I would come after you. Besides, you spent four years sneaking in and out, but I've been doing this my whole life. We'll make our way to the coast and rendezvous—"

"I have to go to Spinner's End."

He gives me an incredulous look. "I trust you'll recall the last time you said that to me."

I cringe but barrel on. "I can't remove his familiar's soul from the talisman. Not without more power—*his* power."

I don't think I need to be in Spinner's End. Our magic connects us. I just need to get inside the Dead Wood. The closer I am to him, the stronger his influence and the deeper his power could root into mine.

"That's a two-day journey," he points out.

"I'm aware." While Vos Talwyn sits at Evewyn's western border, the Dead Wood resides along its eastern. It's a long way to go without getting caught.

Ahead, half-hidden behind enormous magnolia trees, two statues stand sentinel against a section of the garden wall that merges with the palace wall. The left statue is of the Demon Crone. She's hunched, bent by age, her long hair flowing around a withered face and two horns that spiral from either side of her head. The other statue is the Mother Serpent, her long snake's tail coiled in the foliage.

"Is it wise to take that anywhere near the Soulless?" he asks, nodding toward the talisman in my pocket.

"There's no other choice."

Besides, the sooner we get this done, the better. Delay means allowing the queen time to plan her retaliation. And with every passing moment, the Soulless grows stronger.

Prince Meilek frowns. I can tell he has more concerns, but he doesn't voice them. Instead, he tugs me between the two statues, concealing us from view, and then points upward.

"Climb," he says.

Securing my sword with my sash, I climb. I find footholds in the folds of the Demon Crone's robes, the massive staff cradled in the Mother Serpent's elbow, and a stooped shoulder crusted with dead leaves. Once we've climbed past the statue's heads, the thick foliage of the magnolia grove blocks us from view.

"Is this how you and Queen Meilyr used to escape the palace?"

He nods. "Our parents never found out, so we kept the secret. It infuriated them."

My heart hurts as his voice softens with remembrance. "I can go alone," I tell him.

"Hlau Theyen and Kou will make sure the ships retreat to

Kazahyn. My sister won't pursue them. She doesn't have the numbers yet. Besides, she'll focus on following us, which means it'll be dangerous. You need someone to watch your back."

Reluctantly, I nod. I touch the Mother Serpent's cowl. Beneath it, her slit pupils stare ahead, and her full mouth stretches into a serene smile. I murmur, "Thank you for your protection."

When we reach the top of the wall, we linger just below the ledge. The sentinels are looking southward toward the sea and the ships. Silently, we climb over the ledge and scuttle the short distance to the other side. Within heartbeats, we're on the ground, plunging into the bustle of the city.

We find Yandor waiting almost exactly where I left him, finishing off what might have once been a small lizard.

"That's disgusting," I say. Yandor only tosses his head at me.

Fortunately, we find Saengo's drake nearby as well. Drakes don't usually carry two riders, although they're strong enough to accommodate the extra weight for short periods.

We keep to the forests when we can. Every town we pass buzzes with news of the escape from the Valley of Cranes and the brief siege on Vos Talwyn.

On the evening of the following day, while weaving

through the thick underbrush of Evewyn's forests, a foul scent stings my nose. Behind us, gray plumes billow through the trees, accompanied by an acrid, eye-burning stench. The queen's soldiers are attempting to smoke us out into the open. I suspected we were being pursued, but I hadn't expected them to catch up so quickly.

Maybe they're soldiers from the last town we stopped in to water our drakes. We must have been spotted. Still, we remain ahead of them, continuing through the night. It's summer, and the dense foliage provides decent cover. The next morning, the trees begin to thin, making way for farmland and a clear view of the Dead Wood against the horizon.

We cross several farms quickly before ducking into the shelter of a small green wood bordering the crop fields. Our pursuers are close enough that I can spot their figures chasing our trail through the farms' open fields. There are less than a dozen of them, likely traveling ahead of the queen's main force to try and cut us off. They're riding dragules, which are leaner and faster than drakes. No wonder they'd caught up so quickly.

Before long, the cover of trees ends again at another field. This one is wide and empty, grown wild with tall grass and wildflowers. It's been left alone and untended because at its other end lies the Dead Wood.

Behind us, shouts echo through the branches. Our pursuers are nearly here.

I dismount and hand Yandor's reins to Prince Meilek. "You'll have to go now if you want to outrun the queen. Hopefully, they'll think we both went into the Dead Wood."

"You keep finding ways to continue alone," he says. "But you don't have to."

I swallow down the annoying lump that rises in my throat. "I know that," I say, softer now. It means more than I can say that some will risk everything to help me. I don't know if this is what it means to have a family, but if it is, then I can't risk losing any of them. "But I have to do this alone. Please, Your Highness. Please save yourself."

As soon as the words escape me, I know we're out of time. The commotion of multiple dragules trampling through the undergrowth is too close. The glare of armor and the green of soldiers' uniforms flash through the trees. Cursing, I snatch back the reins from Prince Meilek and vault onto Yandor's back.

"Okay, then. We run for it." In an instant, we take off across the overgrown field.

We're exposed, the clear sky providing no shelter, but there's no helping it. Within moments, the queen's soldiers burst from the trees behind us.

Ahead, the decay of the Dead Wood awaits, branches stretching out to embrace us. I grit my teeth and summon my craft. Magic snaps around my fingers, thrilling and eager.

Yandor lowers his head, roaring as he charges bravely toward the trees.

Then, suddenly, he's falling, his strong legs going out from beneath him.

TWENTY-NINE

We crash through the high grass. For brief seconds, there's only pain as my body hits the earth.

Prince Meilek calls my name, but I barely hear it, my ears ringing. I try not to move as I struggle for breath. At last, when my lungs fill with a hoarse gasp, I roll onto my stomach and push to my feet. My hip and knee sting, but I don't think anything is broken. I limp to Yandor, who's still lying on his side, thrashing.

An arrow is lodged in his thigh. He tosses his head, growling as he tries to stand again. Fury closes white-hot around my throat.

"Stay down," I say, yanking on his reins. His claws nearly catch my skin as he thrashes, but I dodge and press my palms to his shoulder. "Please. You're going to hurt yourself."

Yandor snarls, but listens and remains on his side, panting and snuffling at the tall grass. In an instant, the queen's soldiers surround us, cutting off our escape, arrows nocked. The Dead Wood is close, their branches nearly overhead. Only a second longer, and we would've made it.

I close my eyes, resting my forehead against Yandor's neck. His scales are warm against my skin. My hand cups my pocket, the shape of the talisman pressing through the fabric. Am I close enough to the trees? It doesn't take long to realize I'm not. It's hard to sense the souls of the Dead Wood with the talisman's presence thrumming through my skin. It's like a beacon, demanding my attention.

After several minutes, when still no one has said anything, I look up. The half dozen mounted soldiers pen us in, arrows primed to shoot. Prince Meilek remains mounted as well, and he's looking westward.

When I remove my sword from Yandor's saddle, one soldier twitches. I expect an arrow to pierce my hand, but no attack comes, and I stand. I don't know that either Prince Meilek or myself could avoid getting shot at such close range, but we'd put up a good fight. Perhaps long enough for us to get inside the Dead Wood.

But I can't leave Yandor, nor can I risk him getting killed in the crossfire.

Within moments, more soldiers appear, spilling across the

overgrown field, forming two straight lines at either side of an imagined aisle. All of them ride dragules. I look to Prince Meilek, whose expression is inscrutable, and then to the gnarled trees of the Dead Wood.

Everyone is waiting for Queen Meilyr, but the greater threat is at our backs.

I watch the trees shift, their branches twisting and snapping. The soldiers blocking us off from the Dead Wood cast nervous glances over their shoulders. Still, standing within such easy reach makes me uneasy.

The longer we wait, the more those trees stretch ever farther outward. My agitation grows into a sinking sensation accompanied by the constant pressure of the talisman, a vise around my throat. How far behind is the queen? The soldiers' arrows follow me as I take a tentative step toward Prince Meilek. We can't just stay here and wait for the trees to grow bold.

Suddenly, Prince Meilek's chin jerks higher, and I turn to follow his gaze. Crossing the field, looking more harried than I have ever seen her, is Queen Meilyr. Wisps of hair fly about her face, having come loose from her braid. Her robes are wrinkled from long days in the saddle, and her silk train draped over the back of her dragule is coated in dust. Instead of her usual extravagant crowns and headdresses, she wears only a plain gold circlet.

Even after a long, hard ride, the queen's posture and ease in the saddle speak to her experience. Her face is pale from lack of sleep, but she holds her head high, and she's flanked by four members of the Queen's Guard.

To have left Vos Talwyn herself, rather than trusting our capture to her soldiers, she must be livid. Prince Meilek stole half her navy and then sent them to occupy the mouth of Needle Bay so that he could release her prisoners from beneath her nose, all while using the same secret paths they'd taken as children.

Prince Meilek still loves her, though, and if she ever was that girl he spoke of, then some part of the queen still loves him as well.

But love alone isn't enough to bridge what's irreparably broken.

A quick scan of those assembled confirms her Shadow isn't present. I wonder if Yen is all right, or if the queen has decided to move on through Kendara's dwindling list of pupils.

I dampen my lips. Even with the Soulless's talisman commanding the attention of my magic, I still sense the Dead Wood at our back, and the creeping menace makes my skin prickle. We've been waiting here too long. The trees are close—too close.

The queen passes through the brace of her soldiers and stops only when she and Prince Meilek are paces apart. He meets her fury with his own, both of them every bit a Sancor.

This is a reckoning I hadn't expected to come so soon. Not until the Soulless was removed from the conflict, leaving the queen to reevaluate her lack of allies. Not until Prince Meilek had secured his own alliances, when he could face her at the helm of an army, not fleeing like a criminal. This is not the way either of us wanted this to go.

"Hello, little brother," the queen says coolly. "How disappointing you have become."

Prince Meilek's hands clench around his reins, only briefly. His expression softens just enough for the pain to break through.

"Mei." His voice is gentler than his sister's, the affection there hard to hear. Even the soldiers look away out of respect. "What's happened to us? It should never have come to this. Let me help you make things right."

She scoffs, and I marvel at the way her voice catches when she replies. "Help me? You made a promise after they died. Do you remember? You promised that you would always protect me."

Prince Meilek's veneer cracks a little more, pain tightening the corners of his lips. "You know me. I've no desire to be king. I've only ever wanted to support you."

Her chin lifts even higher, her expression hardening with jagged determination.

"Take the counsel of your reiwyn leaders and end the

conflicts outside of Evewyn. Restore the peace," he continues.

She speaks with an eerie calm that belies the barely tempered emotion behind her eyes. "You are no longer my captain, and your words hold no influence. You betrayed me, your sister, the one to whom you swore to love."

"That hasn't changed," he says softly.

"You pledged your life and your sword to me. You betrayed our family, who valued our legacy above all else."

"A legacy of peace and how we can serve our kingdom. I should have been firmer with you earlier, but I'm trying to do right by you now to help you see that the path you've chosen is not what's best for Evewyn."

"As if you would know what's best for Evewyn, splitting our navy and sending ships to assault our capital," she spits.

"Mei—"

"Don't call me that," she snaps. "I am your queen, and I will see justice against all who oppose me."

His shoulders straighten, drawing together the broken pieces of him. "What you call justice, our parents would call tyranny."

She sneers and addresses the soldier at his right. "Arrest them."

The soldier steps haltingly forward. When I lift my sword, Prince Meilek throws me a meaningful look. I frown and give a quick shake of my head. He's going to do something foolish to buy me time to run. I reach up, closing my fingers around his wrist.

He is more than just one man or a friend or a prince. He is the future of our kingdom.

"No," I whisper urgently, but his eyes remain solely on his sister.

A second soldier joins the first as they reach to pull Prince Meilek from his saddle. Yandor growls and snaps at the knees of soldiers trying to reach me from behind.

"No," I say, more loudly, but it's too late. Prince Meilek reaches for his sword, drawing it and steering his drake to the side, swiping the soldiers with the drake's powerful tail. "No!"

"Stop him!" the queen shouts as every soldier draws their sword. Archers pull their bowstrings taut, but they waver, reluctant.

I won't let him sacrifice himself for me. I raise my sword, guarding his back as the first few soldiers overcome their hesitation and charge.

Someone screams, startling the soldiers back before everyone suddenly scatters.

I turn, breath stuttering, to see several soldiers dragged into the trees. Roots tangle their feet, climbing up their legs, as the soldiers scream, tearing at the tall grass without purchase. Branches dip low, sloughing flakes of dead bark as they snare around another soldier trying to escape on a drake, snatching him from his saddle.

Blades pull Queen Meilyr away, shielding her from the mayhem. I spin, searching wildly for Prince Meilek. For a panicked moment, I wonder if he's been taken by the trees. But then I hear his voice and turn to find him waving for me to follow. He's heading back across the field toward the cover of the underbrush.

Swearing, I reach for Yandor, scooping up his reins as soldiers try to wrench me away. I slam my knuckles into the throat of the nearest one and then jab my elbow into the other's eye. Stumbling back, they spy their companions crying out as their legs are crushed by the roots and then wisely choose to flee.

"Okay, my friend, time to go," I say. My heart pounds in my ears, and I flinch every time someone screams. Yandor growls in pain as he rises awkwardly to his feet. Limping, he follows as I lead him away from the archers shooting helplessly into the branches.

The trees groan as they strain and stretch, bark twisting and spilling rot. Roots tunnel beneath the high grass, snaring a soldier trying to help another companion who's shrieking and clawing at the earth.

"Away from the trees!" they shout, as they attempt to flee in terror.

Amid the chaos, I lead Yandor through wildflowers nearly the height of a man. I keep one eye on the queen, who watches the mayhem astride her dragule. Her hair is a wild halo about her face, and her chest heaves with each furious breath. Half of her soldiers have scattered or abandoned.

Though the queen will surely view this attack as a betrayal, I wonder if the Soulless willed this or if this is merely the souls' usual malevolence against fools who linger too close to the woods.

"Find the prince!" she shouts. Two Blades remain at her side as the other two break off to search.

I lead Yandor into the shade of living trees and thick bushes, sheltering us.

Prince Meilek grabs my arm. "You have to go while everyone is distracted. I'll take Yandor."

As Yandor lowers to the ground again, easing the weight on his injury, I glance over my shoulder at the Dead Wood. The indecision claws at my gut, but the presence of the Soulless's talisman remains heavy and oppressive.

I release a quick, frustrated breath as I wrap my arms around Yandor's neck. "I'm sorry, my friend. I keep having to leave you behind."

The moment I release him, Prince Meilek takes his reins. "Hurry."

"Thank you," I say. I straighten my shoulders, steadying my nerves and resolve. My fingers tighten around the hilt of my sword. Then I suck in my breath and break into a run.

I sprint through the high grass, weeds and wildflowers slapping at my legs. Someone shouts, having spotted me. The soldiers who haven't abandoned their positions converge on me. I ignore them, heading straight for those gray-green trees, their trunks bulging, leaking fresh blood.

"Stop her!" the queen shrieks.

Just as I'm about to crash into the trees, a root shoots from the ground. Gasping, I dodge, falling and rolling once before finding my feet again. The nearest soldier isn't so fast. The root latches onto her leg. She cries out as she falls, snatching uselessly at the weeds. Her companions back away, too afraid to reach for her.

Her eyes meet mine, wide and frantic, nails raking the dirt. "Help me!" Her free leg kicks at the roots snaring her, but the limb only tightens, making her shriek with pain. "Please!"

"Damn it," I whisper, rushing forward to grab her hands. Her fingers close around mine. She gasps as her muscles strain, sweat pouring down her face. The roots only pull harder. She screams again, half sobbing as her leg breaks with a sharp *crack.*

Magic rises from me like smoke from flame, reaching toward the trees, the souls that fill them, and that tantalizing darkness that links them all.

"I don't want to die," the soldier says, tears streaking her cheeks. My boots slide over the grass as the roots drag us both toward the hulking trunk of a crooked tree. Hungry faces press through the bark, snapping and snarling, eyes weeping black sap.

Anger flares in my belly. Fear is not a wall, I remind myself. It is a whip. "You won't," I promise.

Heart pounding, I let my fear give me focus as I unleash my craft into the trees.

The souls recoil as if shrinking back from fire, shrieking their hatred. Magic pours from me, reaching through bark and decay, snaring souls like flies on a web.

The surrounding trees crumble into ash. Roots collapse. The soldier whimpers as she releases my hands to crawl away, and her companions find their courage, rushing forward to help her. Her leg drags behind her, broken at an odd angle.

My breaths fill my ears with a muffled rushing sound. All around me, the souls linger where the trees had been, caught within the clutches of my magic. Their rage tries to burrow into mine, to find anchor in my soul. But this time, their voices are muffled, their hatred less potent. The talisman in my pocket shines bright and steady, shielding me from their influence.

I can feel my magic attempting to rupture through my skin. Unlike last time, though, my thoughts are clear. At the end of the souls' tethers, connecting us the way lightning bridges sky and earth, is the Soulless.

His power binds them to the Dead Wood. He uses them to strengthen himself, his magic devouring each soul the way the trees devour their bodies, leaving them forever trapped.

They are a conduit, like familiars, connecting our magic. But just as I feel him there, he can reach me as well. His magic slithers into me, a poison burning up my veins, reaching for the talisman in my pocket. He knows I have it, and he wants it back.

I might be imagining it, but I can almost hear his voice in my head, urging me into the trees, to go to him. His magic is his will, and it infects me with violent persistence.

From behind me, Queen Meilyr snarls, "Arrest her!"

I turn away from the glimmer of souls and face the Evewynian soldiers who've gathered to watch. They keep their distance, some of them clutching small wooden idols of the Sisters. When my eyes meet theirs, they look away, held from fleeing by terror or awe. No one moves.

Furious, the queen jabs her heels into her dragule's flanks. For a moment, I think she means to trample me beneath her mount's powerful legs. But she stops just shy of me, her dragule snapping at my face, its sharp teeth inches from tearing out my throat.

She looks down her nose at me, unafraid. "You cannot win this."

Pain presses at my temples. The Soulless's magic breathes fire through my bones. I let it—I need his power to destroy the talisman, but his will grows as well. I raise my sword with one hand as my other closes around the talisman in my pocket, fingers shaking as I grapple for control.

"Your armies are divided," I manage to say through clenched teeth. "Lord Phang will turn the whole of the north against you. Your kingdom is fractured. You've already lost."

For long seconds, the queen doesn't speak. Her lips thin, whatever she's thinking hidden through years of practice. Then she reaches for her waist and draws her sword.

She looks me in the eye and slashes her blade downward.

But its sharp edge never finds skin. Instead, the queen freezes mid-swing, her soul caught within my grasp. The weapon falls from her hand, her dragule shuffling uneasily at the sudden tension gripping every muscle in her body.

Her soul is a frantic, fluttering thing. Beautiful, like all souls. I'd imagined it rotted with hatred, like the soft, moldering innards of the dead trees.

She's the real infection, a voice whispers from somewhere far off, the words a mere hint of sound. The burn of wicked magic wells my anger to the surface. Look at what she's done to the shamanborn, at what she did first at Ronin's manor house and then at Tamsimno. She needs to be stopped. I've had multiple chances to end this, and I've been too cowardly to take them.

The queen makes a quiet, whimpering sound as my craft constricts around her soul.

Suddenly, I'm struck by the memory of Saengo's hand

closing around my wrist and her soft, firm voice. *Don't.*

With a gasp, I come back to myself. I release the queen's soul as my hand flies to my chest. My heart beats frantically against my fingers.

The queen collapses against her dragule, gasping, before sliding off the saddle. Her dragule snorts and stomps once before abandoning her. She sinks to the grass, wildflowers crowding around her robes.

I take several large steps away from her and into the empty circle of space where the trees had been. Only their souls remain. I stab my sword into the earth, squeeze my eyes shut, and remove the talisman from my pocket.

I thought I would have to get deeper into the Dead Wood to reach the Soulless's magic, but his magic is all around me, bound to the trees. It screams within me, and every soul caught within my grip screams with it.

"No," I say, and pour every drop of magic rushing through me into the talisman. Last time, my craft broke against the talisman's container. This time, it pries past the cage, snapping through the bone to close around the soul trapped within.

It's like holding the sun—radiant and overwhelming, burning through me. A high, enraged howl erupts from the Dead Wood, every soul shrieking and raging.

The remaining soldiers flee for their lives as the trees twist with harsh, jerking movements. Roots lash out. Branches thrash wildly, beating against each other in a terrifying frenzy. They reach for me, disintegrating the moment they're within range.

But the Soulless can't stop me. He's too far away. The souls channel his rage, their faces pressing from within the trees with fractured jaws and hollow mouths. Jagged fingers claw against their prisons.

Nearby, the broken bodies of taken soldiers are heaved out from the depths of blackened trunks. Their bones snap and scrape, blood pouring from their torn lips and crushed skulls as they drag themselves across the grass.

Fear sharpens in my chest, but I don't release the soul. It feels different from what I expected, less tainted by the darkness that has distorted the Soulless's magic.

I back away from the bodies crawling toward me on shattered limbs and say, "It's over."

And then I close my fingers around the soul. It flares, bright and beautiful and powerful as if to remind the world of what it had been, and then it vanishes in a flash of glimmering white.

THIRTY

Every soul seized by my craft vanishes, their fury and violence draining away.

I draw a hoarse, gasping breath. The weight of the souls' presence is gone, leaving a resounding silence.

Looking around, I shuffle away from the bodies of the soldiers lying motionless in the grass like puppets with their strings cut. A low humming rises from the quiet. The trees—they're vibrating.

My skin prickles. Unease ripples down my spine. I brush my craft against the trees' souls and then withdraw at the eerie blankness. The souls are in shock, and beneath that shock lies a still and undisturbed rage.

The Soulless's magic is still intact. I shake my head, confused. The talisman held the Soulless's familiar. Without it, he should be cut off from his magic. Fear trails cold fingers along the back of my neck.

"Sirscha."

I turn at the sound of Prince Meilek's voice, my arm outstretched. "Stay back!"

Kneeling where she'd fallen, Queen Meilyr presses trembling hands to her collarbones as if trying to hold her soul in place. My craft burns hot, almost like a warning. I turn again toward the trees, my nerves wrung taut. The vibrating grows into rattling as that quiet rage boils over.

Roots and branches all converge at once. Prince Meilek shouts my name again as I throw up my arms, my craft blazing, shielding me. Some of the trees' sharp edges scatter into dust, but most slice past me, barely brushing my magic. Behind me, the queen lets out a hair-raising scream.

I whirl in time to see roots close around the queen's throat. Her scream becomes a strangled choking, and then there's a wet, gruesome *snap*. The queen goes limp.

"Mei!" Prince Meilek shouts. Before he can take two steps forward, I snatch up my sword and fling it. The point slams into the earth at his feet, startling him back again.

Branches snag my arms, dragging me off my feet. I let them, watching in horror as they also haul the queen's corpse into the Dead Wood, thick roots wrapping around her waist and legs.

My craft burns through the branches ensnaring me, but

they're replaced by more just as quickly. The Soulless's power surges through the trees, blistering beneath my skin. I grit my teeth. How is this possible? The queen's body slowly rises from the ground, the branches lifting her until she almost appears to be standing before me. Her head lolls on its broken neck.

The queen's eyes open, and I flinch. They're empty, the brown irises flat, the whites veined with red.

"Sirscha," she says. The word is a strangled, scraping sound.

Terror bleeds through me, taking hold of my ribs and filling me with icy dread. I swallow and whisper, "I released your familiar."

The branches squeeze my arms, stinging skin. It worked. The talisman lies broken in the tall grass, empty of its charge.

The queen releases a rattling cry. "You killed him."

Him. My breaths grow quick and frantic.

The terrible truth constricts my chest. "It wasn't your familiar, was it?" I ask. "Who were you keeping in that talisman?"

The queen hisses, lips pulled back over bloodied teeth. "I meant to restore him, but you've ruined everything."

With a soft, horrified exhale, I say, "Your brother."

When he tore his brother's soul, he must have held onto it even through the mindless grief and destruction. Somehow, by whatever strength of love or desperation, he kept his brother's soul from passing on and created a talisman for it. For safe-keeping, for the day he could give back the life he took.

"Is it so impossible?" the queen croaks in that shattered rasp. "You and I might have been strong enough to restore him. But you killed him." The branches squeeze tighter. I grit my teeth against the pain. My bones feel ready to snap.

"I didn't kill him. You did." Sharp edges slice into my skin, drawing blood. "I gave him peace. I want to give it to you too."

"I will never know peace. I am tethered, bound by the souls just as I bind them. My soul is too fractured a thing to exist without the trees."

It's nearly impossible to think through the pain and the shock, but something about his words lingers. Back in Mirrim, Priestess Mia said that they'd experimented with soulrenders to alter the nature of their bond, including binding themselves to more than one familiar in an attempt to amplify their magic.

Could it be possible that the Dead Wood is his conduit? Kyshia had mused that the Soulless had done something to his soul to make himself invulnerable. After the experimentation he endured at the Temple of Light—the ways in which his magic has changed, no longer bound by the rules of our craft—is it so unbelievable that he might have the ability to bond with more than one familiar?

"The trees are your familiars," I say. I want to be sure. No more guessing. No more mistakes.

A branch snakes around my waist, squeezing so hard

that my ribs crack. I gasp through my teeth, the pain singing through every nerve and muscle.

"Yes," the queen hisses. "So long as the Dead Wood exists, I cannot be stopped. But you, Sirscha Ashwyn, are just a girl. I could pull you into the trees and make you my own, just another soul bound to mine, raging against your bonds."

The bitter taste of fear coats my tongue, but I swallow it down. "You're too far away."

The branches constrict around me. I scream through my teeth, head thrown back. My magic pulses against the crushing limbs and they fracture into dust, freeing me. I fall, stumbling as my feet hit the ground, but the Soulless's magic doesn't relent. I duck a branch and then roll to avoid another that stings my cheek, breaking skin.

Roots rise around me as branches descend to form a tangled cage of earth and bark. With a furious cry, I slam my boot against the roots and focus my magic inward, expelling the Soulless's attempt to grip my soul.

The cage shatters. The Soulless's magic withdraws. I press my fists against my aching stomach, breathing hard as if I've just fought a long battle. My entire body hurts, blood dampening my sleeves where the trees tore through cloth and skin.

Queen Meilyr's body sinks to the earth, the roots wrapped tight around her, delicate spidersilk spilling between the dead limbs.

"You and I are the only ones left," she says. Behind her, the bowels of a tree yawn, revealing a wet black pit, stinking of rot. Hands push from within the bark, ready to accept the addition to their forest. "Without you, I am the last. But your betrayal will be paid. Every soul I take, every fool waiting for you to save them will be the cost."

My fingers unfurl, nails digging into my abdomen. I'd told the soldier at Spinner's End we would save them somehow. "Taking innocent lives only proves you're the monster the Empire made you to be."

The queen's mouth stretches into a terrible grin as the trees drag her body into the black crevice. My stomach heaves against my lungs at the wet, sucking sound.

Faces rise from the depths, squinting through the bark as the tree swallows the queen up to her neck, and the Soulless speaks through her one last time. "When the world burns down around you, leaving you no ground, you will come to me."

Emerging from the Dead Wood, I find Prince Meilek waiting. He doesn't look at me. He watches the Dead Wood, eyes wide and red-rimmed, as if expecting to see his sister walk out after me.

I don't know what to say. All I can offer is, "I'm sorry."

He inhales sharply, and his gaze meets mine. The pain there is so stark that my own breath catches. I look away.

"Where is she?" he asks in a whisper.

I don't reply because it would be pointlessly cruel. He already knows. His trembling hands curl into fists. Everyone is silent, even the remaining soldiers. He lowers his head, eyes squeezing shut, something damp tracing a line down his cheek.

There's nowhere to grieve in private, and no time either, but I move past him to return to Yandor.

After a moment, once he's gathered himself, Prince Meilek joins me, and I treat Yandor's wound with herbs and bandages we find among the queen's supplies. The Queen's Guard and the remaining soldiers don't stop us. Some even help, murmuring things like, "My prince," or "Your Highness."

Prince Meilek doesn't acknowledge their words. His eyes are now dry, but his grief is plain to see. Still, he can't break down when he's the only leader Evewyn now has.

Once we see to all of our various injuries, we decide Sab Hlee would be our nearest bet for finding food and shelter, if it's not abandoned.

Although it takes hours with Yandor injured, we arrive at the encampment to find it still occupied. Ronin's former soldiers greet us warmly, but the camp has a quiet, solemn air to it. They explain that while some soldiers returned to their homes, most had no homes to speak of. So they'd remained, banding together to wait out the impending war.

Prince Meilek offers them all a place within Evewyn should they choose, and then we set about the task of alerting everyone to what's happened. We send a falcon north to Falcons Ridge, asking Lord Phang to gather his reiwyn neighbors and lead them south. Their support will be needed when Prince Meilek returns to Vos Talwyn to claim the throne. We also send a falcon to Kou to return the ships to Needle Bay, this time under a flag of peace.

Once everything's settled, I'm eager to find a bed. A shadowblessed soldier shows me to a recently vacated tent, and I'm grateful. Exhausted, mentally and emotionally, I'm asleep the moment my head hits the pillow. My dreams are blessedly empty, save for the distant scratching of fingers against a door as if the souls of the Dead Wood are still trying to reach me.

Sometime later, I awaken to Saengo pulling back the blanket to climb into the small cot with me. When I start to rise, she presses a palm to my shoulder and I gladly sink back into the warm blanket.

"What time is it?" I ask, my voice hoarse with sleep.

Saengo laces our fingers together. "A couple of hours until dawn. Theyen brought me by shadow gate as soon as we received the news. Are you okay?"

My eyes drift shut again, but I can still picture the queen's corpse as she delivered the Soulless's warning that my betrayal would be paid for. "I messed up again," I whisper.

"No one could've guessed whose soul was in that talisman," she says. She's always so poised, even in the worst of times. "If you messed up, then we all did."

I sigh, and she scoots closer on the thin mattress, resting her cheek against the side of my head.

"Theyen had to leave again to report the news to his mother in Penumbria. He's concerned with how the Empire will react once it's known Prince Meilek is sheltering you."

For a heartbeat, anger chases away the cobwebs of sleep. "I'm Evewynian, and they have no power over shamanborn. Queen Meilyr was their enemy, and now she's dead." I'll send a falcon in the morning to the Ember Princess. If House Yalaeng thinks they can attack Evewyn because of me, then they need a reminder that I know their secrets.

Saengo sighs lightly. "Well, you're already a wanted criminal in the Empire. Might as well embrace it."

I smile, but the Empire's secrets have done enough damage. For now, the peoples of Thiy need to be made aware of the danger lurking within the Dead Wood. If we manage to survive the Soulless, then the Nuvali must be told the truth about House Yalaeng. What they do with that truth will be theirs to decide.

But I put away that worry for another time. I don't want to think about whether the Empire will punish Prince Meilek for my lies, or whether Theyen's alliance with the Ember Princess can be salvaged, or whether either kingdom can set aside their differences to face a common enemy.

Right now, all I want to do is sleep and feel relief for Saengo's safety—and Prince Meilek's and Theyen's. This strange, unexpected family that I wasn't given, but that chose me all the same.

"Did you send a falcon to my father?" Saengo asks. I nod. "Good. Once Theyen returns, we'll join with him and return to Vos Talwyn."

My chest tightens at the hope blossoming in her voice, the smile I know she's wearing.

She whispers, "We're going home, Sirscha."

Home. Pain and longing wrench within me. I want it as desperately as she does, every bit of my soul aching for it.

But there is no going back to the way things were. I don't want what we had in Vos Talwyn. I want something better. And we will never have that until the Soulless is defeated.

Every soul trapped within the trees is a conduit. I suppose I've always known what must happen, known the impossible task I must face before Saengo can be safe—before the kingdoms can know peace.

I must destroy the Dead Wood.

End of Book Two

ACKNOWLEDGMENTS

This is the part where I try to find something profound to say, but as I write this, all I'm capable of finding within me is gratitude.

Infinite gratitude for Ashley Hearn, who is both an editorial genius and a delightful geek. Thank you for taking this journey with Sirscha and for lighting my way whenever it was needed (and it certainly was needed). I'm also immensely grateful to the Page Street team for all the time, effort, and love they put into the creation and promotion of this book—I'm blessed to know that Sirscha is in such good hands.

For Suzie Townsend, who has been my champion from the start. Thank you for going above and beyond, and for always being a voice of reason when I'm being perhaps a bit dramatic. I'm so very grateful to have you, Dani, and the entire New Leaf team in my corner.

For Mindee Arnett, who has also been on this journey with me from the beginning. I can't wait to see where we go from here.

For my Fellowship: Lyn, Patricia, Audrey, Emily, Imaan, and Aamyra. You make me smile every day, and I'm so grateful we met. That's one thing Naruto did right!

For my family, who are my best and fiercest cheerleaders.

For the educators, librarians, and booksellers—where would Sirscha and I be without you helping to put her into the hands of readers? Thank you for what you do, for loving books, and for sharing that love with others.

There aren't enough words to express my gratitude for my readers. I hope Sirscha's story resonates with you in whatever way you need, and that she can return even a small measure of the love you've shown this book. Thank you for sharing your time with Sirscha and for accepting her into your hearts. Thank you for giving her a place where she can return home.

About the Author

Lori M. Lee is the author of *Forest of Souls* (Shamanborn #1), *Gates of Thread and Stone*, and *The Infinite*. She's also a contributor to the anthologies *A Thousand Beginnings and Endings* (Greenwillow/Harper) and *Color Outside the Lines* (Soho Teen). She considers herself a unicorn aficionado, enjoys marathoning TV shows, and loves to write about magic, manipulation, and family. She lives in Wisconsin with her husband, kids, and an excitable shih tzu.